CHASING MONA LISA

A NOVEL

TRICIA GOYER and
MIKE YORKEY

Revell
a division of Baker Publishing Group
Grand Rapids, Michigan

Published by Revell
a division of Baker Publishing Group
P.O. Box 6287, Grand Rapids, MI 49516-6287
www.revellbooks.com

Printed in the United States of America

Library of Congress Cataloging-in-Publication Data
Goyer, Tricia.
    Chasing Mona Lisa : a novel / Tricia Goyer and Mike Yorkey.
        p.   cm.
    ISBN 978-0-8007-2046-9 (pbk.)
    1. Art thefts—Investigation—Fiction. 2. France—History—German
occupation, 1940–1945—Fiction. 3. World War, 1939–1945—Confiscations
and contributions—France—Fiction. I. Yorkey, Mike. II. Title.
PS3607.O94C47 2012
813'.6—dc23   2011036155

This book is a work of fiction. Names, characters, places, and incidents are the product of the authors' imagination or are used fictitiously. Any resemblance to actual events, locales, or persons, living or dead, is coincidental.

Published in association with the Books & Such Literary Agency, 52 Mission Circle, Suite 122, PMB 170, Santa Rosa, CA 95409-7953

Page 7—Description from Claudine Canetti, "The World's Most Famous Painting Has the World All Aflutter," *Actualité en France*, http://www.diplomatie.gouv.fr.

Page 211—Material taken from "*Mona Lisa*: The myth of *Mona Lisa*," Treasures of the World, pbs.org/treasuresoftheworld/mona_lisa/mlevel_1/m4myth.html.

Page 277—Description from R. A. Scotti, *Vanished Smile: The Mysterious Theft of Mona Lisa* (New York: Alfred A. Knopf, 2009), 222.

The internet addresses, email addresses, and phone numbers in this book are accurate at the time of publication. They are provided as a resource. Baker Publishing Group does not endorse them or vouch for their content or permanence.

12   13   14   15   16   17   18   7   6   5   4   3   2   1

TO THE READER

The world-renowned Musée du Louvre, in Paris, France, started as a fortress when construction began in 1190. In the fourteenth century, Charles V converted the fortress into a residential chateau, and from the 1660s until 1682, Louis XIV, the Sun King, transformed the Louvre into the grandest palace in Europe. Within its walls today, 35,000 irreplaceable pieces of art are exhibited, including the three most notable—the *Mona Lisa*, Venus de Milo, and Winged Victory at Samothrace.

The *Mona Lisa*, or as she is called in French, *La Joconde*, greets visitors from behind a climate-controlled enclosure fronted by bulletproof glass. Over five hundred years old, the portrait of the most famous woman in the world—Lisa del Giocondo, the wife of a Florentine silk merchant—measures only twenty-one inches wide by thirty inches tall. It is said that her eyes follow—perhaps even haunt—viewers. Her folded hands look smooth, and her smile, forever enigmatic. From the moment the Italian painter Leonardo da Vinci finished this masterpiece in 1519 a few years before his death, no portrait has elicited more scrutiny, study, and even parody in the history of art.

During World War II, the Nazis looted thousands of paintings and art works from the lands they conquered. Armed with the knowledge that their beloved treasures were in danger, the French packed up the *Mona Lisa* before the German Army overran Paris. She was moved from one hiding place to another, and she even hung in a little girl's bedroom for a time. The *Mona Lisa* remained safe throughout the time of the Nazi occupation of France . . .

Until the Libération of Paris.

PROLOGUE

THURSDAY, AUGUST 20, 1942
PARIS, FRANCE, DURING NAZI OCCUPATION

Dressed in soiled blue overalls and pushing a dented trash can, the solitary figure shuffled past two German sentries stationed at the Gare de l'Est's archway entrance.

The brim of a felt hat covered Bernard Rousseau's down-turned eyes, allowing him to avert the soldiers' cold glare. *No one will bother you if you avoid eye contact while performing a menial job.* Cradling that thought, he moved past the guards into the gilded entrance arcade.

Gare de l'Est, one of six train stations in Paris and the main terminus for rail traffic to and from Germany, was moderately busy this summer afternoon. In stark contrast to the pall of oppression in the streets, a festive spirit hung in the air underneath the iron trusses of the train shed where clusters of German officers—flanked by smiling wives and jubilant children—arrived on holiday. Sweating porters toted their luggage, struggling to keep up within the grand structure dominated by decorative columns.

Rousseau ground his teeth at the sight of Germans vacationing in his city. They were the only ones who could afford the haute cuisine at the Hôtel Ritz, the nightly revues at the Moulin Rouge, and the soporific productions at the Paris Opéra. Signs in German plastered the city, including a garish "DEUTSCHLAND SIEGT AN ALLEN FRONTEN" affixed to the Eiffel Tower's first terrace—*Germany Is Victorious on All Fronts.*

Every day at the stroke of noon, German tourists assembled along the Champs Élysées and clapped for three hundred Wehrmacht soldiers goose-stepping toward the Place de la Concorde, trailing a brass band that oom-pahed the strident notes of "Prussia's Glory."

With a sigh of regret, Rousseau refocused on the task at hand. There was only one train that interested him—the 14:05 Intercity to Berlin on Voie 2. He aimed his wheeled trash bin for the voluminous train shed, which covered twenty lines. The departure was an hour away.

He blew out a slow breath, reminding himself to remain calm. Patience and cunning were two of his best assets, and they must serve him well in the next few minutes.

Positioning his cart at the end of the nearly deserted platform, he reached for a long-handled twig broom. Wide strokes gathered food wrappers, strewn newspapers, and used claim checks into a small pile. With the blade of a square-edge shovel, he emptied the debris into his bin.

A pair of German soldiers on patrol passed by with shouldered rifles. They ignored his presence as they continued their slow plod in the direction of the train's locomotive. No passengers were in sight as a three-man crew scrubbed the railway cars and cleaned windows.

Rousseau resumed sweeping, pacing out the mindless task with the enthusiasm of a prison inmate. Fifteen minutes later, a small team of soldiers pushing a pair of flatbed carts passed by. Heavy olive-green tarps, cinched with rope, covered the cargo destined for the heart of darkness—Nazi Germany.

A German officer, dressed in a Waffen-SS mouse-gray uniform with knee-high black boots, seemed unusually intent as he trailed close behind. The soldiers smoothly maneuvered the carts next to a freight car directly behind a tender filled with chunks of black coal. Rousseau couldn't tell what was underneath the tarps, but they looked to be tall, rectangular crates stacked side by side.

He turned his back on the delivery and continued to work his besom broom. When he dared to look again, the soldiers were loosening the ropes on the first cart, leaving the stiff tarp over the cargo.

Rousseau eased closer—close enough to hear the sound of guttural German from the Nazi officer overseeing the loading process. He detested their heavy-handed language—an auditory reminder that German power was absolute. Because of them, the France he knew no longer existed, and the Paris he loved was on its knees.

Hate stirred like untended embers in his gut. Hate toward the Germans' arrogance, their ruthlessness.

Shortly after the Nazis marched into Paris, his father had been picked up off the street. He'd been on his way to return a borrowed ladder when a German patrol stopped him at random, lined him against a wall with nine of his compatriots, and pulled their triggers.

His crime? Nothing. He was murdered in cold blood by a Nazi reprisal squad. Ever since that traumatic event, Rousseau's home had been within the ranks of the Resistance.

The German officer checked a clipboard as the first tarp was peeled back. Four wooden boxes stood side by side in varying heights. Two looked to be about two meters tall, the others slightly shorter. Stenciled in black on the side of the first wooden crate was an eagle atop a swastika and "L-20"—a designation for accounting purposes. Rousseau had seen the same crate yesterday in the basement of the Louvre, where he worked as a member of the maintenance crew.

The famed Chambord collection!

The German Ministry of Culture, now in charge of the Louvre, used the storage rooms to process paintings they had "acquired" for export to the Fatherland. Whether they were buying art or—as the rumors persisted—confiscating paintings, these masterpieces and treasures were being shipped to the Third Reich in inordinate amounts. The Chambord collection, he recalled, included Boucher's *Diana Bathing*, Daumier's *Le Wagon de Troisiéme Classe*, and Pissarro's *Le Quai Malaquais, Printemps*. They were worth a fortune.

Anger at the loss of French art caused the pavement before him to blur for a moment. His hands tightened around the broom handle, and he could feel his heartbeat in his temple. As if German greed hadn't taken enough . . . and now this.

The soldiers hefted the wooden crates into the boxcar as the officer checked off the progress. Then the next flatbed cart was loaded onto the train. This time, Rousseau counted eleven boxed crates—and then *five* more freight wagons appeared!

How much beautiful art was leaving France forever? He dreaded reporting back to Colonel Rol, his Resistance leader, what his reconnaissance confirmed: there were enough masterpieces being loaded onto the Berlin Express to empty a wing of the Louvre.

Anger turned to sadness. His heart ached at the realization

that his country faced more losses than they knew. Their French culture was being stripped, one railcar at a time.

Rousseau stifled a groan as he resumed tidying up the platform. His thoughts returned to an earlier time when, at the age of eighteen, he'd started working in the Louvre's maintenance department. Exposure to the world's great masterpieces had given him a deep appreciation for fine art, especially oil paintings. He admired the way artists conveyed imagination through brushstrokes. Now his knowledge of and appreciation for fine art deepened the sense of loss.

What he saw stenciled on the next set of packed crates stunned him. These wooden boxes were part of the A series—A-1, A-2, A-3 . . . delineating the crème de la crème: Rembrandts, Rubens, van Goghs, Matisses, and Renoirs. He turned away, not daring to look back at the Wehrmacht soldiers loading the carefully packed wooden crates bound for Berlin. He had seen enough.

Rousseau glanced at the round clock overlooking the Gare de l'Est's main hall. The Resistance leadership had asked him to call in his report at one o'clock, which was fast approaching.

He aimed his trash cart toward a side entrance that led to the maintenance shed, where several sweepers were taking a break. They too were part of the Resistance brotherhood.

"Someone wants to see you." The supervisor motioned his head toward the station entrance.

Rousseau recognized Alain Dubois pacing the sidewalk. Dubois worked with him on the Louvre grounds.

Rousseau lit a cigarette as he made his way to Dubois, who immediately pulled him toward the deserted taxi stand.

"Salut, Alain. Everything okay?"

"The art is on the train, right?"

"Much more than we thought. There must have been two dozen A series crates today."

Dubois swore in frustration.

"I know. So many masterpieces—"

"It's more than that," Dubois interrupted. "The FFL wants to blow up the train. They're certain that Reichsmarschall Hermann Göring will be on the Berlin Express when it leaves at 14:05. But he left Paris yesterday. Our people saw him board a plane at Le Bourget."

The picture cleared for Rousseau. Every couple of months, sources at the Louvre told him, Göring breezed into Paris to add to his swelling collection of fine art. The greedy general must have gone on another shopping spree, which would explain today's heavy load-in of wooden crates. But the Field Marshal of the Luftwaffe also had a private plane at his disposal.

"Isn't someone going to stop them?" Rousseau balled his fists at his side. The FFL, Forces Françaises Libres—or Free French Forces—were a rival underground group led by General Charles de Gaulle, even though de Gaulle had been exiled in London following the fall of France.

Rousseau gave Dubois a knowing look. They both belonged to a different resistance group—the Francs-Tireurs et Partisans, or FTP, one of several Communist-led underground groups that spearheaded the Resistance. The FTP didn't see eye-to-eye politically with the Gaullists, but they were united—for the moment—in their common fight against the Germans. "Keep your enemies close and your friends closer" was a motto Colonel Rol often repeated in their clandestine meetings.

Rousseau lifted his fist. "If the FFL blows up this train, they destroy irreplaceable masterpieces. But more importantly, Göring isn't even a passenger. If German soldiers are killed, there will be reprisals. Who knows how many French will die—and for what?"

The usual ratio was 10:1—ten Frenchmen picked randomly off the streets and lined up for summary execution for every German soldier killed in Paris. He had counted at least ten soldiers at the train. If all perished, then at least a hundred innocent Frenchmen would pay the ultimate price, one far too high for failing to kill the Reich's second-in-command.

"Colonel Rol wants us to stop the attack." Dubois rubbed his brow. "Rol is worried about the reprisals, but now there is so much more we could lose . . . our heritage, our masterpieces."

"But how? We don't even know where the train will be blown up."

"One of our people was in the meeting when the decision was made to assassinate Göring. They are wiring dynamite to the track just past the marshaling yards in Pantin."

"Can't anybody get to the FFL and tell them Göring flew back yesterday?" Rousseau asked.

"We got the message minutes ago, and there's no time to get through to them. And what if they don't listen—don't believe Göring flew back? They might go ahead with it anyway. We have to stop the attack ourselves."

"But the Berlin Express leaves in thirty minutes. It has to be four or five kilometers to the Pantin Triage. We'll never get there in time."

Dubois held up a hand. "We must try. Otherwise there will be a massacre for nothing. And the art . . ."

Rousseau didn't need Dubois to finish that thought.

Rousseau flicked a layer of sweat off his forehead and looked over his shoulder. Dubois was nowhere to be seen.

Even though Rousseau's sturdy bike wasn't built for speed, he had pulled away from his fellow Resistance member not long after they departed the Gare de l'Est, Dubois yelling encouragement as he faded in the distance.

Rousseau pumped his legs harder as he flew along the Avenue Jean Jaurés, unfettered by traffic. Gasoline-powered cars, trucks, and taxis had practically disappeared since the Nazis took over.

Fighting to keep his legs driving like pistons, Rousseau rued his smoking habit. He pulled off his hat and tucked it inside his overalls, freeing both hands and allowing him to crouch down, reducing wind resistance. Leaning into turns, he rolled through roundabouts like a truck driver owning the right-of-way and dodged cars at busier intersections.

A glance at his watch told him that the Berlin Express had departed the Gare de l'Est. Most likely, the train had left on time—a testament to German efficiency. Rousseau figured he had less than a kilometer to go. Getting there on time wouldn't be enough; he needed several minutes to find the person detonating the dynamite charge.

The marshaling yard at Pantin was a beehive of activity. Rousseau knew it well. One of the ways the underground confounded the brazen invaders was by throwing a rail switch at the opportune moment, resulting in derailments and devastation but no deaths.

He figured the Berlin Express would be staying on the "through" track once inside the Pantin rail yard. If Dubois' information was correct, then the train would be blown up after the main rail line converged with side tracks at the eastern end of the Pantin Triage.

A loud steam whistle pierced the air, jarring Rousseau's nerves. He looked up, startled. The Berlin Express had arrived, slowing as the long train entered the yard. He had only a minute, if that, to find the dynamite charge.

Rousseau steered his bike to a dirt path between the rail lines, eyes fixed on the convergence point. He kept pedaling rapidly, as if he was sprinting for a finish line.

The Berlin Express bore down, but still at lowered speed. The dynamited rail line had to be somewhere—then it hit him. An elevated bridge crossed a small gorge following the yard. If the wooden supports were blown the moment the engine passed, the momentum of the falling locomotive would drag the remaining cars into the gorge, their combined weight crushing one car atop another. The overpass was just ahead.

Rousseau skidded to a stop and slammed his bike to the ground. Time had run out.

Running to the tracks, he reached for a white handkerchief from inside his overalls. Standing between the rails, he waved his arms from side to side. The immediate release of air brakes split the air. A whistle blew three short blasts as train wheels squealed in protest.

The locomotive neared. Shuddering and groaning, the train pushed a wall of sooty air toward him. Old newspapers rose from the ground, levitating, yet he stood, feet planted. A mere ten meters separated him from the massive machine. Just when he was prepared to jump from its path, the steel wheels of the Berlin Express screeched to a stop. Rousseau leaped aside and bolted toward the locomotive engineer, now leaning from the window.

"What are you doing?" the engineer demanded in French.

"You can't continue on this line. The route is sabotaged."

German soldiers, rifles ready, poured out of the passenger cars and surrounded Rousseau.

A German officer approached—the same one Rousseau had seen checking off the cargo list.

"What is the meaning of this?" he demanded in rapid-fire French that carried a hint of German accent.

Rousseau repeated what he had told the engineer.

"Are you with the Resistance?"

Rousseau ignored the question. "The rail line is dynamited ahead. I am gambling with my life, I know, but I was told that you have valuable paintings on this train. I work at the Louvre and cannot allow irreplaceable masterpieces to be destroyed."

"How do you know about this trap?"

"I overheard a conversation at the museum. People talk."

The German officer pursed his lips.

From the corner of his eye, Rousseau spotted one of the soldiers raising his rifle.

"Halt!" The shout from the soldier caused the hairs on the back of Rousseau's neck to stand at attention.

Rousseau turned. A partisan darted from a nearby maintenance shack, fear distorting his features. One shot shattered the air. Then other soldiers joined in. Gunfire pounded Rousseau's eardrums.

To his horror, the partisan stumbled and then fell into a heap, grabbing the back of his left leg.

Get up!

The man fought to rise and then staggered a few steps, before crumbling again.

"Bring him here!" shouted the officer in charge.

Rousseau's shoulders slumped. His odds of living beyond the next few minutes had just shrunk dramatically.

———

Oberst Walter Heller, hands clasped behind his back, placidly surveyed the Frenchman who had boldly stopped the train. While he was sizing him up, another soldier ran toward him, out of breath.

"Colonel, we discovered a dynamite charge about a hundred meters down the track. We found the detonating plunger in the maintenance shed."

So the Frenchman was telling the truth. But why would he risk his life to stop a German train with this information?

Two soldiers dragged the injured partisan toward Heller. The ashen-faced young man grimaced in pain. His saturated pant leg glistened with blood, leaving an uneven, dark crimson trail behind his limp leg.

"Were you going to blow up the train?" Heller demanded.

The nearly unconscious partisan incoherently mumbled something Heller couldn't understand, although he heard the word "Göring," which caught his attention.

The German colonel directed more questions at the prisoner, now pallid and clammy. There was no response.

"Shoot them both," he ordered in German. He didn't have time to wait for the Gestapo to arrive. They had a schedule to keep.

The partisan hung limp in the soldiers' grasp, showing no reaction to the command.

The other Frenchman gasped and stepped backward, and the two soldiers guarding him clasped his arms.

"No!" He kicked and twisted against their iron hold. "Sir, I risked my life to save you, your soldiers, and your paintings, and this is the thanks I get? My friends and colleagues at the Louvre will find out what happened here. My unjust death will only inspire others to take revenge on German lives."

Heller lifted his chin and approached the Frenchman.

"What's your name?"

"Rousseau. Bernard Rousseau."

"Well, Monsieur Rousseau, I don't think we'll be meeting again."

The German colonel unhooked his leather holster and

drew his service Luger. With arm extended, he moved two steps to his right and placed the tip of the barrel against the forehead of the injured partisan. Nearly unconscious, the young man hung against the soldiers' clenched grip.

Heller pulled the trigger, and a plume of red mist exited the base of the freedom fighter's skull.

Heller turned the gun on Rousseau. The German officer was used to making judgment calls when appraising an artist's talent as well as the value of a painting or sculpture in Reichsmarschall Göring's collection. Now a different type of appraisal was set before him, and a man's life hung in the balance. If what Rousseau had said was true, by all rights he and his fellow soldiers should be dead, lying in a mass of twisted steel.

"Allez," he said to the Frenchman. *Go.* "Before I change my mind."

Relief widened the man's eyes and softened his face. The soldiers released their grasp.

Heller watched for a moment as the man sprinted to his bike. Small clouds of dust and gravel punctuated each stroke as the bicycle tires struggled to find traction.

They were wary adversaries, but he and the Frenchman agreed on one thing: the irreplaceable value of fine art.

For that, he deserved a second chance.

From the back of an empty boxcar on a side track, Antoine Celeste dropped his binoculars to his chest. His lips trembled at the sight, and his breathing became more rapid.

No man should have to witness the execution of his brother, yet he just had. Bile rose in his stomach, and a profound sadness filled his heart. They said that when you joined the Resistance you were signing your own death warrant: sooner, not later, you would join the brotherhood in eternity.

But a fellow Frenchman betraying the cause for liberté in broad daylight—singlehandedly stopping a German train bound for destruction with Göring on board? What explanation could there be?

When he and Philippe had joined the Gaullists' Free French, he expected a fight against Nazi swine, not treachery at the hands of his own people.

Celeste picked up the binoculars and locked on the solitary figure pedaling his bike pell-mell across the rail yard—memorizing his build, mannerisms, and the face that now filled his binoculars' view.

Restraining himself not to act immediately, he slumped to the floor of the boxcar after the bicyclist had passed. Tears streamed down his cheeks as emotions took control.

There, sitting alone in the shadows, minutes passed. Celeste steeled himself. Knowing that his vengeance must wait, he vowed that no matter how long it took, this treasonous dog would be found.

TWO YEARS
LATER...

1

FRIDAY, AUGUST 25, 1944
OUTSIDE OF PARIS

The purr of the four-cylinder engine softened as the dust-enshrouded '38 Mercedes slowed, taking the corner cautiously. A paltry breeze drifted through the windows with little effect on this heat-baked morning.

Eric Hofstadler's eyes swept the serene landscape of the sleepy hamlet of Rozay-en-Brie and then settled on a wooden signpost that bore the words "Nach Paris." The Antiqua script—"To Paris" it said in German—was a stark reminder that Nazi Germany still occupied much of France with a jackboot to her back.

That signpost will be once again in French before the month is out, he promised himself.

Another thought stirred, unbidden. *But the cost in lives is sure to be high.*

Turning his attention back to the roadway, he gently steered the dusty four-door sedan past a panorama of sun-baked walls, vermilion geraniums in windowboxes, and gray slate roofs. Few villagers milled about on this muggy morning in late August.

"How much longer?"

Gabi Mueller flattened the map against her light blue, knee-length cotton dress. "Only twenty or thirty kilometers away. Probably a good hour with the time we're making."

Eric glanced over at Gabi, smiling softly at the way the breeze whipped strands of blonde hair against her cheeks. His gaze drifted to her lips, remembering the last time he'd kissed her. It felt good to have her by his side, knowing she cared for him as much as he cared for her. It had only been three weeks since their first mission together, but the feelings they shared were unmistakable. In these uncertain times, life was measured by the day or hour, intensifying his emotions. Reluctantly, he refocused on the road.

He set his gaze beyond the belfry of a medieval church, where the flowing green fields of the Île de France beckoned him and Gabi toward one of the world's leading cultural centers—Paris. They had been told in their pre-trip briefing that they could expect thousands of Parisians rising up against their Nazi occupiers. Chaos, anarchy, and bloodshed were the inevitable result of warfare between the underequipped citizens and heavily armed German soldiers. Not that anyone could blame the Parisians for mounting an insurrection after four years of simmering frustration and public humiliation that had boiled to a flash point.

Eric slowed the Mercedes—exhibiting a distinctive red cross against a white square on each of the front passenger doors—to a crawl. Outside his dirt-streaked windshield, an older dairy farmer in faded blue overalls rhythmically tapped a tree branch against the red-and-white flanks of a skinny Montbéliarde cow.

"What do you think, Gabi? Looks like neither one are eating very much these days."

"Even the hands of an experienced dairyman like you wouldn't get a liter of milk out of her. Poor thing." Gabi blew on several stray hairs and dabbed the forehead of her flushed face with the back of her hand. "But I sure wouldn't mind a glass of cold, fresh milk." She swished the lukewarm water around in the canteen nestled in her lap. They had been sharing sandwiches of *Weissbrot* and jam, apples, and canteens of water since they left Swiss soil fifteen hours ago.

Eric cocked his head slightly to the right and watched Gabi's eyes follow the path of the lonely farmer and his emaciated cow. A soft smile lifted the corners of his lips.

Gabi set the canteen on the floorboard and unfolded the map supplied last night by Allen Dulles, the station chief of the Office of Strategic Services (OSS) based in Bern, Switzerland. Though she and Eric were both Swiss, they were part of a group of covert agents working for the Americans and the Allied cause.

Eric understood where Gabi's loyalties lay—her father was an American married to a Swiss. As for him, he was a third-generation Swiss dairyman who joined the OSS when he was recruited by Gabi's father, Ernst. While Eric felt a keen sense of mission, if truth be told, working with Herr Mueller wasn't a bad way to spend more time with someone who'd captured his heart.

"And the location?" Eric recalled the memorized address and was ready to repeat it when Gabi looked down at the map and pointed to the Left Bank.

"Right here, just off the Boulevard Saint-Michel. The Resistance controls this neighborhood, so we should be safe."

"*Should* is a word that means little in wartime." Eric

pursed his lips and considered what lay ahead. Paris—seductive and beautiful—had become an active and highly dangerous battle zone nearly a week ago. According to Herr Dulles, Resistance members aligned with General Charles de Gaulle had seized the Préfecture de Police located in the heart of the city near the Notre Dame Cathedral. The Gaullists, also known as the Free French, were determined to bring the Paris police department under their control before the Allies arrived. It was part of their strategy to control the levers of government once the Germans were driven out of Paris.

The wild card, Dulles had said, was the role the Communists expected to play in postwar France, especially since Communists dominated many of the Resistance groups. With all the rival factions—there were at least sixteen different resistance organizations—vying for power, Paris was a powder keg, ready to explode at any moment.

Eric pressed the accelerator and shifted into third gear as they left the village, passing a Rozay-en-Brie road sign with a red diagonal line across the letters. The pimply faced guard at the last German checkpoint told him there might be one more inspection stop between here and . . .

Eric spotted movement ahead to their right—near a cornfield. A German soldier wearing the distinctive coal-scuttle helmet of the Wehrmacht leaped from a roadside ditch. He jumped in their path, leveling his rifle and locking eyes with Eric.

"Halt!" The husky cry exited cracked lips.

Eric slammed on the brakes. The heavy Mercedes skidded to a stop, raising a cloud of dust that settled over the grimy soldier, who repeated his growling *Halt!*

Gabi stiffened in her seat. "Could be a rogue. I don't like the looks of this."

"Me neither." Eric moved his hand to the gearbox. If this was a rogue soldier, that meant he could be desperate enough to open fire on them.

He quietly shifted into reverse, but the soldier moved his rifle away from Eric and toward Gabi. "Hands up, or I'll shoot her!"

The way he uttered that simple sentence in less-than-smooth German . . .

"Did you hear his accent?" Gabi asked.

Eric nodded. This soldier wasn't German. He was part of an Ost battalion—men conscripted into the Wehrmacht from Poland, Czechoslovakia, and Russia. He'd heard about this. Allied troops had been shocked to discover that they were killing Poles, Czechs, and Russians on the beaches of Normandy, as well as Germans.

Gabi pressed her back against the seat. "He's one of those Ost soldiers. I'm sure of it."

"Then we have to be ready for anything."

Herr Dulles had warned them about reports of Ost battalion soldiers either deserting their posts or getting separated from their units. The absence of military discipline created a vacuum, the American director said. They were like caged animals unleashed for murder and mayhem.

Eric sought to defuse the dangerous situation. He leaned out of the open window and adopted a solicitous tone. "Hey, everything's going to be alright," he announced in German. "See, we're Red Cross."

"Hands up! Out of the car! Both of you!" The Ost soldier advanced within a few meters of the Mercedes.

"We had better do what he says, Gabi."

She nodded and moved her hand to the door handle. Before she stepped out of the vehicle, Eric noticed her eyes narrowing and a determined look on her face.

He opened the door, careful to keep his hands up where they could be seen. "Listen, we just need to—"

The soldier's eyes darted to something behind Eric, and his world turned black.

The sound of the rifle butt connecting with Eric's skull filled the air, and Gabi sucked in a breath as Eric tumbled to the ground. The second soldier then turned the rifle, pointing it at the back of Eric's head. He had murder in his eyes.

With no chance of reaching Eric's side before the soldier pulled the trigger, she tried to distract him instead. "No! Stop!"

She darted around the front of the car, toward Eric. Just as she reached his side, the soldier shifted the rifle, lunged, and grabbed her wrist.

"So, you've come to see me?" He snarled as he pulled her toward him, burrowing a sandpaper-like cheek in her soft neck. He reeked of pungent body odor and stale beer. Then he pulled back his leathery face and smiled, showing two rows of rotten teeth. "Juri," he spoke to the other, "this is a pretty one, *ja*?"

Gabi struggled to slip out of his firm grasp. "Let me go!"

Panic rose in her throat. She pushed against him, but he wrapped his free arm around her body and pressed his dirty tunic, caked with white lines of dried sweat, to her chest. She pushed against him hard, then beat him with her free fist, but he was too strong. His arms tightened, making it hard to move. Her power was no match against his.

"You want me, *Schatzi*. I can feel it." His hiss inside her ear brought images of a serpent's tongue.

"Forget it!" Gabi clawed at the hand squeezing her wrist, but his grip felt like iron.

"She's hot-blooded, Juri. I believe I'll keep this one for a while." The swearing soldier yanked on her arm and drew her close again—his mouth nearing hers. His putrid breath caused her to gag.

"Let her go and fetch her purse. This isn't all play," said Juri, who shouldered his rifle and extracted a Luger pistol from his waist belt. "I'll shoot her if she runs." He raised the Luger, fixing it on Gabi.

Juri seemed to be the one in charge. Gabi's knees weakened seeing his gun fixed on her.

"Then you can have your way," Juri added with a snarl.

With a frustrated groan, the other soldier snuggled his bulbous nose one last time in Gabi's ear and then relaxed his grip. Releasing her, he moved around to the passenger's side of the car.

At her feet, Eric lay on the ground, facedown, not stirring at all. She crouched down to check on him, but her shoulders tensed as Juri stepped closer.

Gabi defiantly looked up. "You can shoot me if you want, but I have to make sure he's okay."

Feeling an overwhelming desire to hold him close, she cradled Eric's head and inspected his scalp for a bruise. He moved slightly and groaned, and she released the breath she'd been holding. Her tactile touch discovered a bump the size of a two-franc piece on the back of his skull.

She gingerly separated a thatch of red hairs and inspected the injury. Out of the corner of her eye, she watched the other soldier discover her purse—hidden under the passenger's seat. He rifled through its contents.

"What are you doing?" Anger flared in her eyes. She eased Eric back to the ground and jumped to her feet. Gesticulating with both hands, she knew their only chance was to make a scene. "Get your hands out of there! Those are my things!"

The Ost soldier, nonplussed, looked like he was sampling the summer fruits at a Saturday market. "We need money," he said, unzipping her leather billfold and stuffing all the Swiss and French banknotes into the upper left pocket of his tunic. He dumped the loose change into his pants pocket.

"There has to be more than this." He strode around the front of the car and then approached Eric, kicking him in the backside.

Gabi gasped. Eric moaned, and she saw his eyes open. Seeing the soldier, Eric attempted to rise but stumbled, falling to his hands and knees.

The soldier pointed his pistol at Eric.

"Wallet." He fluttered his free hand.

Highway robbery in broad daylight, but Gabi knew their troubles were just beginning once the soldiers had taken all their money. She helped Eric steady himself so he could reach into his rear pocket. With a shaky hand, he tossed the well-worn billfold toward the soldier.

The Wehrmacht soldier caught the wallet in the air and wordlessly extracted a wad of bills. He pocketed them and flung the wallet to the dirt. "What else do you have?"

She regarded the squinty-eyed soldier with wide cheekbones. His accented German with unstressed vowels sounded Slavic to her ears.

"Just some food, medicine, and clothes," Gabi said. "Take what you want, and then be on your way."

The soldier with the teeth blackened by decay grunted. His emotionless eyes were dark as coal and devoid of any spark. Those same eyes moved over her body, sizing up her curves, reminding her of what he really wanted.

He swung his carbine off his shoulder and approached. Then he slowly circled behind her and used the tip of his rifle to hike up her skirt.

Gabi clenched her jaw and remained ramrod still, sensing that he wanted her to lose control—so he could lose control. She reached down and straightened her skirt. *Show no fear. You are Swiss. You are neutral.*

"When's the last time you ate?" Gabi brought her right hand up to her mouth to mimic the eating motion toward the soldier in charge.

"Gestern." *Yesterday.*

"There's food in the car." She pointed to the backseat. "Can I get it for you?"

The soldier nodded. Apparently hunger inside the stomach trumped a different type of ravenousness.

Resisting the urge to look at Eric, she took several steps to the passenger side door and leaned inside. The soldier with the carbine came up behind her and ran the tip of his rifle up her leg again. She shivered against the feeling of the cold metal against her skin but willed herself to ignore him. She would not acknowledge her fear.

Gabi grabbed the handle of a wicker basket. "We have some sandwiches with butter and jam you can take with you." She forced a half smile.

She lifted the wicker basket out of the backseat and set it on the road. She lifted one flap and then moved her hand underneath the red-and-white napkins, feeling what she was after. Her hand wrapped around the grip. Her finger on the trigger. "We also have apples. I picked them just yesterday."

The salacious soldier bent down for a look. With a rapid swoop, she lifted her arm and aimed the snub-nosed pistol.

He lunged, and her finger pulled the trigger. The bullet tore into his upper chest, next to the heart. Both hands involuntarily grasped at the massive wound as a burst of crimson immediately stained his gray uniform. A look of surprise, a strained wheeze, and within a long second, the soldier fell forward in a heap, legs twitching as blood pooled on the dirt roadway.

The gunshot lifted the fog from Eric's mind and gave him an immediate boost of adrenaline. At the same instant, he dove for the other soldier, Juri, who had trained his pistol on Gabi. Jostled, Juri missed his target, but a metallic thud left a small hole in the back of the Mercedes. They fell into a heap. Rage consumed Eric—rage that Russians or Poles or whoever they were wanted to rape Gabi and then kill her.

The soldier's pistol bounced away in the dirt. Eric put his years of gaining muscle from baling hay to work and wrestled him away from the weapon. When a fist crashed on his temple, he replied by pummeling his foe with blow after blow.

"Get away from him!" Gabi screamed. He knew she held her fire because she didn't have a clear shot. Out of the corner of his eye, he saw Gabi kick the soldier's pistol into a clump of weeds.

The momentary distraction was to the soldier's advantage. He threw himself on Eric, pinning his arms to his side. They rolled through the dirt, with Eric trying to push himself away and the soldier digging his hands into his torso, as if he knew that once distance was put between them, Gabi's close-in shot would kill him.

Then a bloodcurdling scream—this from the Wehrmacht soldier. With ferocious determination, Eric had reached the broad hunting knife in his ankle sheath and plunged the razor-edged steel blade upward. The sharp knife had slipped through the coarse military uniform and under the sternum. Eric's knuckles blanched white as his grip tightened around the handle.

Eyes wide with shock and disbelief, the Wehrmacht soldier pushed his boots hard against the road. Heels furrowed the soil, but there would be no escape. Eric kept the tension strong until the soldier's arching body collapsed against hardpan. With a deep breath, he drew the knife out, wiping the heavy blade against the German uniform.

Rising on shaky legs, a feeling of intense relief came over him. Lifting his pant leg, he slid the knife back into his ankle sheath with finality. Neither of these soldiers would ever take advantage of the girl he loved.

Gabi watched, as in a trance, while Eric retrieved the Swiss and French bills from the dead soldier's upper left pocket. Then he grabbed the soldier by the ankles, dragged him across the dirt road, and chucked his lifeless frame into the roadside ditch. He could keep the change.

The other lifeless soldier received the same brusque treatment.

Eric hustled back to Gabi, and the emotions she'd been holding in overwhelmed her. Memory of the soldier's breaths close to her lips caused her hands to tremble. If he'd had his way . . .

"No," she whispered. She buried her face in her hands. Even though she knew she had the right to protect herself—and Eric—her stomach sickened at the realization that she'd taken a life, however justifiable the cause may be.

Eric stepped toward her, anger still flaring in his eyes. She wasn't used to seeing him like this. She was both drawn by his strength and overcome by the image of Eric's knife plunging into the man's chest. Yet this was Eric . . . she looked into his face again.

His gaze softened as he neared, and Eric reached around

the back of her waist and drew her close. "Thank you for saving our lives. You know that's what you did, don't you?"

Gabi struggled for the right words. "They were going to kill us and take the car after they got everything they wanted." Her voice sounded flat. Her throat felt thick, making it hard to swallow.

Fear of death, fear of being so *violated*, had prompted her to do what she had never done before—shoot a man and take a life.

2

Colette Perriard studied the faces of her fellow travelers on the Métro like one would study a great work of art.

Normally, Parisians were content to stare straight ahead or bury their faces in one of the collaborationist newspapers like *Paris-Soir* or *Le Petit Parisien*. On this Friday morning commute, however, perfect strangers eagerly shared morsels of gossip they'd heard on the street. Hope lighted thin and pale faces. Chins were held higher, like in the H. de la Charlerie engraving, *The Women March on Versailles*.

Bus service had been canceled because of the Paris insurrection that started almost a week ago, but below ground on the Métro, rumors buzzed like a swarm of locusts . . .

French tanks were seen passing through May-en-Multien during the night.

The Americans want to free Paris, but Montgomery doesn't want to put British troops into harm's way.

They're waiting for de Gaulle to arrive from London.

Colette listened impassively, not sure what to believe. Someone even claimed that the Germans had decided to begin mass executions, starting at dusk.

She let out a slow breath. For her, the meaning of life

was tied to the art she worked hard to protect and preserve. The liberation of Paris and the ultimate defeat of the Nazis would mean the recovery of priceless treasures and the restoration of sanity in the world of fine art.

She alighted at the Palais Royal stop and hurried from the tomblike oven. She climbed the last of the stairs and stepped onto a broad sidewalk shaded by pavilions and baroque buildings with colonnades. Here on the Right Bank was the center of contemporary Paris, home to palaces, government buildings, and museums, including the Louvre, where she worked as a curator.

Most pedestrians avoided eye contact as she walked a brisk half block to the Rue de Rivoli, one of Paris's grand boulevards. The optimism of the underground Métro had given way to the reality of the streets: Paris would soon be under siege. Gazing toward the western horizon, she viewed pillars of brown and white smoke curling to the heavens, signs of skirmishes and pitched battles in the distance. Her stomach clenched, and she quickened her pace.

She reached the corner, preparing to cross, when a convoy of German troop trucks rumbled her direction. She stiffened, pausing her steps. Truck after truck thundered past—more than a dozen vehicles in each of three columns. The air thickened with plumes of sooty exhaust. As each truck passed, rows of seated German soldiers cast cold stares at the knot of Parisians waiting to cross the boulevard. Colette's eyes met one soldier's narrowed gaze, and a shiver traveled up her spine. Death was landscaped in the soldier's look.

Perhaps the rumor about summary executions was right.

"I haven't seen this many *boches* in one place since June 1940." The observation came from someone she recognized from the Louvre's Antiquities area. Several Louvre employees had gathered at the corner, patiently waiting to cross.

"Where do you think they're going?" asked another.

"Probably the Hôtel Meurice." The man from Antiquities rubbed his hands. "That can only mean one thing—the German High Command knows the Allies are coming to liberate us."

The Hôtel Meurice, located half a kilometer west of the Louvre, housed the top German military brass as well as the commanding governor, General Dietrich von Choltitz.

As Colette crossed the boulevard, she looked toward her office on the third floor of the Richelieu Wing. Working at the Louvre had been a wartime balm and had given her an opportunity to live adequately amidst the food and fuel shortages the last four years, comfortable by comparison to most Parisians.

With Paris on the cusp of liberation—or unruly revolution—every able-bodied employee had been called in to the Musée du Louvre. It was all hands on deck after Gaullist forces stormed the Préfecture de Police nearly a week ago and set Paris down a path of no return. No one knew what the next day or even the next hour would bring.

Colette drew in a heavy breath. She had a feeling that history would be made very soon—and she had a front row seat.

"Bonjour, Anne."

Colette set her purse on the file cabinet and approached Anne Chavanette, who, like Colette, was twenty-seven years old and a Louvre curator. Anne stood up from her desk, and the pair leaned forward and lightly touched cheek with cheek—once for each side.

"Hear anything on the Métro?" Anne asked.

"The rumors get wilder each day. At least no one spoke of the Louvre getting blown up this morning."

"You'd think the Allies would be here by now. I heard that Patton's tanks turned in our—"

Colette held up a hand. "Right. And General de Gaulle will be parachuting into Paris to storm the Hôtel Meurice single-handedly and drive out the Nazis with a cowboy six-shooter."

Anne waved her off. "You and your imagination. Can I pour you some tea? It's a bit weak."

"Sure." Colette held out a chipped china cup for Anne to fill, then sat down at her desk and opened the top right-hand drawer. A small glass jar half filled with honey was still there. Colette picked it up to appraise how much was left. "I see you're being a good girl."

"I wouldn't imagine using any of your honey. But since you're here—" Anne walked over, and Colette handed her the small jar with a smile.

Time to get to work. She retrieved a set of keys from her purse, one of which she used to open the top drawer of the wooden file cabinet. The worn folder of Paul Cézanne, the Post-Impressionist painter, was the closest—right where she had left it yesterday. Inside the file were pages of information about his paintings and where they were located.

Cézanne apparently fancied himself as a philosopher as well. Several pages of his writings were included in the files, including this quote that leaped from the smudged pages: "Right now a moment of time is passing by. We must become that moment."

Colette sat down and took her first sip of sweetened tea. She was certainly in the moment now. A liberated Paris and no longer working for the Germans were tantalizing prospects. She'd been hired in the summer of 1940 after her predecessor had fled for Vichy France because of Jewish ancestry. Since then, Colette had faced all sorts of pressures from the occupying victors. The Germans had been distressed to learn that Cézanne's works as well as the Louvre's priceless "show pieces"—led by Winged Victory of Samothrace, the Venus de Milo, and the *Mona Lisa*—had been evacuated the moment Hitler unleashed the Nazi blitzkrieg on Poland. What remained in the Louvre's depleted basements were minor collections and lesser-known odds and ends—but all were valuable.

If only she'd had a chance to see the *Mona Lisa* in her position as curator, but the painting had already been safely hidden away for six months by the time she'd arrived. Of course now . . . if stories of liberation were true, she might soon get her chance. The prospect of planning the return of the *Mona Lisa* to her rightful place in the Salle des États thrilled her.

Colette sighed. She couldn't think of that yet. Her work wasn't done. The victory was not yet theirs.

She looked up from the file, turning to Anne. "Do you remember when someone from Reichsmarschall Göring's office came here? I saw a soldier on a transport that reminded me of him today. Maybe it was the hard look in his eyes."

"Colonel Heller?" Anne refilled her cup with weak tea. "He's the one snatching up art pieces for Göring—that fat hunk of sausage. Come to think of it, we haven't seen the colonel in a while."

"Good riddance." Colette looked down at her file. She hadn't forgotten the time when Heller asked her to go to the storage basement to identify a half-dozen paintings confiscated from Jewish families. He wanted an expert opinion about their worth. When she confirmed their authenticity and incredible value, Heller replied that the paintings and sculptures were destined for the *Führermuseum* in Adolf Hitler's hometown of Linz, Austria. The conceit of those Nazis! Soon France would be rid of them. She wished for nothing more.

Until then, she had to appease types like Heller. Government-run museums like the Louvre fell under the control of the German Ministry of Culture and were subject to their whims and desires. Seeing German soldiers load their loot into trucks caused her heart to break.

"Liberation can't be much longer." Anne set down her cup of tea and inserted a piece of paper into her typewriter. "Is anything happening out there?"

"I'll take a look." Colette stepped over to their third-story vantage point overlooking the busy thoroughfare and pushed open the window to gain a better view.

"German tanks are coming this way, two or three blocks to the east." A trio of Panzers ate up pavement in single-file fashion and would soon pass on the street below.

Her colleague stopped typing and rose from her desk to join Colette at the window. "Where do you think they're going?"

Colette's ears tingled from the exhaust notes of the powerful diesel engines. "When I got off the Métro, we saw a huge convoy of troop trucks. They had to be heading to the Hôtel Meurice."

"Yes, I heard them pass too."

"And now these tanks are moving in the same direction. Maybe an Allied attack *is* imminent."

As a rule, Colette kept her distance from where the German High Command was posted. Most Parisians did the same, although some parents still visited the lovely sculptured Tuileries Garden opposite the hotel, where their children played by the pond with wooden sailboats. She leaned out the windowsill and regarded how the tanks purposefully maintained a straight line down the middle of the boulevard, which had emptied in the last twenty minutes. The few Parisians out and about skirted underneath the alcoves or slipped into the background.

Easy now, she thought. All it took was a Resistance member to fling a Molotov cocktail at one of those tanks, and a trigger-happy tank gunner could punch a grotesque hole in the nearest building—or her office.

Anne stood on her tiptoes and leaned out the window. "I'm looking for Allied tanks, but I'm not seeing anything."

Colette mirrored her movement. "Me neither. I'm sure we'll hear shooting once the Allies are in Paris. This certainly is nerve-racking, waiting for something to happen."

"What are you going to do when the shooting starts?"

"Stay here as long as I can. I would imagine that the Louvre would be one of the first places the Allies want to secure."

Colette closed the window, which cut down the cacophony of sound considerably. Anne returned to her desk, while Colette turned to the wooden file cabinet and unlocked the second drawer. The file she sought was one she could find blindfolded. She bent over, let her fingers count off six files, and pulled out a binder marked *La Joconde*.

She carried the thick file back to her desk and untied the string holding its contents. Henri Rambouillet, her department head and senior curator, had given her a promotion that carried responsibility for the *Mona Lisa* back in 1942, one which raised eyebrows among other Louvre curators since she only had two years of experience. The hallway gossip was horrible. Some said the German cultural minister pressured Rambouillet because she had slept with him, but that was a filthy lie. It was her mother-tongue fluency in German that leapfrogged Colette over other applicants.

Colette skimmed the first few pages, which she could practically recite by heart. When Hitler was rattling sabers in the summer of 1939, at least one segment of the French elites believed him—the arts community. August vacations were canceled at the Louvre, and packing and crating started in earnest. A plan was formulated to safeguard priceless works of art like the *Mona Lisa* and Venus de Milo by removing them from the Louvre and hiding them outside of Paris for safekeeping.

Over the next four years, the famous painting moved more often than a green pea in a shell game. Currently, she was resting in a chateau outside the medieval town of Annecy, not far from Geneva.

Colette smiled and gathered the papers in the file and straightened the bottom edges. Keeping up with the wry smile of a Florentine merchant's wife and her constant moves caused Colette to rub her temples. But based on the events of the last few days, soon she—and all of France—could breathe a collective sigh of relief.

Colette looked up from her file. "It will be nice to get *La Joconde* home where she belongs," she said to Anne.

The phone jangled, which Colette picked up.

"We have a problem," a voice announced.

She immediately recognized the voice of Monsieur Rambouillet, her superior, a few offices away.

Rambouillet cleared his throat. "There's a German major in my—"

The phone line went dead. Seconds later a commotion of guttural German shouts and heavy boots filled the hallway.

"What's happening?" Anne asked, the color draining from her face.

"I'm not sure." Colette set the black handset back in its cradle and stepped out into the hallway. Monsieur Rambouillet scrambled her way. A German officer and a soldier holding a bayoneted rifle followed with heavy steps.

Rambouillet, pale and clammy, mopped his brow with a handkerchief. "I can't understand a word this crazy German is saying!" he cried. "You have to help me."

Colette stepped in front of her superior. She squared her shoulders and gathered her courage. "There seems to be a misunderstanding, Herr Oberst. How can I help?" she asked in crisp German that bespoke authority.

"I'm here to move a few paintings."

Colette regarded the intruder. His uniform was all starch and shiny brass. Slight of build with a face pockmarked from scarred acne, the Prussian exuded arrogance. His pinpoint eyes made her skin crawl.

"Sir, this is the Louvre, and we work under the German Ministry of Culture. May I see your requisition documents, please?"

"Will this suffice?" The major unbuttoned his leather holster and pointed a pistol at Colette and then Rambouillet, who instinctively held up his hands at chest height.

Colette's heart skipped a beat, then she steadied her nerves and took a long moment to study the German major, whose exertion had prompted two lines of perspiration to roll down his craggy face. To Colette, he reeked of desperation, which was the picture of a proud and boastful enemy teetering on defeat.

"But Herr Oberst, how will I explain this to the Cultural Minister?"

Without moving his gaze from Colette, the major aimed his Luger in Rambouillet's direction and fired a single round. Rambouillet winced as powder stung his bald head. Behind him, wood splintered and scattered to the floor. Shock hung in the air with the acrid aroma of spent gunpowder filling the hallway.

Colette maintained her composure. "Herr Major, surely you're aware that I'll need to answer to the Ministry for any pieces of art released without the proper paperwork."

This time the major slowly lowered his outstretched arm and pointed the pistol directly between Rambouillet's eyes. "I'm sure the Ministry has more pressing matters to tend to at the moment . . ."

Colette stiffened. "Very well," she said in a steady voice that surprised even her. "What do you have in mind?"

"A few souvenirs of my time in Paris. I'd like to see what you have in the Sully Wing," he replied, while returning the sidearm to his holster.

Colette's gaze narrowed. "Yes, let me see what I can arrange. You can follow me." She turned to Rambouillet and switched back to French. "You may go back to your office. I'll handle this."

She had never seen a more grateful look in her life. Anne, who'd watched the encounter from the doorway, slipped away and joined Rambouillet down the hall.

Colette had trained for moments like this and knew exactly what to do. She stepped back into her office, and with a demure smile to the major, she lifted the phone. "I'll just call the custodian and ask him to meet us at the storage area."

The connection was made after two short rings. "Je cherche Monsieur Monet. J'ai besoin de le recontrer dans l'aile Sully," she said. *I'm looking for Mr. Monet. I need to meet him in the Sully Wing.*

A brusque, deep voice replied that Monsieur Monet wasn't available. She hung up the handset. "He wasn't there," she said in German to the two men occupying her office. "I can try someone else—"

The German officer placed his left hand over hers before she could lift the phone to place another call. Her body shivered in response to his cold touch.

"That won't be necessary. I'm sure you know the way."

The major had good information, Colette thought. The Sully Wing was the easternmost annex of the Louvre, ringed by a thirteenth-century moat, and showcased invaluable eighteenth-century paintings from French artists like Fragonard and Watteau. Many had been wrapped, boxed, and shipped out in the fall of 1939, but with 15,000 works of art in the Louvre's possession at the start of the war, thousands of paintings had to be left behind in the Louvre's basements.

And now some rogue Nazi was treating the most famous museum in the world like a shopping gallery. She wished her boyfriend, Bernard Rousseau, had picked up the phone when she dialed Maintenance.

She led the Germans from the Richelieu Wing into the main palace courtyard, which was empty except for a pair of gardeners clipping potted hedges to the left of the Sully Wing entrance. The German major was a step behind her, followed by the soldier who had shouldered his carbine.

As they approached the ornate double doors, the German major called to her, "Fräulein, one moment."

Colette came to a stop in the magnificent courtyard and turned to face him. The major paused his steps and leaned in slightly.

"We will keep this our little secret, *ja*? If not—" The officer tapped his black leather holster, a visual reminder to Colette that he was prepared to use his Luger.

Colette did not respond. Her attention was directed elsewhere—to movement behind the Wehrmacht soldier. In one fluid motion, one of the gardeners swung a short-handled tool into the back of the unsuspecting infantryman.

With a muffled grunt, the soldier fell face-first to the cobblestone square, the blunt end of a pickaxe extruding from his back.

The German major swiveled and fumbled for his Luger as a shadow of a shovel darted across the walkway ahead. The broad blade of the tool struck him square in the face. The sharp crackling of bone and cartilage was muffled by splitting skin. The dazed officer covered his face and doubled over in agony, blood dripping between his fingers. Colette placed her hands over her mouth and stepped back.

Windmilling the shovel, the gardener brought the blade down hard against the back of the major's head, flattening the base of his skull. The German crumpled to the ground. Colette stared in horror as the gardener delivered the coup de grâce—a pair of hedge shears ferociously driven between the officer's shoulder blades.

A grotesque sucking sound caused her stomach to lurch as the long-handled shears were pulled from the dead officer. The gardener quickly removed the Luger from its holster and tucked it under his belt.

"Et voilà," he said, breaking the silence with his gruff voice. *There you have it.*

Colette felt her world spinning. She knew that her code phrase—"Je cherche Monsieur Monet"—would alert the maintenance crew that she was in danger, but up until today, she had never needed to make that call. She moved to a nearby bench and sat down, taking several deep breaths to steady herself.

"Quick—help me load this pig." The gardener beckoned his partner to give him a hand.

Within seconds, the second gardener wheeled a wooden

handcart out from behind the potted hedges. Together, they heaped two bodies onto the cart and covered them with a green canvas tarp.

"Go back to your office," the gardener said to Colette. "We'll tell Bernard you're okay."

"Where is he?"

He adjusted his brimless beret. "I'm sorry, Mademoiselle, I don't know where he is, but he is fighting for our liberation. Vive la France!"

"Oui, vive la France."

Colette looked up at the summer sky, tarnished with smoke and haze in the distance. She could only wonder what Bernard was doing at that moment.

3

Four years of Nazi rule in Paris had not sanded off the corners of Bernard Rousseau's resolve.

For this member of the Resistance, fighting back against evil was a core value firmly lodged in the center of his being. That's why he had volunteered for this early morning mission in the 6th arrondissement not far from the Latin Quarter.

As the cool morning air caressed his cheeks, his thoughts turned to Colette. He knew it wasn't wise to have allowed himself to fall in love, but he could not deny the solace, the comfort he found in her arms. In the moments when he looked into her gentle gaze—or when his lips touched hers—he could forget that their nation was no longer their own.

Or maybe it was because each day could be his last that he allowed himself the pleasure of her company. It was selfish, he knew, especially since he never let his mind wander to the future. He never offered Colette more than today. She never asked.

As Bernard quickened his steps, he mentally prepared for the possibility of sacrificing everything for a higher ideal—a Communist France where the proletariat was no longer exploited by the bourgeoisie. Where common man could determine his own future, and all men care for their neighbors as seemed only right.

And kill as many Germans as he could along the way.

On a brisk June afternoon in 1940, Bernard had stood stoically on a crowded sidewalk along the Champs Élysées and cursed under his breath while the victorious German Army marched on cobblestones that hadn't yielded to the leather soles of a foreign invader since the Franco-Prussian War of 1871. Their synchronized goose steps and collective smugness nauseated him that dark day, but it wasn't until his father's shocking death that he was motivated to fight the Aryan conquerors.

He eagerly fell in with the Francs-Tireurs et Partisans, a Communist-run Resistance group that sabotaged German capabilities, fabricated false identity documents, and generally made themselves a pain in the derrière to the occupying force. The FTP and other confederate Resistance groups kept the candles of *liberté, égalité,* and *fraternité*—the tripartite motto of liberty, equality, and fraternity—lit during France's darkest days.

Their illumination was increasing with each hour. On this cloudless Friday in August, four years and two months after the fall of France, the *libération* of Paris was imminent. He could feel it in his bones. If things fell as planned, the hated Nazis would be driven out, setting the stage for France's Fourth Republic to become the world's second Communist nation, united under Russian hegemony.

"When do you think we'll see the first patrol?"

The question from Alain Dubois startled Bernard, who willed his mind back to the task at hand.

"Not too much longer." Bernard smirked. "You know *les boches.* Regular as clockwork. Since they clocked in at 8 a.m., we should see them stirring at any moment."

Their perch inside a second-story apartment overlooked the Jardin du Luxembourg, where symmetrical gravel footpaths and scrawny lawns ringed the Luxembourg Palace. Luftwaffe Field Marshall Hugo Sperrle—one of Hermann Göring's subordinates—commanded this stronghold for German forces that had occupied Paris like an iron fist in a velvet glove. Bernard was directed by his superiors to keep an eye out for anything beyond the usual troop movements. He and Dubois were positioned along the Rue de Vaugirard, which bordered the Luxembourg Garden's northern flank.

Bernard pulled back a light curtain and held up a pair of binoculars. He scanned the palace grounds before locking on a wooden barrack situated in a rectangular orchard of apple and pear trees about a half kilometer in the distance. Clusters of German soldiers, with rifles slung over their shoulders, milled around a lineup of troop trucks. They were undoubtedly waiting for orders of the day. Or maybe they were being held in reserve to put down the latest insurrection hot spot.

Bernard inhaled a quiet breath of warm summer air— and then heard the unmistakable sound of a diesel motor. He didn't need binoculars to spot a gray Panzer rumbling toward their position, crawling in low gear and making a racket from the metal caterpillar treads grinding on the granite cobblestones.

"A Panzer III," he announced. He and Dubois were quite familiar with the medium-sized enclosed armored military vehicle, an obsolete battle tank of the German forces that was seriously outgunned by Russian T-34s on the Eastern Front. In urban hot spots like Paris, however, the Panzer III proved to be a formidable foe against a relatively unarmed citizenry. The only weapon available to partisans was Molotov cocktails.

The next sight caused Bernard's stomach to tighten. Lashed to the tank turret was a French hostage. This wasn't the first time he'd seen Panzers use a human shield to protect themselves from crude homemade fire bombs.

Bernard looked down at a wooden crate containing a half-dozen incendiary devices. "I guess we won't be needing those."

Dubois swore in frustration. He leaned in for a closer look as the Panzer approached at low speed. "It's Louis Michaud!"

Bernard nearly pushed Dubois to the floor to get a better look. Louis Michaud worked on the same maintenance crew at the Louvre Museum, but he had disappeared four days earlier. One of the guys at work said he had answered the call of the French Forces of the Interior—the Resistance group loyal to General Charles de Gaulle. The apolitical Louis, loyal and brave, had bounced from one Resistance group to another during the Occupation. The Germans must have captured him. And now this indignity—being used as a human shield to stop any attacks from the Resistance or citizenry.

"I'll wager a *sou* the Panzer is headed toward the Sorbonne." Bernard mopped a layer of sweat off his forehead with the back of his grimy hand.

"That's a sure bet," Dubois said. "Probably going over there to smash a few barricades set up by the students."

They watched the German tank pass below their perch and rumble east toward Boulevard Saint-Michel. The Panzer commander stood in the gun turret to direct the driver. All tanks had notoriously restricted views when buttoned up in battle, which meant the tank commander was the eyes and ears when the Panzer was on the move. One of the gunners had opened the escape hatch, no doubt to help with circulation of air.

Louis Michaud came into focus, a black armband of the Resistance on his left sleeve. His face was a mask of fright. The Panzer crew members had secured his torso with ropes to the main turret and pinned his arms behind him. At least they weren't dangling him from the 75-millimeter howitzer, letting him hang like a pig on a pole being led to the fire. Bernard had seen Panzer crews do that before, often for the sport of it. He shuddered at the memory of watching one of his comrades fall off the gun barrel, only to be chewed up by the metal tire tracks like a hand-powered meat grinder.

"What are we going to do?" Dubois pulled back from the window as the Panzer passed underneath their second-story aerie.

Bernard considered their course of action, but there was really only one option. "The same thing Michaud would do if one of us was lashed to a tank turret—he'd save us."

"But how? We can't chase after him. We could be shot if we run into a German patrol—"

"Here, grab one of these." Bernard reached for a Molotov cocktail housed in a dark green bottle that had once held 750 milliliters of red wine. He tossed it toward Dubois.

Dubois snatched the bottle out of the air and placed it in his satchel, as well as a second fire bomb.

Bernard grunted. "Here's the plan. We're not going to launch any Molotovs from here. There's a good chance we'd hit Michaud and burn him to a crisp. Plus we'd expose our position." He spread the curtain to check the tank's progress. "The Panzer is headed for the Sorbonne. He's not moving fast, though. We can cut him off and save Louis."

"Bernard, think this through. What if the flames get out of control or the tank blows up?"

"Louis would tell us to take that chance. Don't you think they're going to kill him anyway?"

Dubois shrugged. "Probably. I guess we owe it to Louis to give it a try."

Bernard filled another satchel with two more Molotovs. Then he checked the pockets of his navy workpants. A French military revolver and six bullets in his right pocket. A lighter and pocketknife in his left. No identification.

He assessed Dubois. His comrade was similarly armed, except his rusty Belgian Pinfire pistol looked like it had last been fired in the Great War. Not much firepower against an armored tank. Still, they had maneuverability in their favor.

Bernard figured they were as ready as they'd ever be. "It looks like he's heading over to the Boulevard Saint-Michel because it's a wide boulevard. Panzer tanks don't like tight quarters. We can still cut him off."

The pair of partisans hustled down the building's central stairwell. Bernard held up his hand when he reached the apartment building's main entrance and leaned forward and listened. Hearing nothing, he slowly opened the door. A glance up and down tidy Rue de Condé revealed a deserted street: no cars and no people. Those with the resources had left this neighborhood days ago.

Bernard hurried onto the sidewalk, followed by Dubois. He felt awfully exposed, knowing that a German patrol would shoot first and ask questions later. They scurried down the street, and Bernard took a breath and slowed his gait when he spotted his first pedestrian—an elderly woman out walking her white poodle.

He tipped his navy beret as he passed by, and then the pair broke into a sprint toward the street corner. When they reached Boulevard Saint-Michel, he saw the gray tank heading in their direction, about 150 meters from their intersection. They had successfully headed off the Panzer.

"Here's our chance." For the next minute, Bernard

outlined a plan. They would remain hidden, and when the tank passed, they would each rush the armored vehicle from behind and dump the burning gas bombs into the open escape hatch. Once the tank's hull was ablaze, Bernard would jump on while Dubois would provide cover by shooting anyone exiting the turret.

"Once I'm on the tank, I'll slice through the ropes binding Louis. Then it's a matter of jumping off before it's too late."

Dubois cocked an eyebrow and nodded.

Bernard ignored his friend's concerned gaze. "We have to work quickly. No more than thirty seconds."

They took cover inside an apartment stairwell and listened for the approaching Panzer. Bernard wondered if these were his last minutes of existence.

He reached for the silver Zippo in his right pocket and noticed a slight tremor from the adrenaline rush. Nonetheless, in one smooth motion, he flipped open the lighter and lit the strip of white undershirt stuffed into the neck of the wine bottle. Then he held his flaming weapon steady for Dubois to ignite his own incendiary cocktail.

From his crouched position, Bernard peered around the corner of the stairwell at Boulevard Saint-Michel, where the sycamore and poplar trees that lined the broad sidewalk partially blocked his view. From afar, Michaud looked resigned to his fate, strapped to the tank turret.

He knows this isn't going to end well for him. He and Dubois had to try. They were his only chance. Even if they weren't successful in saving Michaud, then at least another Panzer tank would be taken out of commission.

The rumble of the diesel engine reverberated through the neighborhood as the Panzer III drew closer. The tank, Bernard noticed, had started to veer toward the far side of the broad boulevard, perhaps anticipating a right turn into the Sorbonne. This would make for a longer sprint—and give the tank commander more time to spot any partisans approaching from his left flank.

Bernard held up his left hand while his right gripped the flaming bottle. Louis Michaud, he noticed, happened to be looking in their direction—and their eyes locked.

We're coming to save you!

Bernard waited . . . waited . . . and at the right moment, just as the Panzer passed, he sprinted toward the moving tank. Dubois was in his wake.

Michaud was yelling something, but Bernard couldn't make it out over the noise. He raised his right arm, closing the distance between him and the Panzer. He needed to get as close as possible to the open escape hatch.

Michaud cried out, shaking his head vehemently. This time Rousseau could make out his words. "Bernard, don't! Don't throw it! It's our tank!"

Bernard paused for a split second—enough time for the tank commander to draw his sidearm and place him in his sights. The tank lurched to an awkward stop. Rousseau and Dubois froze in their tracks, holding flaming bottles in their right hands.

The tank commander, wearing a garrison cap and radio earphones, lowered his pistol and turned to the partisans.

"Michaud's right," he called in the accent of a Parisian, eyeing the burning bottle in Bernard's hand. "We stole the tank this morning. One of their Panzers has our boys pinned down at the Sorbonne. Michaud volunteered to be a hostage so we wouldn't get hit."

Bernard looked at the blazing wick—and had to get rid of the Molotov cocktail *immédiatement*. He waved Dubois to follow him, and they stepped away from the tank and tossed the Molotov cocktails curbside. Two explosions shook the ground, and he wiped the perspiration beading on his brow. Only then, Bernard released a heavy breath and watched the small explosions burn harmlessly.

Bernard slapped his hands and hustled back to the tank, realizing how close he'd come to hurting their own.

"Do you need help?" he asked Michaud.

"I'm just hanging on to these ropes until the right moment to jump off." Michaud looked like he was counting the seconds.

Bernard sized up the Panzer again. "Unbelievable. Do you guys know how to fire these things?"

The "commander" answered for Michaud. "I don't, but we've got two gunners below with tank experience. You two could help us by creating a diversion. If you have any other Molotovs, put those on the tank and walk in front. You might be able to use them yet."

Five minutes later, Rousseau and Dubois—with hands held high—walked before the stolen Panzer III into the Quartier de la Sorbonne, where a Panzer IV had parked at the end of the open square. The tank commander trained a pistol on the walking pair to maintain the ruse that Germans were in command. They were just a hundred meters away, surrounded by university buildings, when their tank came to a stop.

"The other tank is calling us on the radio," the tank commander announced from the turret.

"Don't answer it!" Bernard yelled.

"We won't, but the other tank is pleased to see us," the tank commander said. "Tanks always work in pairs, so he's probably been waiting for reinforcements before he storms the student barricades. That's a Panzer IV, which has fewer vulnerabilities."

Bernard turned back around to face the Panzer IV. From

his vantage point, the howitzer gun barrel was pointed at a nine o'clock position—toward the main student square.

The tank commander ordered Michaud to get ready to jump. The partisan loosened the knots and poised to free himself. "Thirty seconds, guys. When I give notice, run for cover."

Michaud, though he was no longer bound, remained in the hostage position. The commander crouched, and Bernard heard all sorts of bearing numbers being exchanged with the gunner, who was working to bring the main gun and sights in line with each other. The gun barrel twitched from slight adjustments.

"Allez vite!" *Go quickly!*

Michaud didn't have to be told twice. Rousseau and Dubois dropped their raised arms and bolted toward the tank hull, where they grabbed their satchels and gathered up Michaud, who had leaped to the ground. Together, the three sprinted for a nearby alcove. They had nearly reached safety when a deafening explosion rocked the Panzer III. With a white flash, the first cannon shot streaked toward the Panzer IV. The turret storage box on its rear exploded, scattering tools, sleeping rolls, rations, and even pitching underwear and uniforms into the plaza. Scraps of laundry hung from nearby tree branches.

Time stood still for a long moment until the enemy tank crew began swinging their turret in the direction of the Resistance tank. Bernard watched the scene unfold from his perch behind a column. "They're turning in our direction!"

"Reload, reload!" screamed the tank commander.

Bernard held his breath. He figured the Panzer III gunner was struggling to set the point of aim by mentally calculating the error margin. The delay only prompted more pandemonium inside the tank as shrill voices pleaded for him to fire off another shot. Precious seconds passed. The howitzer of the wounded Panzer IV continued to swing around, but the German armored vehicle didn't have the renegade tank in his sights yet.

"Shoot! Shoot!" The partisan tank commander was clearly panicking.

The "French" tank lurched as a second projectile exited the howitzer barrel—but missed completely. Bernard reached into his satchel and drew out both Molotovs.

"What are you doing?" Alarm creased Dubois' face.

A quick flick of his Zippo, and a pair of cloth strips were ablaze. Bernard set off for the Panzer IV, the voices of his comrades yelling for him to come back. He ran like the wind, closing the distance just as the Panzer IV's cannon was in position to fire. From a distance of twenty meters, he lobbed one flaming bottle after another.

The first Molotov struck the back of the turret, and the second smashed into the escape hatch, dousing the occupants within and exploding into an orange inferno.

Screams erupted from the tank's interior. The gunner, his gray uniform on fire, managed to haul himself onto the hull, then fling himself upon the concrete. He cried in agony and rolled his burning body to put out the flames.

A third projectile whistled across the square and struck the center of the German tank, underneath the caterpillar tread. The Panzer IV burst into a giant fireball. A column of flames funneled up from the open turret like a giant Roman candle. The shock wave from the blast knocked Bernard into the air. Pain shot up his arms as he tumbled to the concrete.

The partisan covered his head as chunks of metal peppered the square. Scrambling to his feet to escape the rain of shrapnel, he sprinted back toward the Panzer III, which was already backing out and turning around.

"Let's go!" the tank commander yelled over the din.

Dubois and Michaud dashed for the relative safety of Boulevard Saint-Michel.

Bernard looked downrange at the inferno. Already, several students had come out of the shadows, their arms raised to shield themselves from the searing heat—the tank now enveloped in a whirlwind of flames. They also kept their distance from the burning soldier, who—summoning his last ounce of strength—failed to tamp out the flames. His body contracted unnaturally.

The grotesque smell of charred flesh and fumed diesel wafted past Bernard. Grasping his stomach, he leaned over and disgorged his breakfast.

It was a smell he would never forget.

4

So this is Paris.

From the passenger seat, Gabi gaped at the Gothic-style churches and the cream-colored stone buildings accented with sidewalk cafés and red awnings. The spacious parks looked threadbare and left her wondering how lush the grass and flowers had been before the war.

Has God abandoned Paris? Abandoned all of us? She pushed the thoughts out of her mind as quickly as they had come. Many voices had muttered such things over the previous years. She'd heard them among her father's congregation, but she'd never allowed such foolish ideas to enter her mind, until now.

Eric took his eyes off the road and glanced over at her. It was easy to do since only the occasional delivery truck and a few bicyclists vied for space. "How are you doing?"

They had barely said two sentences to each other in the last hour.

"I feel like I'm waking up from a bad dream." Gabi's voice quivered, surprising her. She folded her hands on her lap and clenched them together. She couldn't see blood on her hands, but she could feel it. Even the anticipation and excitement of entering Paris—a city she'd wanted to visit since she was a child—hadn't gotten her mind off the brutal incident they'd just survived.

Lifting her eyes off her hands, she looked out the window, forcing herself to push the images of the dead men out of her mind. If only the ache in her heart and the pain deep in her gut would let her forget completely.

"Arriving in Paris is helping." She sighed, hoping her voice sounded convincing. "Even under the thumb of German occupation, she's still a jewel."

Gabi picked up the apple on the seat next to her—the one she'd promised Eric she'd eat but still had no appetite for. She tossed it from one hand to another. "I don't think I'll get over our run-in with those German soldiers—or Russians, or whoever they were—anytime soon."

Eric reached over and squeezed her left knee. "You did what you had to do. I was wondering how we could get to that pistol. Your quick thinking saved our lives."

She cocked her chin, repeating aloud the words that had been replaying in her mind. The words she was trying to reassure herself with. "It was him or us. That's what they taught us at the Bern firing range. I have no regrets."

Her stomach churned again, and an icy chill traveled down her spine as she remembered the man's face inches from hers, his foul breath moistening her cheek.

Willing her mind elsewhere, she turned her attention back to the passing scenery. Through the windshield, Paris seemed calm at this late-morning hour, but she wondered what lurked beneath its serene surface. The grand boulevard was framed with broad, leafy trees and fronted by soft-colored stately buildings. Shops were shuttered, and only a handful of cafés had opened, their tables dotting the sidewalks. A solitary waiter wearing a long white apron served demitasse to two customers.

She'd spotted the spindly Eiffel Tower before Eric, but her excitement was tempered by an enormous red flag with a black swastika fluttering atop the landmark, a tangible symbol of an oppressive regime shackling the spirit of the three and a half million Parisians.

That was the only Nazi swastika she'd seen so far. In this neighborhood, other flags—some tattered and faded, some homemade from bed sheets—hung from windows and rooftops. "I'm surprised to see all the French flags. I wonder when they came out of hiding."

Eric leaned out the car window and looked skyward at the numerous displays of blue, white, and red vertical stripes that had symbolized France since the Revolution of 1789. "They're definitely showing defiance. Since Hitler's armies marched in, it's been illegal to show the *tricolore*, but that's going to change."

"The French flags are a good sign. That means we're in a neighborhood controlled by the Resistance, correct?" She sat straighter in her seat.

"You'd think so. Take a look at that poster." Eric pointed toward his right.

A tall placard, plastered on a building, showed a rendering of a clenched fist with the proclamation *"A chacun son boche!"*

" 'To everyone his Kraut,' " Gabi translated. "Must be a word play off *A chacun son goût.*" To each his own taste.

Eric grunted. "They're saying it's open season on German soldiers."

Gabi shivered as memories of the road outside Rozay-en-Brie returned. Of the cool metal of the soldier's rifle tip sliding up her leg. She did what she had trained for. *They* had decided their fate.

She returned the apple to her seat and picked up the

map, trailing her finger to where they were headed—the Latin Quarter. Eric slowed their vehicle slightly as they came upon makeshift barricades the local populace had erected to stop—or at least slow—German tanks and troop trucks. The resourceful Parisians had thrown old bedsprings, refrigerators, bulky cabinets, and even kitchen sinks into the jerry-built fortifications. At the entrance to one neighborhood, a long line of women and children passed paving stones ripped up from the street to each other. Under their pile of stones, the burnt hull of a German troop truck formed the main bulwark.

Even though the citizens appeared thin and their clothes threadbare, cheeks were flushed. Mostly from the work, but also from the hope that their efforts would make a difference. Chins lifted as their vehicle passed, and tired eyes met Gabi's for a fraction of a second before they turned back to their work.

"What's that green thing?" Gabi pointed toward a rectangular stall leaning against the barricade. The rusty green edifice, which looked like an outdoor telephone booth, lay atop a barricade that included cobblestones, old furniture, and even an upright piano.

"Ah, you may not want to know. Might ruin your impression of Paris." Eric's humored smile made her want to find out even more.

"Come on." She enjoyed teasing him, especially when his cheeks colored.

"Uh, French men and German soldiers use them to relieve—"

"Got it," Gabi interrupted, then wrinkled her nose in disgust.

She returned to scanning the tired faces of Parisians who'd ventured out. More glances followed their Red Cross sedan, one of the few cars motoring down the Avenue d'Italie. The locals probably wondered what a Mercedes bearing Swiss license plates and Red Cross markings was doing in Paris. They passed an old Citroën huffing and puffing to keep up with a half-dozen bicyclists pedaling along the right-hand lane.

"That car looks as if it's about to explode."

Eric raised his eyebrows as he peered through the windshield. "That's because it's fueled by a wood-burning engine. You need a permit and plenty of money to bribe the Germans to drive a car, especially with the petrol shortage. The wood-burning conversion is the only option—unless you want to pedal a bike."

Gabi's eyes moved from the strange vehicle to the map in her lap. "We're coming up to a roundabout. Look for Boulevard Saint-Michel. It should be straight ahead."

Eric weaved his way through a half-dozen bicyclists and smoothly entered the roundabout. They swung onto the spoke leading to Boulevard Saint-Michel, which took them toward the Sorbonne.

"A left here at Rue Racine," Gabi directed.

They turned into a narrow street, where the urban fabric changed dramatically and tall buildings cast deep shadows. Gabi remembered learning about these medieval fortified houses known as *hôtels*, a French term dating back to a time when wealthy merchants sought a solution to defending their homes—or at least closing them off from the street. The residences were built with walls and buildings that lined the edges of the property, leaving a courtyard in the middle.

The address led them to a two-story gated wall. An older man with gray frizzy hair stepped out onto the street to greet their car.

"The Red Cross?" he said, stating the obvious.

"Yes, we're here to deliver medical supplies," Eric replied.

"Password?"

"La gloire de Paris," Eric said. *The glory of Paris.* "And yours?"

"Jean has a long moustache."

Eric chuckled. "Glad you heard our coded message on Radio London." He thrust his right hand through the car window and exchanged a brief handshake.

"Right this way, monsieur." The guard whistled, and a massive gate opened, revealing an arched passage that opened to a courtyard and an imposing four-story residence.

A pair of men dressed in sweat-stained shirts and long pants watched Eric steer the Mercedes into the large courtyard—where he was shocked to see a Panzer tank pointing at him. Eric's heart pounded and his fingers stretched, preparing to go for his pistol. Then his eyes darted to the faces of the men, whose eyes drooped in weariness. Only then did he relax, guessing the tank to be booty.

With a cigarette dangling from his lip and a carbine slung over his shoulder, one of the men lazily gestured for him to park next to the tank. Eric lifted his hand in affirmation and slid the Red Cross vehicle between the Panzer and some rusting bicycles. In the shadow of the tank, a small flock of chickens flapped their wings and scattered for safety.

Eric hopped out and opened the car door for Gabi. They approached the unshaven freedom fighters, who each wore soiled navy berets and looked like they hadn't slept in a week. Their brimless felt caps were nonetheless swept jauntily to one side.

The taller one approached Eric. "Welcome to Paris. I'm

Bernard Rousseau, and this is Alain Dubois. I believe you know who we are, correct?"

"Yes, Mr. Dulles filled us in." Eric regarded Bernard, dressed like a scarecrow in fraying olive green pants and matching long-sleeved shirt. Four years of lean rations had left a gaunt face under a beak nose. His sallow brown eyes, however, contained a spark that spoke of quiet optimism.

"The Panzer was a surprise greeting." Eric gestured toward the long-barreled tank marked with an Iron Cross. "Where did that come from?"

"We liberated the German tank this morning." Rousseau exchanged a knowing look with Dubois. "Almost out of fuel, though. You have the supplies of medicine?"

Before Eric could answer, the faint sound of church bells pealed in the distance. All four tilted their heads and perked their ears.

"Mon Dieu." Bernard's cigarette dropped from his gaping mouth as he crossed himself. "We haven't heard church bells since . . . the Occupation began."

"Not even for Christmas or Easter?" Gabi asked.

"Not once. Turns out the Nazis aren't very religious. The only assemblies they ordain are those in front of firing squads. But the bells can mean only one thing . . ." Emotion caused the man's voice to tremble.

He didn't need to finish. Eric understood. The people were winning the streets, and neighborhoods were being liberated.

Bernard found his voice again. "The *boches* must be retreating like stuck pigs." He slapped his palms together, clearly more energized than a moment ago. "But the fighting is sure to be heavy. Let's get these medicines unloaded now!"

Rousseau unshouldered his rifle, as did Dubois. Together, the four of them returned to the car, where Eric opened the sedan's trunk. Four crates stuffed with medicines and supplies were cached inside. He handed out each crate one by one. The two partisans stacked them outside the entrance.

"We have one more small gift for you." Eric reached inside the trunk for a small tool chest. Then he sat down in the driver's seat and turned toward the inside door panel. Rousseau and Dubois moved for a closer look. Eric loosened a series of screws until he could pull down the top of the door panel. The cavity was crammed with stacks of French francs and American dollars, each wrapped in a rubber band.

"Gabi, can you get my backpack? It should be on the backseat."

Gabi handed it to him, and Eric deposited the bundles of cash into the leather-lined bag.

"Sacré bleu. Where did you get—?" Bernard, clearly astonished, left the sentence unfinished. Color filled his weary face.

"Don't ask, but we almost didn't make it here."

"How so?" Though Rousseau raised the question, he and Dubois' eyes were fixed on the stacks of bills that Eric jammed into his backpack.

"We had a run-in this morning with some German soldiers, except they were Polish or Russian." Eric clucked his tongue. "Let's just say they weren't looking to see if our travel documents were in order."

"What happened?" Bernard's eyes finally moved to Eric's, a look of concern clouding his face.

"Gabi saved us." Eric's hands paused, and he fingered a bundle. He again questioned whether he should have let Dulles talk him into bringing her to Paris.

He shook his head. "Quite a story, and I assure you that they are no longer a threat." His words sounded cockier than he felt.

"I understand this problem. We've heard about those Ost soldiers." Bernard reached for a pack of cigarettes, placing one in the corner of his mouth. "Extremely unpredictable. The German officers put them in front-line trenches and shoot any man leaving his post. Caged, wild animals, every one of them."

As Bernard spoke, both anger and pain filled his gaze. Anger Eric understood, but the pain? There could be a thousand reasons for the emotion. Memories the freedom fighters carried with them were no doubt equally as graphic and painful as he and Gabi had just experienced.

Eric was nearly finished fishing out the francs and dollars from the door when Gabi cleared her throat.

"Excuse me, but are you in charge here, Monsieur Rousseau?" Her eyes were fixed on his.

The Resistance leader gave a slight nod and pulled at his navy beret.

Gabi pursed her lips. "We were instructed to convey a message along with the money and medicines. The message could not be written down. We must deliver it verbally." Gabi looked over to Eric and then back to Rousseau.

Bernard flipped the lid of a silver lighter and lit his cigarette. "Please continue," he said, blowing a line of smoke to the side.

"Do you still have the capability to pass along messages to your leaders?"

"The Resistance works through various networks, but I'm part of the senior leadership."

"What I have to say may not be what you or the Resistance want to hear."

Bernard stroked his stubbly beard. "And who's the message from?"

"The highest levels of the United States military." Gabi

paused for dramatic effect. Then she plunged ahead. "First of all, the Allies do not want to be pulled into bare-knuckle street battles to dislodge the German garrison. That would be destroying a city in order to save it. The plan from General Eisenhower at Supreme Headquarters is for the Allied armies to bypass Paris and drive for Germany. Let the Nazis chase after them." She spoke with confidence.

Eric held his breath, anticipating Bernard's response. Anger flashed on his face, just as Eric had expected. Somehow the medicine and cash they'd just unloaded seemed like a paltry offering compared to what these men needed.

"That's crazy!" Bernard growled. "Paris will become a mound of rubble, a diamond smashed into a thousand pieces. Surely this General Eisenhower can be persuaded that history will severely judge such a folly—"

Eric broke in, lifting his hands as if to calm the man. "Here's how Dulles explained it to me. If the Allies were to rush into Paris, there would be firefights in the streets, and that would favor the Occupation force. They know these streets, they are well-armed, and they can make use of fortified defensive positions. Even if the Allies rushed in, they do not have enough food and petrol to supply Paris. Those critical supplies are earmarked for Patton's tanks, which are sweeping across the plains south of the city and driving for Germany at this moment. We beg you to keep your powder dry for a little bit longer."

Bernard held up his right hand. "*C'est impossible*. You can't stop us from throwing out the *boches*. The situation will come to a head very soon."

"Tell the Resistance leaders to wait," Eric continued. "Our intelligence tells us that the German garrison is 20,000 strong. A full-scale rebellion means they'd have open season to destroy this beautiful city block by block. It would be a bloodbath."

"No!" Bernard pulled his beret from his head, balling it in his fist. "They must die. They must pay!" The pain in his voice was fresh. His loss was an open wound.

Gabi took a step closer to Bernard. She dared to place a soft hand on his arm. "Learn from the Warsaw Uprising. At this very moment, Polish insurgents are being crushed underfoot by their German captors, who are defending 'Fortress Warsaw' and counterattacking the Russian Army."

"We heard the same thing from the German propagandists," Bernard conceded.

"So you know," Gabi whispered. "The Warsaw Uprising started three weeks ago with high hopes, but the Nazis are ruthless. They're torching neighborhoods, mowing down civilians. I fear Warsaw is a model for how Hitler's armies will leave nothing but dead bodies and scorched earth behind."

Eric caught the look between Rousseau and Dubois that revealed how they thought things would be different in Paris. He reached out and placed a hand on Gabi's back, urging her to continue. Pride again filled him at how capable she was for a young woman in her mid-twenties—and how dedicated. Even though she was shaken from today's events, he knew it would not hinder her from performing the task she'd been asked to do.

She glanced to him and then pointed toward the western horizon. "You need proof? Take a look at the smoke. Who knows what that's from? German reinforcements could be pouring into the Parisian neighborhoods where those church towers may have heralded *libération* a bit too prematurely. I wouldn't put it past them."

Bernard effected a wan smile. "I'll pass your message up the ladder, but nothing's going to change. Our leader, Colonel Rol, declared that 'Paris is worth 200,000 dead.' That's how far the Resistance is willing to push to rid ourselves of this national humiliation."

Eric regarded Bernard's confident body language, which confirmed his belief that the liberation of Paris was part of his destiny. Like the sound of a clanging church bell that could not be unrung, he knew there was no turning back for Rousseau and his Resistance members.

5

The impact of the shovel echoed in Colette's mind, and she grabbed the stair railing and paused. She stared at the marble step before her, knowing if she closed her eyes, she'd see it again—the sight of hedge shears being yanked from the major's back.

Throughout four years of German rule, she'd heard stories of war, about the bloodletting and barbarous battles. She'd heard about men who'd received a worse fate, but never so near. She covered her mouth and nose with a quivering hand, sure the scent of blood was still in the air.

You have to get ahold of yourself. Those men are no longer a threat. But that was only half of her worries. As Paris was drawing closer and closer to liberation, she wondered if other high-ranking German officers would have the same idea of pillaging the Louvre of her priceless artwork while they still had the chance.

Will I be able to handle their request so calmly next time? She had to believe she would react in the same way. She longed for the hour when she could relax and release the breath she seemed to have been holding for years.

She continued up the marble staircase, and with each

footstep she felt her composure returning and confidence building. Years of kowtowing to the Germans would soon be over, and life would return to some semblance of normalcy.

When she opened the door to her office, Anne jumped out of her chair to greet her.

"You poor thing!" Anne reached out and pulled her close, and Colette felt her body slump. She expected tears to come, but they didn't.

She pulled back from Anne and pressed both hands to her temples. "The sound. It was horrific—"

"Don't say anything. Push that out of your mind. It had to be done," Anne rambled. "Here, have a cup of tea." She poured her a cup from the ceramic teapot.

Colette sipped her lukewarm tea and could tell that her fellow curator had doubled up on the honey. "That's very nice of you," she replied unconsciously, lost in thought. Colette was no innocent when it came to man's inhumanity to man. She had seen the same themes in the works she cared for. The artists of the past understood the human condition—the desire to conquer and subjugate others.

Anne's voice startled her out of her reverie. "Monsieur Rambouillet wants to see us. We saw the entire incident from his office. When I'd heard you'd used the Monsieur Monet alert code, I feared for what would happen next."

"If only Bernard was there. When it wasn't his voice on the phone, I feared—well, I could barely walk across the palace courtyard. I knew that the German major wouldn't hesitate to kill us. When he fired a shot in the hallway, I was sure both of us were next."

"They are dead and gone, thank goodness. Let's not dwell on it. You showed great courage."

"*Merci*. That's very nice of you." Colette sat at her desk, feeling the strength that had carried her up the stairs ebbing away. She lifted the cup with both hands. "Give me a moment, and then we'll go see Monsieur Rambouillet." Though Anne had encouraged her not to dwell on the incident, she did not see the cup of tea before her eyes but rather the dark red pool of blood seeping from the major's skull.

A few minutes later, after informing Anne that she was ready, the pair walked together into the senior curator's spacious and well-appointed office. A light cabaret tune hummed from a mahogany-cased radio perched on his desk, its bouncy tune conflicting with the dull pain filling her chest.

Rambouillet reached over and lowered the volume, then hurried around his desk, opening his arms wide to embrace Colette. "You saved my life. When that *boche* officer walked into my office and waved his Luger in my face, I thought today would be my last. You followed the plan to perfection."

The music stopped, and Colette pulled back from his embrace, turning her head to the radio. Perhaps there was an announcement forthcoming from the German Ministry of Propaganda. The Germans still held control of the major radio stations in Paris, and everybody knew what the announcers *didn't* say was more telling than what they *did* report. Usually the pronouncements on the radio were the opposite of what was really happening.

Rambouillet raised the volume in time to hear the familiar voice of Roger Villion, the infamous collaborator, echoing through the speaker:

> The following is an important announcement: The authorities are appealing for calm. Do not believe the rumors that you are hearing on the streets. You are urged to stay inside your homes, where you will be safe.

Rambouillet lowered the volume as an accordion-driven folk song came on. "My brother called ten minutes ago. A friend told him that French tanks were seen passing through Porte St. Cloud."

Colette's lips parted. Porte St. Cloud was on the south-western periphery of Paris. "French tanks? I thought the Americans were coming to rescue us."

"At this point, who cares? This really could be it." Rambouillet smiled at the women. His eyes narrowed into thin half-moons as his cheeks pressed upward. "I know. What can you believe? But this one makes sense to me. The Métro shut down an hour ago, so something major must be happening."

"Great news." Anne clasped her hands together, a wide grin brightening her face. "Just to think, after all this time—"

"No time to celebrate yet." Colette tucked a wayward curl behind her ear. "Until we see that swastika come down at the Hôtel Meurice, the Germans are still in charge."

"I agree." Rambouillet strode back to his desk and pressed his hands on the surface. "Which means you must leave."

"Leave? But why?" Colette felt the weakening of her knees once again. To stand up to the German major was hard enough, but walking away was impossible.

"You know how it is with informants these days," Rambouillet stated. "Someone could have called the Germans and told them about today's incident in the courtyard. The *boches* pay good money for information like that. Whom can you trust?"

He glanced to his window. "I don't think we should take any chances. It's more dangerous for all of us—and for the art—if you remain here. You need to leave now."

Colette reacted with mixed feelings. On one hand, it was the best plan for her personal safety, but then again, it was her job to be here. She didn't want to leave the Louvre at this momentous time in history.

"You said the Métro stopped running. I'd have to walk,

and who knows how safe the streets are." Colette hoped that sounded like a good enough excuse for her to stay.

"That's why I'm authorizing Anne to go with you. We can't take the chance of a German staff car pulling up to the front door looking for a missing major. I'm requesting this for your safety as well as ours."

Colette realized that she couldn't put her colleagues at risk. She looked at Anne, who nodded. "I'll go get my things."

Five minutes later, Colette and Anne stepped outside the Louvre's front entrance. The courtyard was deserted. The museum had been officially closed all week because of the wartime uncertainty.

Colette scanned the horizon, marred by a thin film of smoke. She noticed a piece of white paper, burned black around the edges, floating to the ground. Looking skyward, a light rain of ash fell from the hazy sky.

"My place?" Colette asked.

"I don't think that's a good idea. You're more than a ninety-minute walk away. Same as me. I doubt we'll find anyone to give us a ride on the Rue de Rivoli. It's like everyone has disappeared."

Colette's face brightened. "My mother lives off the Rue de Madrid in the 8th arrondissement. No more than forty-five minutes on foot. But we'd have to walk in the vicinity of the Hôtel Meurice." She bit her lip, knowing they'd pass by the heart of the German command. "I don't think anyone will bother us if we stay in the Tuileries Gardens."

"Good idea. And we wouldn't know what we'd run into if we took a detour."

The two women departed the Louvre courtyard, linked arm in arm, in the direction of Napoleon's Arc de Triomphe du Carrousel. They passed by the monument and continued along the gravel pathways into the Tuileries Gardens, staying on the left side of the park, parallel the Seine.

Barely a ripple moved across the river's emerald-colored surface. Barges, flat-bottomed boats, and Bateaux Mouches—the famous open-air tourist boats that roamed the Seine—were cinched tight to their moorings. The dozens of love-struck couples who normally lingered along the banks were absent.

Anne followed her gaze toward the empty stone embankments. "You miss him, don't you?"

"How did you—?" Then again, Anne knew she and Bernard often sought solitude along the Seine during long lunch breaks.

"I haven't seen Bernard all week." Colette swallowed hard, attempting to hold down her emotions. "I'm worried sick."

Anne drew Colette's arm closer, patting it. "I'm sure you'll hear from him soon."

They continued along the southern outline of the Tuileries Gardens, the largest and oldest public park in Paris. Colette looked through a cluster of deciduous trees toward the octagonal Grand Basin. No mothers had taken their children out to play with their small wooden sailboats, not on a day like this.

Many of the green lawns had turned to dirt. Brown weeds infested the formal flowerbeds. Straggled new growth splayed from the famed hedges that outlined each rectangular quadrant of the park. Through the hazy air, she spotted a tendril of smoke rising from the Hôtel Meurice not far away.

Then the sound of idling diesel engines caught her ear. She studied the source of the noise, and up ahead a half-dozen Panzers formed a phalanx in front of the Hôtel Meurice. Several German troop carriers were parked in the gardens. Others were positioned across from the front entrance to the hotel.

Colette stopped in her tracks. "You see what I see?"

"Yeah. I've never seen troop trucks parked there before."

"Or so many tanks on the Rue de Rivoli."

Anne paused, clutching Colette's arm. "I don't know about this. Maybe we should go back. Find another way—"

Colette considered returning. Surely someone would be looking for the major by now. Her throat tightened as if squeezed by an invisible noose. She patted Anne's hand and took another step forward. "No one's going to bother a couple of women in the middle of the afternoon."

Against Anne's protest, the two continued past the disheveled gardens, hooded by broad centennial chestnut trees. There was no sign of activity near the troop carriers, but as they drew closer to the Hôtel Meurice, she saw soldiers exiting the lobby and carrying boxes—toward a bonfire. Soldiers one by one dumped reams of paper into the flames.

"You see that, Anne? The Germans are packing up—"

"Qu'est-ce que vous faites ici?" A sharp voice split the air. *What are you doing here?*

Colette turned in the direction of the voice and gasped at the sight of a rifle pointed at her heart. Anne, momentarily frozen, squeezed her arm in fright.

"Qu'est-ce que vous faites ici?" the soldier repeated in a horrible French accent. "Vous êtes des espions, non?" *You're spies, aren't you?*

Colette sucked in a breath. Her legs urged her to turn, to run. Instead, she transformed her mask of concern into a warm smile. "Ist das wie Sie alle jungen Damen des Reiches behandeln?" *Is that how you treat all young ladies of the Reich?*

The soldier lowered his carbine. "You're Germans?"

"Yes. My friend here"—she nodded toward Anne, whom she could tell didn't understand a word—"and I are on holiday in Paris. We were supposed to leave Sunday, but things have been rather chaotic. All trains are canceled to Germany. So what should we do? And what about the bonfire?" Colette nodded in the direction of the plume of smoke.

The soldier's gaze fixed on her, and she broadened her smile. Though her heart pounded in her chest, she mimicked the flirtatious looks of the American movie stars she'd seen in the cinema.

Gradually the soldier's look turned to one of interest. Of protection.

"The only thing I know is that we were ordered to burn documents and keep our eyes alert. It's getting more dangerous by the minute. I wish I could walk you back to your hotel. It's not safe."

Colette placed a hand over her heart, feigning horror. "Have the Allies arrived?"

"They don't tell us anything. Just that it's dangerous to be wearing a German uniform on the street. Listen, you need to seek shelter. We could be attacked any minute by Sherman tanks."

Colette turned to Anne. "Let's go back to our hotel," she said in German, knowing her friend understood the universal word *hotel* and not much more. Anne, lips sealed, nodded her approval.

"Good, then it's decided." She thanked the soldier, and they retraced their steps. When enough distance had been put between them and the German troop carriers, Colette spoke in French.

"I told him we were Germans on holiday. We better return to the Louvre. The *boches* have better things to do than worry about a German officer going AWOL. I'll feel safer there." The worries over the possibility of someone coming to the Louvre now paled compared to the fear Colette experienced facing the soldier.

"No argument from me," Anne replied. "The sooner we're in the palace, the sooner I can start breathing normal again. Besides, there are plenty of places to hide within those walls."

"You're back."

Colette and Anne stood inside Monsieur Rambouillet's office.

"It's getting crazy out there." Colette removed her scarf and folded it in her hands as she related the unexpected confrontation with the German soldier in Tuileries Gardens.

"Thinking quickly on your feet has served you well today. Perhaps it's fortuitous that the both of you returned. Radio France is back on the air."

"Radio France?" Colette's eyes widened. How long had it been since she'd heard a friendly voice over the airwaves? Too long.

Rambouillet reached over and turned up the volume on the radio. "Parisians, rejoice! You will soon be liberated!" a voice shrieked in joy. "A column of tanks led by General Leclerc just passed through—"

A burst of static cut off the transmission. Rambouillet tapped the radio several times in frustration. "Radio France has been in and out since it returned to the airwaves, but our season of shame will soon be over."

Liberation! She squealed and hugged Anne.

Warmth flickered inside Colette, as if the rays of sun shining through the window had pooled in her chest. With a deep chuckle, Rambouillet wrapped his arms around them both.

"This time it's true." Colette's words released as a breath, otkeysoningand she wiped the tears that had started to pool on her lower eyelids.

"I really do think so," Rambouillet replied. "Perhaps the next voice we hear will be that of the man representing the new French government." He chuckled again. "We've nearly made it."

It was the word "nearly" that caused a thousand needles to travel up Colette's spine. *Surely the worst is over now . . .*

Back in her office, Colette's emotions rose and fell like the English Channel on a stormy day. Hope battled with fear. Uncertainty threatened to drown out excitement. She opened the file in front of her and then closed it again. It was impossible to focus. She turned her mind to the most interesting task on her desk, hoping that would do the trick.

Seeing the file marked "Salle des États Exhibitions," she set her mind on a new course. Very soon the priceless treasures that had been scattered across France would be brought back. The minor pieces now on display would return to basement vaults for storage and reassignment—which meant many of the world's greatest paintings would once again fill the grand halls.

A few weeks ago, when it became apparent that the Allies had finally broken out of hedgerow country and were moving west steadily, Monsieur Rambouillet had asked her to select paintings that would join the *Mona Lisa* in the Salle des États. What paintings should go on her left and her right? What mix of paintings would enhance the *Mona Lisa* experience rather than detract from her smile?

Colette had eight pieces in mind. They were Old Masters that deserved to be in the same room as the genius of Leonardo da Vinci.

83

A distant telephone ring pulled her back. After the third ring, Anne looked up from her typewriter. "Do you want me to get that for you?"

"No, I'll take the call." Colette picked up the black handset. "Allô? Mademoiselle Perriard."

"You may continue to speak in French in case anyone is in the office with you," a male voice said *en français*. "But I will now speak in our mother tongue."

The voice from Germany was weak over the static. She was surprised that phone service between Paris and the outside world was still possible.

"Oui, monsieur. Continuez." The warmth in her chest seeped out, and an icy chill filled its place.

"You know who this is, yes?" the distinctive voice said in German.

"Oui, monsieur."

"Then I will get to the point since we cannot be sure how long the connection will hold. We are entering an era of great uncertainty, but my colleagues and I desire to continue our relationship. The Reichsmarschall asked me to tell you that since the situation is more fluid, he is willing to reward your cooperation in a more tangible sense."

"Oui, monsieur. D'accord." She tightened the grip on the handset, anger pounding in her temples.

Got it. Instead of threatening to arrest and torture Bernard, you're going to bribe me.

"You will hear from us soon. I wish you a pleasant day." The static-filled phone line suddenly clicked.

Colette set the phone down, a bit dazed.

"Who was that?" Anne came around to her desk.

"My landlord. He said a German tank is roaming the neighborhood, so I should stay away."

Anne bought the story. "That was nice of him."

"Very nice."

Colette bit her lip and lowered her head. She'd assumed when Paris was liberated, Colonel Heller would be out of her life forever.

She was wrong.

6

Bernard Rousseau's quotation from Colonel Rol echoed through Gabi's mind: Paris is worth 200,000 dead.

She released her fists, attempting to comprehend the Resistance leader's words. She couldn't imagine such destruction, such loss.

If you just sit back and wait, she wanted to tell him, *the Allies will come.*

Yet she knew her words would go unheeded. A sense of urgency crackled through the Paris courtyard, and the fixed gazes of the men told her their minds were set. They would fight for their city, for their pride.

"Let's get these crates inside." Bernard picked up the first box of medical supplies, and Gabi grabbed a box and fell in step behind the others, telling herself to be strong. The Frenchmen and Eric hefted the packed cases of medicines and bandages and mounted a set of stairs leading into the imposing entrance, dominated by a pair of marble columns. She kept pace behind them.

Bernard led them inside a foyer that opened to a long hallway. "This is my aunt and uncle's place." The first door to the left was slightly ajar, which Bernard propped open with his foot. He motioned them inside the anteroom, where they set their boxes next to his.

Gabi looked at her dirty hands. She still felt the soldier's sweat on her skin and swallowed down disgust. "Where can I wash up?"

"Down the hall and second door on your right." Bernard held up his hand. "Let me direct you."

She followed him to a hallway door, and as Bernard opened it, the odor of barnyard assaulted her. A half-dozen cages filled with roosters and hens were haphazardly stacked in one corner. Two wooden cages, lying on a bed of tawny straw, filled the porcelain claw-foot bathtub. Gabi counted a half-dozen white and gray rabbits inside.

Bernard stuck a finger through the cage and scratched the furry forehead of a rabbit with a frosty white coat and black rings around his eyes. "Each morning, the older ladies chop a few forbidden blades of grass at a nearby park. It's all we can do to keep our menagerie alive. When they don't make it . . . into the soup pot they go. With the rationing, at least it's protein."

He offered a low chuckle. "We joke that our meat rations are so small that you can wrap them with a Métro ticket, as long as it hasn't been punched. Otherwise, the meat will fall through."

Gabi smiled and nodded in understanding. She thought about the few times a month when they had enough butter to spread on Mother's baked bread. "We have rationing in Switzerland for butter, eggs, and that sort of thing."

"We hear about the Swiss rations. In Paris, we get two eggs, 100 grams of cooking oil, 100 grams of margarine, and a kilo of flour each month. Sugar is nonexistent. For many of us, the staple is boiled rutabaga. Before the war, rutabaga was cattle feed. I've lost ten kilos since Hitler danced his jig at Compiègne." Bernard patted his flat stomach for emphasis.

When Gabi finished washing up, she found everyone in an oversized dining room, where three women occupied a rectangular table topped with empty wine bottles, corked flasks, and strips of shirts. Copies of collaborationist newspapers rested next to underground flyers blaring the war-cry headline "Aux Barricades!" *To the Barricades!*

"Our weapons factory," Bernard announced. "If there's one item we'll never run out of, it's empty wine bottles. These Molotov cocktails are quite effective against German Panzers, except when they tie one of our own to the gun turret."

"Seriously?" Eric inquired.

With a twinkle in his tired eyes, Bernard relayed the morning's drama.

After listening, Gabi approached the women at the table, taking an empty spot. The pungent smell of turpentine permeated the dining room. She watched as one woman poured a liquid into an empty wine bottle and stopped it with a cork. Then a strip of cloth was dipped into a bowl of the same liquid and tied to the bottle's neck.

"All you have to do is light the rag, toss the bottle at the tank, and *whoosh*, you're in business," Rousseau said. "We heard about them from the Finns, who put them to good use against the Russians and Commissar Molotov earlier in the war. Now we're doing the same. Otherwise, we'd be attacking the Germans with our bare hands. Look at our weapons, such as they are."

Gabi and Eric redirected their attention toward the far corner, where a dozen rifles were loosely stacked.

"We fight with what we can," Bernard said. "Rusty rifles from the Great War, even muskets from the days of

Napoleon III. And our ammunition supplies are dreadfully low. Without our fire bombs, we're no match against Panzers and machine gun nests."

Gabi noticed a house safe perched at one end of the long table. "Where did you get the Bauche Brevete safe?"

Bernard's eyes widened. "How do you know the make and model? Women are more interested in silk stockings than in security safes." He leaned forward, eyes fixed on her curiously.

Gabi smiled to herself.

"Not all women." She regarded her nails, then met his gaze once more. "My grandfather was a locksmith. So where did you find this classic?"

Bernard removed his beret and ran his right hand through his jet-black hair. "We pilfered the strongbox from the Jardin du Luxembourg. It was in a Nazi accounting office, and we thought it might contain cash. We haven't figured out how to open it."

Gabi looked at Eric, who rubbed a slight smirk from his face. She approached the cast-iron safe and gave its combination dial a gentle spin. "Mind if I try?"

An incredulous Bernard waved his arm like a Moulin Rouge maître d' sweeping a showroom. "Please, be my guest."

Gabi leaned her ear against the combination dial and concentrated. All eyes turned to her as a hush fell over the room. She turned the dial slowly to the right, her eyes closed and her ears detecting vibrations to reveal whether she had "hit" either side of the notch on the wheel. This particular model, though, was a safecracker's delight: each click was confirmed by a tactile lurch in the wheel. In less than two minutes, she stood up.

Bernard grinned. "Too tough for you?"

"I don't think so. Let me know if you find any silk stockings inside." Gabi reached down and pulled the lever handle, and with a hard metallic clunk, the safe door swung open, accompanied with an immediate burst of applause from the women around the table. The safe, the size of an artisan breadbasket, was crammed with folders bound with thin brown strings.

Bernard, nonplussed for a moment, theatrically bowed and reached into the safe to retrieve the contents. "You're one beautiful surprise after another."

The Frenchman sorted through the stack. "Unfortunately, no money or stockings." Scanning the folders, he mused, "I recognize German efficiency, but I don't recognize the German words."

"May I?" Gabi held out her hand and received the folders from Bernard. "The first one is a list of purchase orders for what appears to be artwork."

Thumbing through the stack, she paused. "Now here's something that may be of interest." She pulled a folder from the stack labeled *Informanten*—informants—and extracted five or six pages, which were filled with columns for names, addresses, and telephone numbers. "Looks like a long census."

She handed the sheaf of papers to Bernard, who scanned the column of names. Watching him, she could tell he recognized a few. Then his finger paused on one name.

She barely detected his whisper.

"It can't be . . ."

Suddenly, an explosion rattled the windows, followed by distant bursts of small arms fire. Then the sound of heavy footsteps as Dubois stormed into the room. "A German troop truck has smashed one of our barricades a few blocks over! They could be heading here next!"

Bernard jerked into action. "Everyone out!" The room was filled with bodies in motion, then the sound of more partisans descending three flights of stairs coming toward them. A half-dozen beret-wearing Resistance members bolted inside, grabbing up rifles, boxes of ammunition, and each a Molotov cocktail or two.

"Wait—what about the files?" Gabi gripped them in her hands.

"And your money?" Eric took the backpack off his shoulder.

"Leave everything on the table—with them!" Bernard motioned toward the three women, who were hurriedly packing Molotov cocktails in wine crates. "I trust them with my life. We have to help!"

As they swept up their belongings, Gabi glanced back at the empty safe. There was something about this Bauche Brevete that caught her eye.

"Let's go!" Eric waved his arm. "They're waiting!"

"Just a second." Gabi's eyes quickly scanned the interior of the safe as the older women dispensed freshly made Molotov cocktails to partisans rushing down the hallway.

She reached inside and knocked on the base . . . detecting a false bottom.

"What are you doing?" Eric asked, waiting impatiently.

Gabi's fingers worked the slider, and underneath the lid she discovered a small book. It was black, the size of her palm.

She slipped the thin volume into the pocket of her dress and ran toward Eric. Grabbing his hand, they sprinted out of the main building.

By now, a dozen Resistance members had gathered in the courtyard, each gripping small arms and Molotov cocktails.

"Where's the patrol, Dubois?"

"They're gathering like cockroaches near the Pont Saint-Michel. Perhaps they're heading our way, or maybe they're going over to the Sorbonne after what happened this morning. I'm not sure how long our comrades can hold out."

Gabi's heart raced. The French call to rush the roadblocks—"Aux barricades!"—and her sense of duty meant they had to do *something*, even if it was manning the rear guard or tending to the wounded. "We're coming with you," she announced, her jaw set. "We can help with first aid."

The Resistance leader shrugged. "It's very dangerous on the streets. I am concerned for your safety."

"It's dangerous *anywhere* in Paris. A tank shell could come through that window any second."

"Too true," Bernard agreed.

Gabi regarded Eric. He gestured his support with a slight nod.

Bernard reached for a knapsack filled with first aid supplies. "À chacun son boche," he said quietly as he led them out of the courtyard.

To everyone his Kraut.

7

Gabi slipped her hand into Eric's grasp before the Swiss couple reached the two-story entry gate, which opened onto Rue Racine. She needed the reassuring touch of his calloused fingers wrapped around hers.

Eric paused just inside the gate and turned to her. "Are you sure you want to do this?"

Gabi closed her eyes for the briefest second. She opened them and looked over his shoulder to the smoke rising in the distance. Then her eyes darted to his gaze—seeing the concern there.

"Yes, I'm ready." She took a step forward, leading him through the gate. The prospect of participating in Paris's liberation was dangerous, but the desire to help those who had been suffering for so long propelled her beyond the safety of the courtyard.

A dozen Resistance members fanned into the neighborhood, sprinting along Rue Racine and turning left at Boulevard Saint-Michel.

A concussive boom ricocheted off the Baroque-style buildings. Gabi flinched, and Eric instinctively tightened his grasp of her hand. Together, they searched the lilac-colored sky. The hazy canopy grew smokier by the minute.

"They're heading north," Bernard explained. Then he described where the grand boulevard transformed into a bridge connecting the Left Bank with the Île de la Cité, the island home of the Notre Dame Cathedral. "Word on the street is a Panzer's attacking a partisan barricade in the area."

Rousseau, clutching a rifle in his left hand, tossed a cigarette into the gutter. "Sounds like that Panzer is knocking over some china at Pont Saint-Michel."

"Is that where we're headed?" Gabi whispered to Eric. She tried to picture facing off with a Panzer. A shudder moved down her spine.

"We can always turn around—"

"No, I want to help." Gabi locked eyes with Eric, searching for his thoughts.

"If the situation is too dangerous, or Bernard says we have to go back, that's what we'll do."

They looked back to Bernard, hunkered down by a brick wall and peering around the corner. "Stay low and follow me," the Frenchman said.

When they reached Boulevard Saint-Michel, rifle-toting citizens darted behind the broad trunks of poplar trees lining each side. There was no rhyme or reason to their movements, but that was the nature of urban warfare. Through the leafy environs, she couldn't see the German tank.

"Just a few blocks up." Bernard jerked his head toward the Seine. "Maybe one of our Molotov cocktails will get him and we won't need these medicines." The Resistance leader adjusted the shoulder pack he'd stuffed with bandages and sulfa drugs—just in case.

As the threesome set off, Gabi sensed the mood of the city had changed. Despite the defiant gestures of tattered and improvised French flags hanging from windowsills, a menacing and sullen air hung over Paris like a gathering thunderstorm.

The grand city was past the point of no return, and events were unfolding exactly as Dulles had predicted: pitched battles between a lightly armed but determined local populace with everything to lose, and a well-equipped but morale-whipped Occupation force. No one had expected the insurrection to play out for nearly a week. The lives of thousands of Parisians, and their treasured city, hung in the balance, especially if the Americans bypassed Paris in a race for the Rhine.

Gabi reminded herself to breathe as they crept along Boulevard Saint-Michel, ducking into doorways and storefronts. In the murky distance, popping sounds of small arms fire competed against the intermittent bursts of a machine gun. Judging by the sounds of the pitched battle, they were only a few hundred meters away.

Bernard stopped to catch his breath. "We set up one of our biggest barricades at the end of Boulevard Saint-Michel, where it meets up with the Quai Saint-Michel."

They continued their advance, and ten minutes later, Gabi got her first good look at a barricade composed of paving stones, bedsprings, hutches, dining room tables, and the like. Behind the makeshift barrier, a dozen men—many cradling hunting rifles or clutching pistols—clustered behind a gimcrack fortification that reached only two meters high.

Gabi and the two men approached within fifty meters and huddled inside the alcove of an abandoned flower shop. Several minutes passed without gunfire. Bernard looked around the corner, then motioned for Gabi and Eric to follow him. Shoulders hunched, they sprinted for the relative safety of the barricade, crouching behind a heavy wooden tabletop.

"Who's in charge?" Rousseau barked.

A young man with curly blond hair and pink cheeks that glowed with adolescent fervor looked back toward the new arrivals. "I am."

Gabi looked around. Every partisan appeared as young as her twin brothers serving in the Swiss Army. They had to be students at the Sorbonne.

Bernard eyed him. "Status report?"

"Several partisans ambushed a troop carrier with Molotovs. Direct hit on the engine. The *boches* ran and hid behind the walls on the Île. A Panzer tried to rescue them, but our Molotovs forced him to keep a healthy distance. Then the Panzer backed up and disappeared. Everyone was wondering if he might do an end-around on our position, so I sent a runner into the neighborhood. We haven't seen the tank since—"

The unmistakable metallic sound of tank tread devouring pavement caused the discussion to stop in its tracks. The Panzer had returned and was advancing slowly along the Quai Saint-Michel, a frontage boulevard that paralleled the Seine.

"Here he comes!" The young leader pointed toward the advancing Panzer.

Gabi looked up to see one of the partisans, a schoolboy no older than seventeen or eighteen, picking his way to the top of the barricade. He poked his head above the firing line.

Just then, rapid machine-gun fire shattered the calm. Gabi watched in horror as blood splattered around them. The boy's arms raised in the air as he tumbled back, hitting the paving stones and exposing the remnants of his shattered skull.

Gabi stifled a scream and was the first to reach the young man. Her stomach lurched at his shocked, lifeless expression.

She felt a hand on her shoulder. She didn't look up to see who was there, but he handed her an overcoat, which she draped over his pale face and the growing pool of dark blood.

———

More gunfire sounded, plinking the top of the barricade. The men ducked and made themselves the smallest targets possible.

"Where are the Molotovs?" one of the commandos screamed. "Panzer dead ahead, attacking our position!"

Eric ducked his head as machine gun fire erupted from the German tank. The tank rumbled forward slowly, maintaining a healthy distance from any thrown firebombs. Several partisans—the brave ones—inched up the rampart and argued about the wisdom of firing off a few rounds, although Eric knew their bullets had no hope of penetrating the armored hull of a twenty-five-ton tank.

"How far away is he?" Bernard shouted over the din of the battle.

"A hundred meters—still too far for our Molotovs!" one partisan replied.

A tank blast rocked the barricade, jettisoning cobblestones into the air. Eric threw himself on top of Gabi to protect her from the flying rocks. A jagged chunk of concrete landed on his back with a thud.

The jolt of sharp pain between his shoulder blades focused his thinking. This motley band was about to be overrun by a superior military force—and if he and Gabi hung around, the tank would crush them.

"Bernard! We can't stay here! We have no chance against this Panzer. He is staying out of range of our Molotovs."

The Resistance leader nodded in agreement. "I'll lead you out!" he shouted over the din.

Gabi leaned closer. "No, you stay here with your men. We'll find a way."

"I can't let that happen." Bernard took off the shoulder pack of medical supplies. "I have my orders too, and they were to make sure you return safely to Switzerland. We can leave the bandages and medicines here."

Eric looked at Gabi, then back at Bernard. "So what are we going to do?"

"Get you back to the safe house. Follow me."

The three crouched and took off, staying low and keeping the barricade between them and the tank. Eric took one last look over his shoulder. The rest of the student brigade ran for the exit doors, as well. Tanks versus rifles would always be a mismatch.

The trio retraced their steps. Fifteen minutes of stealth movements returned them to where they started—Rue Racine. They were within steps of the medieval hotel when the *klack-klack-klack* of a throaty diesel engine filled the air. This time it wasn't a Panzer. Eric's throat cinched down at the sight of a troop truck 150 meters away, bouncing in their direction.

Spotting them, the driver accelerated. Bernard, rifle in hand, beckoned with his other arm. "He's not stopping to ask for directions. Quick!"

Bernard pounded the wooden gate. "Let us in! Uncle George, it's me!"

Within seconds, the frizzy gray-haired pensioner who owned the large property cracked it open.

Bernard dove inside. "The *boches* are coming! Warn the others!"

"Everyone's gone," George replied. "Just the wife and a few other women are left."

"You tend to them. We'll take the underground route."

Bernard set a wooden post across the back of the double gate while George hustled toward the house. Eric and Gabi followed Bernard toward the parked Panzer, where the Frenchman grabbed a long rod with an S-hook that was leaning against the house. They watched as he immediately began working the steel pole into a manhole cover set in front of the German armored vehicle.

"What are you doing?" Fear raised Gabi's voice an octave.

"You'll see." Bernard grunted as he put more force into the pole.

Eric crouched next to the manhole cover, ready to lend a hand. He heard the diesel truck slow to a stop outside the fortified entry, and he wondered again why he'd put Gabi in this position.

The truck's engine shut off, followed by the sounds of troops landing on pavement and an animated Germanic exchange. From what Eric could make out, they were squabbling about what they would find on the other side of the wall. One insisted they were walking into a *Hinterhalt*—an ambush—while another soldier reminded everyone they were in the army to fight.

Bernard popped the manhole cover, lifting the heavy lid high enough for Eric to clear it away.

The Frenchman dusted his hands and motioned into the dark cavity. "Our escape route. Like I said, I'm responsible for your safety."

"What about the others?" Gabi looked behind her. Rifle butts battered the gate, pounding incessantly.

"George and the women can take care of themselves. Time to go, before the *boches* make a move."

Rifle slung over his back, Bernard stepped onto the first metal rung inside the manhole and descended into the dark, subterranean opening. The distance to the bottom rung wasn't insignificant: about five meters. Bernard stepped off the bottom rung and found his footing.

Eric leaned over and looked closer. It looked like Bernard was standing next to a river of brackish water. He hoped this was runoff from the storm drains, but the latrine-like smell told him otherwise.

Gabi came up alongside him. "Is that what I think it is?"

As a dairy farmer, Eric knew excrement when he smelled it. "I'm getting a good whiff of rotten eggs."

The banging of rifle stocks against the oversized gate rose in volume.

"Down you go," Eric directed.

Gabi clasped her summer dress around her thighs. She moved athletically and began her descent. Bernard assisted her to the landing.

Eric had just stepped onto the first rung when the German troop carrier crashed through the oversized wooden gate and careened into the courtyard. The Swiss reached for the heavy iron cover as he ducked into the manhole opening, but he struggled to move it back into place.

"Leave it!" Bernard yelled. "There isn't time."

Eric worked the heavy cover into the opening, but it wasn't completely seated in its circular casing. His effort would have to do.

Grabbing both sides of the ladder, Eric hurtled down the dark passage. He landed with a thud that echoed inside the damp tunnel.

"Over here," Bernard said from the darkness. There was a spark, and his face was illuminated by a flickering yellow glow. He held up his lighter to reveal a handheld lantern hanging from a hook. "We keep a kerosene lamp down here. Just in case."

Eric looked back toward the thin vein of light coming from the opening. Had the German soldiers seen him?

"This way." Bernard lifted the kerosene lamp to head height. "Watch your head, and watch your step. You don't want to be falling in the drainage channel. Might ruin your day."

What Eric saw under the lantern's luminescence surprised him. An underground passage nearly as large as a Métro tunnel stretched before them. A central channel, wide and deep enough for a boat, appeared to be draining runoff water and raw sewage.

They moved quickly along a meter-wide brick walkway. Overhead, leaky pipes and communication cables lined the ceiling. Still there was adequate headroom. Eric followed Gabi, who followed Bernard.

Gabi moved with quickened steps. "Seems like it would be easy to get lost down here."

"Let me show you." Bernard slowed next to a blue enamel sign with white-lettering that looked very much like a Paris street sign. "Each sign mirrors the streets above. Clever, *non?*"

Resuming their hurried pace, they moved quickly and then stopped to catch their breath. "Our sewer network is a technological marvel extending more than 1,500 kilometers beneath the streets of Paris," Bernard said with pride. "Growing up, every schoolchild took a field trip through the Paris sewers. We even had to pass a test afterward."

Eric could tell by the look on Gabi's face that she didn't share the same appreciation for the eighth wonder of the world. "Where are you taking us?"

"We'll skirt the Jardin du Luxembourg," Bernard replied. "It's a German stronghold. I know a safe house on the Rue de Vaugirard. I was there this morning. We should be there—"

A shaft of light fell on the paved walkway fifty meters away. Someone had opened up the manhole cover. Voices could be heard—German voices.

They were coming.

8

Bernard extinguished the flame inside the kerosene lamp. The cavernous passage was instantly cloaked in total darkness.

Eric strained to hear the voices coming through the manhole.

"Ich habe die drei in diesem Schach verschwinden gesehen," said one.

Bernard sidled up next to Eric. "What did he say?" he whispered in French.

Eric drew close to Bernard's ear. "He said, 'I have seen the three disappear in this manhole.' Now they're discussing what to do. The leader is saying there's no way he's climbing into a dark cesspool to chase us, but one of the soldiers said there's a lamp in the truck."

From their accent, these were real Germans—not Poles or Russians shanghaied into the Wehrmacht.

"Wait. They're still talking." Eric cupped his ear.

"One is saying that he wants to kill some frogs before he leaves Paris. Another soldier said he'll join him. They're basically volunteering." Eric realized both soldiers were trigger-happy and itching for action. "I suggest we get going."

The Frenchman grunted his approval. Bernard relit the kerosene lamp, and they scurried along the walkway, the sound of their quick steps echoing inside the underground passage. When Eric—last in line—looked behind, he could barely make out the shaft of light in the distance. Then he saw one soldier land on the walkway, illuminated by the deep yellow hue of a kerosene lamp.

"They're coming!" Eric laid a hand on Gabi's shoulder.

"Stay with me!" Bernard whispered loudly. Ten meters ahead was the first intersection. Instead of crossing on a wooden plank, Bernard turned right with Gabi and Eric in close pursuit, taking them out of the Germans' line of sight.

A report from a rifle reverberated down the concrete passage. The bullet ricocheted off the metal pipes hanging from the ceiling. A second and a third shot followed, then silence.

Eric checked his pocket and felt the smooth metallic finish of the Schmidt 7.5mm revolver. There wasn't anywhere to hide in these tunnels. The German's rifle carried a distinct advantage. Only at close range would Eric have a chance. Maybe Rousseau, who had a rifle draped over his back, was a sharpshooter, but in this catacomb-like setting, they couldn't let the Germans get them in their sights.

———

Gabi held her side and gasped for a breath, longing for fresh air and wondering if she'd be able to keep up the pace.

They raced along the underground walkway with Bernard stopping periodically to check the street signs. At another intersection, more wooden planks were strewn across the bisecting channels of human waste. Bernard held up a hand and studied his options.

"This way." The partisan stepped across a makeshift bridge, then he beckoned for Gabi and Eric.

Gabi hoped Bernard knew where he was going. The stench was getting to her. Leaky walls closed in, and with each step, the intense, claustrophobic oppressiveness wrapped its coils around her, threatening to pull her into the endless stream of raw sewage. She glanced down. Thick sludge and bits of tissue paper floated by. Gabi choked back a gag and continued putting one foot in front of the other.

The German soldiers weren't giving up. Their leather boots clamored in the distance with persistence. So far, Bernard's changes of direction hadn't shaken them off their tail.

"Keep moving. Keep up," he prodded.

They pressed ahead in the dark tunnel. At the next intersection, Bernard ordered a left turn and followed a new channel. Minutes passed.

He stopped suddenly and Gabi almost ran into him. Bernard placed his forefinger against his lips. They listened for their pursuers. Ten seconds of silence gave them their answer.

Two Germans talked somewhere in the darkness. They had closed the gap. Gabi guessed them to be just beyond the last corner. They were making up ground.

Bernard drew close to Eric and Gabi. "Change of plans. We have to get to street level now. I don't want a bullet in my back—not at this late stage of the war."

"Will it be safe? You said we could be near a German garrison." Eric's voice was barely a whisper.

Bernard shook his head. "I don't know."

Gabi held her arms tight, attempting to stop them from quivering. "Do you know where we are?"

"Near the Jardin du Luxembourg, I believe. We could open the manhole cover and discover an entire *boche* battalion on patrol, but I say it's worth the risk."

Behind them, the plodding of the soldiers' footsteps grew

closer. They still hadn't turned the last corner. Gabi held her breath, waiting.

"How much longer?" Eric reached for his revolver. "If we have a ways to go, I think we're better off surprising them when they come around the corner."

"It's not much further. Our chances are better up above than down here."

Gabi nodded and covered her nose. "I agree." Any plan that allowed her to escape this fetid hole was her first choice.

Bernard turned and continued on, blazing a trail on the stone walkway. Gabi scrambled to keep up.

Returning to her quickened pace, her head felt light. Was it from the fumes? The running? The fear? Maybe all three. She focused on Bernard's back, pushing herself on. Just then her right foot slipped. She stumbled and before she could catch herself, her foot dipped into the churning sewage.

"Yeech," she hissed through clenched teeth as she yanked her right foot out of the dirty water.

Eric took her arm, helping to right her. "Don't think about it. Keep moving."

Bernard hadn't stopped. He glanced over his shoulder, his eyes widened in fear. "They're gaining on us. The next manhole shaft is just ahead."

He picked up his pace, sprinting with the kerosene lamp held aloft.

Ten seconds later, Bernard found the set of metal rungs leading to the street. "Here, hold this." He handed the lamp to Gabi and scampered up the ladder. She looked up to see the Frenchman pressing both palms against the manhole cover. He pushed harder, grunting, but without success.

"She won't budge," he groaned. He pulled the rifle from

his shoulder and slammed the butt against the cast-iron cover. A dull thud echoed off the walls of the tunnel.

Gabi glanced behind her. The German soldiers' pace had quickened. Time was running out.

"Let me up there!" Eric grabbed a rung and flung himself up the manhole shaft. Bernard shifted to one side to give Eric some room.

Eric's jaw fixed and his eyes narrowed in determination as he pounded his shoulder against the manhole cover. Bernard joined in, hammering the edge with the rifle stock.

Gabi looked back. In the dim light, she saw the silhouette of a coal-scuttle shaped steel helmet belonging to the Wehrmacht. He couldn't have been more than seventy-five meters away. As the soldier knelt and shouldered his carbine, Gabi climbed the metal rung with her right hand, steadying the kerosene lamp in her left. She shimmied up the vertical shaft as two gunshots ricocheted off the metal ladder with a flash of sparks.

The gunfire reverberated through the sewer tunnel, intensifying Eric and Bernard's efforts.

In seconds they would be shot like fish in a barrel.

"C'mon, Eric," she whispered, while holding up the kerosene lamp.

She watched Eric lean into the steel cover with his back, using his legs against the ladder rungs to leverage himself, but it appeared the heavy iron cover had been sealed shut with cement.

The German soldiers took off in a sprint.

"They're almost here!" Gabi called.

Eric strained and a primordial cry burst from his lips. A grating sound hummed through the tunnel, and dust and small bits of sand showered them. Next came the scrape of metal on metal and the heavy cover tilted slightly.

More sand and dust tumbled down. Gabi lifted her face and watched with squinted eyes. With renewed energy the men pushed harder.

Just then, the manhole cover disappeared. A commotion of voices and cries filled the air, and suddenly Eric and Bernard were gone. Vanished.

Daylight flooded the sewer shaft, temporarily blinding Gabi. Dropping the lantern to free her hands, she grabbed the ladder and scrambled toward the street surface. She heard the lamp carom down and sounds of breaking glass as it smashed into the stone walkway, splashing kerosene across the walls and in the path of the advancing soldiers.

Seconds later a swirl of heat and black smoke propelled Gabi upward into waiting hands that wrapped around her arms and launched her past the street level. She fumbled for her footing like a marionette on a string.

Righting herself, she looked around to see that she stood among dozens of Parisians. Loud cheers echoed in her ears.

Just then, the crack of a rifle sounded and a bullet scorched the air behind her head. The noise of the crowd silenced. Some darted away from the hole. Others crouched down, looking for the source of the shot.

Like a gopher emerging from his hole, a German helmet popped out. In a single motion, Eric pulled Gabi aside. Then with all his weight, he stomped on the helmet with his heel. There was a crunch as cervical vertebrae compressed, then gave way with a loud snap as the soldier's head fell awkwardly to the side. His dead weight, propelled by gravity, slammed into the second advancing infantryman. With a clattering of metal on concrete, both fell into the river of sewage with a deep, heavy splash.

Eric looked at Rousseau. "What now?"

"Leave the rats to their bath. Quick, help me with the cover."

Sounds of Germanic swearing became muffled as the heavy cast-iron cover slid back into place with a hollow thud. The crowd, swelling in size, cheered with approval. Another round of applause erupted as a Frenchman with a pencil-thin moustache took Gabi in his arms and kissed her full on the lips.

"Je m'excuse, mademoiselle. Paris est libéré!" *Paris is liberated!*

Eric, bent over with hands on his knees and breathing heavily, looked up at Gabi with a knowing smile. They'd barely cheated death.

Gabi peeled herself from the Frenchman and rushed into Eric's waiting arms. As he drew her close, she could palpably feel their hearts pounding against one another.

As her pulse slowly returned to normal, Eric looked into Gabi's eyes. "Have you taken a look around?"

Without releasing her grasp on Eric, Gabi turned to see a boulevard adjacent to one of the largest parks she'd ever seen—and a parked tank.

"That's one of ours!" she exclaimed in surprise. Adoring Parisians surrounded a French tank with the tricolor and Cross of Lorraine stamped on its armor plate. The tank commander stood in the open turret. He took turns swigging gulps from a wine bottle and laying kisses on a beautiful young woman wrapped in his left arm.

"This is amazing." Gabi filled her lungs with fresh air. Thousands of people had poured into the streets, mad with exhilaration. Church bells pealed across the city, heralding the departure of the hated Germans and the return of liberty. France was once again France.

Gabi took in the unrestrained joy beaming from the

Parisian faces. The city was proud and alive again, and they were eyewitnesses to it. Eric pulled her tighter.

An accordion player tapped out the first bars of "La Marseillaise," and the Parisians quickly drowned out the musician as they sang their national anthem with fervor.

> *Marchons, marchons!*
> *Qu'un sang impur*
> *Abreuve nos sillons!*

Eric led her to a low stone wall and patted the surface, motioning for her to sit. She did, leaning into him. With breathless wonder, her eyes took in the frenzied, joyful scene. What appeared to be perfect strangers kissed with abandon. Many guzzled from green wine bottles. Accordion folk music picked up again and the crowd waved miniature French flags from side to side.

Gabi met the eyes of Bernard. He clapped his hands to the squeezebox beat. She waved him over. "When did the tank arrive?"

"I was told just fifteen minutes ago. The 2nd Armored Division of General Leclerc rolled into Paris this morning, and even though the Germans had promised to defend Paris to 'the last cartridge,' resistance was isolated and sporadic. That's why we heard the church bells earlier. Then the 2nd Armored captured the German commander of Paris, General von Choltitz, at the Hôtel Meurice. Once word got out about von Choltitz's surrender, the cowards put their tails between their legs and stormed out of Paris."

"So the Germans are gone?" Gabi's eyes widened.

"See over there?" Bernard pointed through the park of the Jardin du Luxembourg toward two sets of wooden barracks. "That's where the *boches* were bivouacked. Too bad. They missed their day of reckoning."

Gabi did her best to understand what Bernard must be feeling after four years of hated Occupation had finally ended. "Be grateful that Paris did not become another Warsaw."

"Touché, Mademoiselle Mueller." Bernard returned his gaze to the accordion player, segueing into another French folk song.

Gabi watched him mouth the words to "C'est Magnifique" with a smile growing wider by the minute.

Paris est libéré!

She sealed the memory in her heart, grateful to be a witness—and not the last casualty in Paris.

9

A light breeze failed to dispel the uncomfortable sultry pall that hung over the Schorf Heath, a low-lying forested area northeast of Berlin.

Carinhall, a palatial hunting lodge with vaulted ceilings and thatched roof, could not shield the August mugginess from its owner, Reichsmarschall Hermann Göring, who was feeling the oppressive heat in more ways than one. The second-in-command of Nazi Germany tugged at the gold Luftwaffe insignia attached to the collar of his pastel blue summer uniform while his aide-de-camp, Oberst Walter Heller, trailed in his wake.

"How did the Führer receive the news?" Heller cautiously inquired as they strode down the hall of the sumptuous residence.

Göring slowed his gait and came to a stop inside an ornate drawing room, where he surveyed the French cut-glass and ormolu chandeliers that hung from beams of oversized timber. The pair stood flanked by anterooms named Gold and Silver. Inside, hundreds of the finest Italian, French, German, and Dutch paintings and floor-to-ceiling Flemish tapestries occupied every available square centimeter.

"I'm afraid our beloved leader did not accept the latest situational report very well." Göring let out a heavy sigh. "Just hours ago, the Führer asked General Jodl, 'Is Paris burning?' When told that the Commander of Gross Paris had surrendered with barely a fight, the Führer shrieked and flew into a rage. He called von Choltitz a mutinous cretin for disobeying direct orders."

Göring had witnessed the volcanic eruptions before. He didn't need much imagination to envision the Führer, with neck veins bulging and bloodshot eyes, working himself into a good lather. Direct orders from Hitler were not to be ignored, and the Reichskanzler had been specific, telling von Choltitz that the French capital "must not fall into the enemy's hands except lying in complete debris." Von Choltitz was lucky to be taken prisoner by the Allies. Whatever the conditions, a far less hospitable fate awaited him back home.

For Göring, the Teletype message from Berlin an hour ago declaring that Paris had fallen was distressing, though not unexpected. A silver lining in the gloomy transmission was that the most beautiful city in the world hadn't been turned into a smoldering slag heap.

A week earlier, a source on General Jodl's staff had told him that the 813th Pionierkompanie—Engineer Company—had strapped U-boat torpedoes underneath forty-five bridges spanning the Seine. A cache of dynamite had been also set aside to blow up the most recognized landmark in the world—the Eiffel Tower. *Sheer lunacy!*

"Let's look at some of my paintings," Göring said to his aide, attempting an upbeat tone. Sometimes in low moments like this, he needed to be close to his art. The works of Old Masters gave him perspective and a chance to think clearly. On occasions, he believed treasures of the past spoke directly to him.

They continued along the white arabescato marble flooring he had personally selected from an Italian quarry. He had approved every detail of Carinhall's construction, right down to the lavish door handles. The memory caused his heavy chest to swell with pride. No residence in the world housed as many pieces of exquisite art, all chosen by him.

"Each day that I'm here gives me immense satisfaction, Heller." His gaze focused toward the masterpieces hanging on the walls, many having come from—or through—Paris, where Heller had traveled at his behest to purchase the very best art available on the market. Yes, purchase, because he could afford them. As Prime Minister of Prussia, Minister of Aviation, State Foresting and Hunting Master of Germany, Field Marshall of the Luftwaffe, and director of the Four-Year Economic Plan, his bank accounts overflowed with Reichsmarks.

Of the eight homes Göring owned, Carinhall was the one he loved most. He had intended to build a simple hunting lodge, but one remodeling project beget another—plus the need for more wall space to display his art. A small army of carpenters worked for nearly seven years, adding high-ceilinged atriums, oversized sitting rooms, and wood-paneled studies until his country home reached Versailles-like proportions.

"What do you think of our latest Cranach?" Göring stopped in front of a tall, rectangular oil painting that had replaced an inferior piece traded to an unsuspecting dealer.

Together, Göring and Heller took a long moment to study *Cupid Complaining to Venus* by German Renaissance artist Lucas Cranach the Elder. The tableau depicted Cupid as a naked, potbellied preschooler complaining to Venus, a long-limbed nude, that bees had stung him when he stole a handful of honeycomb.

"It's certainly allegorical," Heller replied. "It speaks to the idea that life is a mixture of pleasure and pain."

"I see your point, Heller. Pleasure. Pain. A metaphor for these times." For pleasure, Göring took great delight from indulging his appetite for masterpiece paintings, valuable jewels, and exquisite objets d'art, just as he satisfied his palate with sumptuous meals, expensive French wines, and Dutch cigars. He rather enjoyed the role of bon vivant and grand patron of art, music, and theater—mantles that underscored his exalted position within the Reich. He was a Renaissance man, the only member of the Führer's inner circle with an upper-class upbringing who moved smoothly within sophisticated international society.

But today was one of those painful days—the loss of National Socialism's crown jewel. At one time, Paris represented the Reich's future, the inauguration of their *belle époque*—beautiful era. The loss to the Allies was further proof that the Third Reich's trajectory was tilting back toward Earth. A horrific and deadly crash was inevitable unless Werner Heisenberg and his nuclear physicists could come up with a *Wunderwaffe*, a wonder weapon.

They approached a masterpiece by Flemish painter Jan Brueghel from the early seventeenth century.

"Ah, *The Vision of St. Hubert*, one of my favorites," Göring declared.

They regarded Brueghel's composition of a heavily wooded forest scene. At stage center, a proud stag stood before St. Hubert, bent on one knee and gazing at a light and a crucifix between the deer's antlers. A white steed and hunting hounds surrounded the huntsman.

"Because of your love of hunting, Reichsmarschall?"

"St. Hubert is the patron saint for hunters—particularly deer hunters. His intercession was said to ward off rabies. Not that I believe any of that superstition."

Göring studied the painting. He had never counted the

number of tracking dogs in *The Vision of St. Hubert*, but today he enjoyed the diversion, which took his worried mind off the funereal dispatches from both fronts. He regarded the five beautifully drawn hunting hounds and thought about how they had nothing to worry about except for loyally serving their master.

If only life were as simple for him. He had joined the Nazi Party in 1922 after hearing Adolf Hitler deliver a mesmerizing speech about the great injustices of the Versailles Treaty. He ingratiated himself to the former Austrian corporal, who appointed him to command the Sturmabteilung (SA)—the brownshirts. A year later, he took a bullet in the groin for Hitler after Bavarian police broke up the Beer Hall Putsch. He nearly died, but he had proved his mettle.

There was no one more loyal to the Führer, yet at this present time, he was in the Führer's doghouse. Ever since the Battle of Stalingrad ended disastrously in the spring of 1943, Hitler had blamed him for the Luftwaffe's deficiencies. He was shuttled to a side rail and replaced in the National Socialism hierarchy by Heinrich Himmler, the toadyish bootlicker of the Gestapo. Göring knew that he no longer had the ear of the Führer, who had been acting more and more erratic. The Führer's nerves were kaput, evidenced by the trembling of his left hand.

Heller interrupted his thoughts. "The legend goes that Hubert, a Frankish courtier around the year 700, went hunting deep in the Ardennes forest on a Good Friday. A stag appeared before Hubert with a crucifix glowing between its antlers, and a heavenly voice reproached him for hunting on Good Friday."

"Ach—more superstition. I would have never guessed that side of you." He regarded Heller and his close-cropped black hair. The colonel was twenty years his junior and considerably more trim. "Heller, how long have we known each other?"

"Let's see. In 1937, you plucked me out of my art studies at the University of Berlin. I have served you faithfully ever since."

"Yes, indeed. You have undertaken many sensitive tasks for me over the years."

Heller registered surprise. "That's correct, Reichsmarschall. It has been my honor." The aide regarded him with a wry smile. "Can I be of service to you in some manner? I assume that's why you invited me."

"Very perceptive. The fact is, I want you to contact our people in Zurich. For a sensitive mission. One that could determine my fate—and yours." He let the thought hang in the summer air.

"I'm listening, Reichsmarschall."

He looked over Heller's shoulders, then glanced behind to ensure they were alone in the main hallway. "What I am about to say to you must stay within these walls. This is for your safety as well as mine. Do you understand?"

"Jawohl, Herr Reichsmarschall." The officer clicked his boot heels.

"How many paintings are in my possession?"

"Total? Including the paintings in all your homes as well as the special works kept in Switzerland for safekeeping?"

"Yes, all of them."

"I can't give you a highly accurate number, but it's close to 2,000."

"Are any of those paintings priceless?"

Heller assumed a quizzical look. "We purchased them at prices you were willing to pay on the open market. Then there are the confiscated pieces in the inventory, which came at no cost. That doesn't mean they aren't quite valuable. The Jews have an eye for art."

"But nothing in my possession could be placed in the priceless category."

"Correct. Priceless paintings, by definition, are national treasures that cannot be bought or sold at any price. May I inquire why you are asking?"

"Because I desire to add a priceless piece to the collection."

"Excuse me? I'm not sure what the Reichsmarschall—"

"I've been giving this some thought, and I have a particular piece in mind."

"But sir, as I just said, priceless paintings do not have a price. There is *no* purchase tag."

"Which means we'll have to acquire it . . . by other means. There is more at stake here, Colonel Heller, than just another addition to the collection. Our very survival may depend on this."

Heller muffled a cough. "What priceless work did you have in mind?"

"The *Mona Lisa*."

10

Gabi glanced over at Eric, his head thrown back in laughter, immersed in revelry. She couldn't believe they were really here, celebrating Libération—lucky to be part of this, and even luckier to be alive.

Last night, while loading up the Red Cross sedan for their journey to Paris, Gabi contemplated her love for Eric, and how much it had grown. Her days before becoming an OSS agent seemed like a lifetime ago, when her feelings for Eric paled by comparison to what she felt now. Thoughts of almost losing him made her shiver involuntarily.

Her instincts to stand by the man she loved had been tested, more than most would experience. Now, seeing him safe, happy, and basking in the warmth of the moment filled her heart with a peace greater than she had ever felt. She understood better that true commitment meant being together in the good times . . . and the bad.

She entwined her arm with Eric's as they strode past the medieval hotel's oversized gate, bent and broken by the Nazi troop carrier. Beyond the entry, hundreds of celebrating Parisians from the surrounding neighborhood had poured into the cobblestoned courtyard, drawn by festive music and news that George Beaumont had opened his wine cellar.

"Isn't it great that the accordion player brought the party over here?" Gabi clapped in rhythm to "Fleur de Paris" as the setting sun was about to dip below the Paris skyline. Orange light swept their faces one last time on a day that would never be forgotten by history.

"Shall we dance?" Eric placed his left hand on the small of her back and swept his right arm like d'Artagnan of the Four Musketeers. The only thing missing was a cape and feathered hat.

"I'd love to." Gabi curtsied. "But first I have to change my shoes and put on fresh clothes."

Fifteen minutes later, she emerged from the house and smiled demurely at Eric.

His eyes scanned her new outfit. "You look beautiful."

"Thank you. I was hoping . . ."

"Hoping I'd do this?"

He approached her and opened his arms to her, and then pulled her into a hold. They lost themselves in the throng of revelers. Gabi's eyes locked with Eric's, and she leaned into his hand supporting the small of her back. The movement felt safe and secure and made her hope that she would always feel this way in days to come. When he drew her close, she lay her head on his right shoulder. The tension that had bottled up all day evaporated in his embrace.

She closed her eyes and let the soaring music take her to a tranquil place. A thousand flutters—like ripples on the Seine—stirred as he gently led her around the littered cobblestones of the courtyard. It seemed right that she was here, sharing this moment with Eric and those around her. Never before had people opened their hearts as the Parisians did that afternoon. Streets flooded with joy, the people were intoxicated by unsuppressed freedom, hugging and kissing anyone within arm's length.

Gabi knew this party would not be over anytime soon. Every face was etched with pure delirium—joyous women dancing on their toes, schoolgirls once again—while their laughing partners held hands aloft. Those who weren't gamboling about were clapping to the lively beat, savoring the moment.

"Excuse me, Mademoiselle Mueller?"

Gabi looked over. It was Alain Dubois.

He gestured for her to come closer and motioned for Eric to follow. "You have a telephone call."

"It must be Mr. Dulles." Gabi looked to Eric.

Eric steered her away from the music. "I sent him the phone number in my transmission an hour ago."

Gabi straightened the pleats on her dress, as if the OSS chief were waiting inside the front door. "How'd he get through?" Gabi wondered aloud. "The phone lines must be jammed."

Eric looked pensive, as carefree feelings faded. "More importantly, *why* is he calling now?"

They followed Dubois to the second-floor apartment, which earlier that morning had been a Molotov factory. Boxes of empty wine bottles were still stacked in a corner, and strips of clothing—the wicks—were piled in an open box.

A Resistance member held the telephone's handset. He shrugged his shoulders as if to say—*Who wants to take the call?*

Eric motioned to Gabi. "Your English is better," he said in Swiss-German.

"Hello?"

"Gabi, wonderful to hear your voice."

"And yours as well, Mr. Dulles."

"I understand the Parisians are painting the town red tonight."

"I don't think I heard you correctly—" The connection was garbled.

"Sorry. American slang. What I meant to say is there must be quite a party in Paris. I want to thank you and Eric. You risked your lives for others, and we are proud of you."

"It has been an interesting day. But we're safe now."

The American chief in Switzerland affected a more serious tone. "Thanks for delivering my message to the Underground. We were a day late and a dollar short since Leclerc's tanks stormed into Paris today. Ike was livid when he heard what happened. He ordered the 4th U.S. Infantry to assist but felt his hand had been forced by the Free French. History will be the judge, but it looks like the Gaullists have won control of Paris, at least for now. How are Rousseau and his Communist pals taking the news?"

Gabi paused. "I haven't seen Bernard for several hours, so I'm not sure."

"That's okay. If you hear anything, let me know."

"We'll stay in contact." Gabi smiled and nodded toward Eric, who was straining to follow her side of the conversation.

"So when are you coming back?"

"Eric and I talked about that earlier. We don't want to be on the road until after the Germans clear out, so not for several days. There's a problem finding petrol too. Plus, we heard there's going to be a victory parade down the Champs Élysées tomorrow."

"That's fine, but be alert. The war isn't over, and you might learn something useful. If I need to reach you, I'll either call or transmit a message at the usual times."

"We'll be in touch." Gabi thanked Dulles for the call and hung up the phone.

Eric pressed closer. "What did he say?"

"He approved of our plan to stay in Paris, to be his eyes and ears. A lot is happening right now."

"He's right. Things are very fluid."

Another raucous cheer rattled the windows overlooking the courtyard. Eric took Gabi's hand in his and led her over to the view. There, in the corner of the room, was the empty safe, still ajar.

Gabi reflexively felt for the black book that she had slipped into her pocket earlier, but the small volume wasn't there. In an instant, she realized that she left the black book in the pocket of her soiled skirt upstairs. She'd check into it later.

Outside, the party had picked up intensity. Another accordion player had joined the mix, swelling the ranks of partying Parisians. Celebrants of Libération covered every cobblestone in the courtyard. Gabi pointed to the half-dozen revelers jitterbugging on the Panzer. She couldn't help but smile at the irony.

"Shall we get back out there?" Eric tilted his head. "I'd like to finish our dance."

Before Gabi could answer, the musicians broke into "La Marseillaise"—the fifth time she heard the French national anthem since they were pulled out of the Paris sewers. The memory required fresh air. She opened the window a little farther as the opening stanza permeated their thoughts with emotion:

> *Allons enfants de la Patrie,*
> *Le jour de gloire est arrivé!*

Yes, children of the Homeland, your day of glory has arrived: Friday, August 25, 1944, a date that would forever be etched in French history.

Colette turned the corner onto Rue Racine and heard the rhythmic clapping to the patriotic music. Her eyes glistened in happiness. Excitement rose in her throat. She was sure that Bernard, and what sounded like a good part of Paris, awaited her at the Maison Beaumont.

An hour ago at the Louvre, a dozen American troops had rolled into the Cour Napoléon in a half-track troop carrier escorted by two French tanks. For Colette, their arrival signaled the end of a dark era. With the palace secured under Allied guard, there had been a collective sigh of relief as Rambouillet told everyone to go home. She tried three times to call Bernard, but the line had been busy. The Beaumont residence was a Resistance gathering point, and she figured Bernard would be there, or his aunt or uncle would know where he was.

On her way from the Louvre, she saw Parisians bang open their shuttered windows. They'd poured into the streets and threw themselves into the arms of total strangers, howling in happiness. Men and women embraced her, kissing both cheeks. From balconies, windows, and doorways, from plazas, boulevards, and barricades, Paris pulsated with unrestrained jubilation. The sound of church bells, building in depth and intensity, rang over the city.

Colette's feet glided effortlessly over the cobblestones during the half-hour walk to the Left Bank. She could see the Maison Beaumont in the distance. Neighbors milled around the entrance—still a couple hundred meters away—when the sound of footsteps following her on the sidewalk caught her attention.

A chill crawled down her back. She hesitated. The footsteps were gaining on her, raising the hair on the back of her neck. Something told her not to look back. To pretend she didn't hear.

She picked up her pace again, remembering the warning from French soldiers at the Louvre. They'd told her to expect German stragglers—snipers and soldiers separated from their units. Was one of them after her now?

She was a mere fifty meters from the Beaumont residence and thought to call for help, but realizing they wouldn't hear her, she started to run—

Strong hands grabbed her shoulders and spun her around. A paralyzing scream stuck in her throat while she pushed hard into the man's chest.

"Colette . . ."

She found herself looking into a face she recognized.

"Bernard!"

He held her to his chest, and their lips met. Never before had a prickly beard felt so good.

She pressed against him, joy replacing fear. "You scared me. I didn't know who was following me." Colette touched his cheek, his neck, reminding herself it was really him, awash with relief.

"Sorry. I wanted to surprise you."

"Mission accomplished." Colette playfully thumped him on the chest. "I've been worried sick about you. It's been a week since you disappeared. I didn't know what to think."

"I answered the call of duty—for France. For our future." Bernard outstretched both hands and took hers. "I heard about what you did at the Louvre today. I'm sorry I wasn't there to save you myself, but I'm glad you're all right."

Colette looked into his eyes and held them. Something was different; he seemed a bit aloof. She held his gaze, willing to lose herself in the security of his embrace. "Is everything all right?" she asked.

Bernard stroked her cheek. "I'm fine. Just a very long day, and I have many things running through my head."

He reached into his right pocket. Then he held out a closed hand. "I have something for you. My grandmother gave this to me before she died. She wore it every day. I want you to have it." He opened his hand, revealing a heart-shaped gold locket.

"Bernard—I couldn't."

"Today is special in many ways, but it is mostly a new beginning—the freedom to live and to love again. My grandmother would approve." He unclasped the necklace and fastened it around the nape of her neck.

"It's lovely." Colette fingered the pendant and opened the small ornamental case, revealing a snippet of black hair.

"I didn't have a photo, so I included a lock of hair. I hope you don't find it too sentimental."

She wrapped her arms around his neck. "No, not at all. It's perfect. I'm seeing a different side of you. Thank you, Bernard." She tipped on her toes and their lips met again. Stepping back, she admired the locket, then looked to him.

Studying him skeptically and noting his fresh olive shirt and dungarees, she said, "You look so . . . what I mean is . . . you don't look like you've been fighting Nazis."

"Believe me, I was a couple of hours ago. You have no idea."

She chuckled. "So what happened?"

"Not now. Maybe later. Tonight, we celebrate."

Colette noted the evasive tone but let it go. He was right. Tonight was a time to celebrate and forget. He'd always hidden his involvement in the Resistance, but then again, she had her secrets too.

The sight of a couple hundred revelers, swaying to the music and draining dust-covered bottles of Bordeaux, greeted Bernard and Colette.

"Would you like something to drink?" he asked. "It seems Uncle George is emptying the wine cellar tonight."

"A glass of red would be fantastic."

He returned with the drink and then took her hand. "Let's go upstairs. Maybe my aunt will have something to eat besides boiled rutabaga."

Bernard grasped Colette's hand as they threaded their way through the crowd. He was grateful for the break to gather his thoughts. His emotions were torn, and he wasn't sure what to believe after seeing Colette's name on the list of informants. They were lovers, but a horrific war had forced them to hold back parts of their lives from each other. Presently, nothing made sense. If she had been talking to the Germans, why had he never been picked up and taken to the Gestapo prison at Fresnes? It didn't make sense, but now was not the time to bring up the subject.

They climbed the stairs and turned into the dining room. Several members of the Resistance had gathered around the long wooden table, sharing boisterous exploits.

Seeing them, Aunt Irene stepped out of the kitchen and dusted her hands on her apron. She greeted Colette with two kisses and a hug. "One of the neighbors brought over some Camembert and three loaves of *pain rustique*." She reached for a wooden board with wedges of the soft, creamy cheese and chunks of dark rye bread.

"Thank you, I'm quite famished." Colette spread a sliver of Camembert on a slice of bread and handed it to Bernard.

"No, after you. Please, eat."

Colette crunched into her first bite, pausing as the creamy delicacy melted into her taste buds. "This is so good! I haven't had cheese in a month."

"Then have another." Madame Beaumont passed the

wooden board to Colette. She accepted the offer without hesitation.

Irene Beaumont, her gray hair gathered in a bun, turned toward her nephew. "Do you want to ask the Swiss over there if they would like some?" She tilted her head toward the couple gathered at the window overlooking the courtyard.

"Good idea."

Bernard stood, but Colette motioned to him, drawing him closer. "Who is she talking about?"

"Eric Hofstadler and Gabi Mueller." Bernard nodded toward the couple on the other side of the living room. "They're with the Red Cross. Arrived today with medical supplies from Switzerland."

"So that was their car I saw parked next to the tank. Why would they come here?"

Bernard smiled—and shrugged. He reached for the wooden board of cheese and bread from his aunt. "You can ask them yourself, but to be honest, I'm not really sure."

Bernard and Colette crossed into the living room, hand in hand. Eric spotted them first, and introductions were made as cheese and bread were passed around.

Gabi waited until she finished chewing her first morsel. "Nice to meet you, Colette. We saw you walk in together. How did you two meet?"

"We both work at the Louvre." Colette's cheeks flushed. "We've known each other a couple of years."

"Bernard told us he worked with the maintenance crew. I know the Louvre's a big place. So what do you do?" Gabi asked.

"I'm a curator, but really, in title only. The extent of my work and our exhibitions were quite rudimentary after the German Ministry of Culture was in control."

"What was that like, having the—?"

The phone next to the kitchen entrance rang. The four turned. Bernard watched his aunt answer the phone and then wave him over.

"Excuse me," Bernard said. "I should only be a moment."

Grateful to escape the small talk, Bernard held the telephone to his right ear.

"Rousseau?"

"Oui," he replied.

"Twenty-two hours, Meeting Point B," the deep voice said, followed by a click.

He'd been expecting the phone call after the liberation of Paris. The message meant the war wasn't over for the Communists in the Resistance.

The battle lines had merely shifted.

11

"An excellent *Wiener schnitzel*. My compliments to the chef."

Colonel Heller lifted a bite of the Belgian veal, coated in seasoned breadcrumbs, to his lips. They never served this type of repast in the officers' mess.

Heller let his eyes drift around Carinhall's cherry-wood dining room. There was a lot to take in since this one room was three times as large as the house in which he was raised. Everything about Carinhall was out of scale, massive—in keeping with the image of its owner.

"It's good you stayed for dinner, Heller. Somehow, it didn't seem right to be entertaining a large crowd on an evening of such distressing news."

An hour earlier, Göring had told his valet to cancel the usual dinner party, a nightly occurrence whenever the Reichsmarschall stayed at Carinhall. Between twenty and fifty were usually invited to these affairs—a glittery mix of captains of German industry, local politicians, film stars, socialites, and sycophants, sprinkled with the occasional Luftwaffe general or fleet admiral passing through. Heller was a regular invitee, but he preferred his perch on the periphery, biding his time while the Reichsmarschall held court. When summoned, Heller knew he would be given an assignment or be asked to do a favor on Göring's behalf.

"I can only imagine the chaos on the streets of Paris, sir." Heller knew his comment was like setting the ball on the pitch for a penalty kick. He hoped the Reichsmarschall would boot it in for a goal.

Predictably, Göring's countenance brightened. "We'll see if the Gaullists turn on their Resistance brothers, or vice versa. If the cheesers thought they had problems with us in charge, wait until they discover what it's like dealing with the Bolsheviks. I have a feeling their 'liberation' is just the beginning of their next war. After all, Stalin has killed many more Russians than we have. Uncle Joe won't hesitate to exterminate anyone standing in communism's way, especially in France."

Heller watched Göring set down his silver fork and knife and fidget with one of the half-dozen bejeweled rings attached to his sausage-like fingers. He could foresee what was coming next—a diatribe against the Jew-infested Communist "rabble" seeking world domination. But lately, such harangues had given way to a different topic that stirred his passions—art. This time, Göring chose the latter route, although he took a conversational detour to get there.

"The distressing news on the war front prompted me to do some diversionary reading. I found an old diary of mine from 1911, right after I graduated from Gross Lichterfelde." Göring patted the quarto-sized volume beside his plate.

Heller was surprised. The Reichsmarschall *never* spoke about himself in a personal matter, unless it was an opportunity to boast about his genealogy, exploits, or collection of art. He could trace his bloodline back through most of Germany's emperors as well as Bismarck and Goethe.

He was the last commander of the legendary Richthofen Squadron in the Great War, a celebrated fighter ace with more kills than any German pilot save for the Red Baron. He was one of the founding fathers of the Nazi Party and more: after Hitler consolidated power in 1933, Göring created not only the concentration camp penal system, but he was also the architect of the Gestapo, the secret state police. Heller had heard it all so many times . . .

Heller harbored no illusions for whom he worked. Underneath the bonhomie and pretense of art connoisseur, Reichsmarschall Hermann Wilhelm Göring was ruthless, vicious, and self-centered, and operated under two principles: National Socialism defined morality, when convenient; and money could buy everything and anything you wanted—including the world's greatest art. His appetite to accumulate was centered somewhere between his ego and his stomach, and it was getting hard to tell which was bigger.

"Excuse me, Reichsmarschall. You mentioned Gross Lichterfelde. This would have been when you were eighteen or so?" Gross Lichterfelde, the Prussian military academy, ranked with Sandhurst and West Point.

Heller waited in anticipation for what he envisioned to come. His foot tapped softly on the wood floor, impatiently hoping that his hard work and dedication would pay off soon and he'd be the man Göring would usher into unimaginable power and wealth. He understood that if the Reich continued to fall, the Allies would have Göring in their sights. The goal for Heller was to be close enough to hold the keys to the kingdom, but recluse enough to remain hidden in the shadows. For his plan to succeed, maintaining trust was imperative.

The Reichsmarschall set down the diary and sectioned off another portion of his schnitzel. "Correct. I sailed through my finals and scored 232 points, the highest in the academy's history. I graduated summa cum laude."

Here it comes, the self-inflating windbag. So far, the Reichsmarschall hadn't said much that was new, but he dare not interrupt Göring's soliloquy.

"Back then, some of the boys and I decided to take a springtime trip to Italy." Göring leaned back in his chair and crossed his legs, revealing an ankle clad in a fine woven red sock. "Our first stop was Milan, where we found Leonardo da Vinci's *Last Supper*. The mural that da Vinci painted was so faded and cracked that it had lost its original beauty. I wasn't impressed, but that changed after we arrived in Rome. My pals and I came upon famous works by Raphael, Titian, and Bellini. Here's what I noted in my diary:

> *The paintings we saw at the Sistine Chapel today were magnificent, as well as the sculptures inside St. Peter's. We spent hours gazing at each piece of art, but the passage of time never moved so quickly. Nor had I been so moved.*

"I know, Heller, scribblings of an immature schoolboy. But I must say that my time in Rome was when appreciation for art stirred for the first time. And now look where I am. Thirty years later, I have become the world's most discerning collector."

Was there no end to the self-praise? Heller knew where the conversation was heading—and the Reichsmarschall determined its timing.

Göring uncrossed his legs and reached for a handbell. "Care to share a cognac or a schnapps after dinner?"

"Cognac will be fine, Reichsmarschall."

Göring's bloated fingers flicked the bell, and a butler dressed in a black suit stepped through a swinging door. Once the Reichsmarschall finished his instructions, he resumed his ravenous attack on what remained of his second helping of *Wiener schnitzel*. After the manservant had departed, Göring declared, "I want to return to our conversation about the *Mona Lisa*."

"Yes, I was hoping we would." Heller dabbed his lips with his starched napkin. "I must admit that I was taken aback by your idea. We're not 100 percent sure where the *Mona Lisa* is, although we have a good idea."

"But you could find out, correct?"

Heller nodded. His chest tightened within him, not with anxiousness, but with excitement. Was it really possible to find the painting? To behold it? To claim it?

"Yes, Reichsmarschall. Our informant in the Louvre has kept us apprised of where the French are hiding their national treasure." He pictured beautiful Colette and was disappointed their relationship had been all work. "If my memory is correct, the *Mona Lisa* is resting at a chateau outside of Annecy. The exact location is in my file."

"Annecy?" Göring stopped chewing. "That's right outside Geneva."

"Correct. Less than fifty kilometers from the Swiss border."

Heller regarded the Reichsmarschall, who was lost in thought.

Göring leaned back with fingertips pressed together and stared into the distance. "So once we get our hands on the *Mona Lisa*, we could get the painting into Switzerland rather quickly."

"It would seem so, yes. But we're relying on the resourcefulness of Schaffner and Kaufman to 'get' the *Mona Lisa*. For all we know, the French may have the local police guarding the chateau."

"Offer Schaffner and Kaufman ten times what we normally

pay them. They're creative. Tell them they'll receive a generous bonus once they deliver the *Mona Lisa* to Zurich."

Heller considered Göring's idea. Hans Schaffner and Rolf Kaufman were a two-man team—both Germans and both Party members—living in Switzerland's largest city. They acted as the Reichsmarschall's personal emissaries in Switzerland. Armed with diplomatic passes and guile, they'd been performing various "errands" over the last decade, from depositing knapsacks of cash in numbered accounts to hand-delivering some of his most prized paintings for storage in Swiss bank vaults. They weren't averse to performing the occasional "muscle work" when warranted. Schaffner and Kaufman were resourceful, calloused—and well paid.

Heller adjusted himself and leaned in toward Göring. "What's working to our advantage is that the *Mona Lisa* is a small painting, so it's easy to transport. Also, the chaos of the last few days will work in our favor. The French will have their guard down, still hung over from celebrating our departure."

"Excellent." Göring tinkled the bell one more time, a signal that he was finished eating and ready for dessert and his daily *digestif*. "You know what to do?"

"Yes, but one question remains. May I ask how you intend to use the *Mona Lisa*? Were you thinking of using her as a bargaining chip, should the war . . ."

Heller let the question hang. It was too risky to speak in a defeatist manner.

At that moment, the butler entered the dining room carrying a bottle of Rémy Martin Cognac and two silver plates adorned with plum tortes crowned with fresh cream. They waited until the butler departed before resuming their conversation.

"May I be candid with you?" Without waiting for a reply,

Göring continued. "As you know, unless there is a somewhat unlikely turn of events, the Third Reich will be overrun by the Allied forces. Many have made plans for a life after the war and its uncertainties. There are few desirable locations, but fewer that offer anonymity without significant travel. The nearest port would be through France, which could present problems for a man of my stature. I propose we have a passport that would make the French welcome my departure from their beloved Marseille. Once safely on foreign soil, we turn over the whereabouts of their national treasure."

What Göring told him made all the sense in the world.

He was crazy—like a fox.

—————

With a gracious *auf Wiedersehen* to the Reichsmarschall's valet, Colonel Walter Heller departed Carinhall through the front door, welcoming the warm evening air. His black leather boots crunched a path across the gravel drive toward the gray BMW motorcycle with attached sidecar. With a single kick, his driver brought the engine to life. Two white-tailed rabbits scurried across the lawn, seeking shelter from the distinctive exhaust notes.

He had first dismissed Göring's idea about the *Mona Lisa* as coming from someone intoxicated with gluttony, but as they talked through his plan over dessert, Heller saw the merits—and the possibilities.

South America. That was a new one, but Göring mentioned that those in the know were already making plans for the future—probably in Argentina. The more Heller thought about disappearing in untamed South America, the better he liked the idea. He had his future to think about too. Thankful that his nest had already been partially feathered, he was grateful not to be completely dependent on Göring when it would be every man for himself.

Though he was well-versed in art, Heller viewed himself as a pragmatist—and yes, sadly, an opportunist, but only out of necessity, he rationalized. Long before Göring would admit the obvious, Heller recognized that the Third Reich's ambitious plans were faltering and saw a need to protect his future. Göring's appetite for exquisite art had provided the solution. The sheer volume of purchases on Göring's behalf had left ample room for creative accounting, the tangible fruit secure within a numbered account at the Dolder Bank of Zurich.

The Reichsmarschall was right about another thing as well: the glorious Reich was slowly sinking. He didn't come right out and share such treasonous talk, but he nibbled at the edges. If others were already making plans . . . there was less time than he had estimated.

The Reds were pushing from the East, and the Allies hadn't been stopped since the invasion. It was like being aboard the *Titanic*, but on this ship, there were no lifeboats.

They needed to construct one while there was still time to act.

12

"I'm telling you, de Gaulle has no right to speak in the name of the French nation!"

Bernard Rousseau watched Marcel Bertille pound the wooden table with his right fist, furious with the news that the Free French leader had tried to exclude Colonel Rol—their commander in the Resistance—from signing German General von Choltitz's surrender document.

Bertille, face flushed, wasn't finished. "I see through de Gaulle's gesture," he hissed. "This is a move by our rivals to take credit for Paris's deliverance. I can assure you that this is not what we envisioned for our future or the future of communism!"

Shouts of agreement echoed through the smoke-filled back room of the Brasserie Lipp—the Left Bank establishment with an art deco interior that dated back to 1926. A Veronese-style painted ceiling complemented by mosaic panels and decorated mirrors allowed Bernard to view everything happening in the banquet room. What the Frenchman saw, following his arrival at Meeting Point B, was frustration building at a time that had been only a dream prior to D-Day.

"Keep your wits about you, Marcel." Bernard looked

around the table where the Resistance leadership had gathered. "Yes, it's true de Gaulle said that Colonel Rol's name had no business being on that document, but in the end, his signature was part of the proclamation."

"Barely." Bertille shook his head. "The Colonel had to gate-crash the meeting between Leclerc and von Choltitz and insist that he be party to signing the surrender documents. I, for one, say that we are lions led by donkeys. We have been hoodwinked by the Free French. Their greedy hands control the police and the government buildings, but I will not forget the struggle of the last four years, paid for in our comrades' blood for a socialist tomorrow!" Bertille punctuated his outrage with a clenched fist.

Heads around the table nodded in agreement. Bernard's too, but the truth was that the dozen or so Resistance groups, including their Francs-Tireurs et Partisans and de Gaulle's Free French—had varying political outlooks and class compositions. They had united collectively to drive out the Nazis, but now that liberation was a fait accompli, fissures were sure to appear once the dust settled onto the cobblestones of Paris's majestic boulevards.

"You seem to have Colonel Rol's ear," Bertille said. "What do you think he's going to tell us tonight?"

The eyes of more than a dozen Communist leaders bore into Rousseau. He met their gaze and nodded in respect toward the more senior members. "As I look around, I see comrades who have fought for the working class and against the French imperialist state since 1936. I joined this great struggle long after many of you answered the call. For the last four years, together we circulated copies of our manifestos, sabotaged trains and electricity stations, and conducted an urban guerilla campaign. Fascist repression was vicious, and we paid a heavy price. On average, a member of our *bataillons* lived only seven months. Yet, somehow, we have survived to carry on the banner of communism and fight against the oppressive bourgeoisie. As to Monsieur Bertille's comments, I agree. We must remain vigilant over the course of the next few weeks, days, and even hours. This is our chance to claim the seat of power."

For the next half hour, Bernard listened as the group debated France's future. Most agreed the Gaullists had out-maneuvered their cause when they beat the Communists to the Préfecture de Police a week earlier—the flash point of the Paris insurrection. Others recommended they take the fight for the working class to the streets.

The discussion and the room were heating up when the red velvet curtain behind Bernard parted. Two men armed with MAS-38 submachine guns framed the passage. There was an immediate screeching of chairs as all who had gathered leaped to their feet. With straight shoulders and a lifted chin, "Colonel Rol"—the *nom de guerre* for Henri Tanguy—strode in. Hands that had instinctively reached for sidearms now saluted their commander.

Although Colonel Rol was only in his mid-thirties, Bernard looked up to him as a father figure who possessed all the qualities he admired: patriotic Frenchman, devoted and disciplined Communist, and above all, a brave, ambitious leader.

The Colonel, red-eyed, weary, and dressed in his Spanish Civil War uniform, demurred. "Please, sit down. Rest your feet. It's been a long day."

A place was cleared at the head of the table, and the fatigued Rol accepted the offered chair.

"Would the Colonel like to toast our victory?" one of the lieutenants asked.

Rol waved off the offer. "Not after the news I learned." His expression darkened as he surveyed the silent room.

The Resistance leader rose to his feet. "Upon de Gaulle's arrival in Paris this afternoon, he told several people I know that he expected a direct, Communist-led challenge to his authority in Paris, so he decided to receive us when he was ready to—and not a minute before. The first thing he did was visit the Préfecture de Police to inspect the start of the uprising, and then he was driven over to the Hôtel de Ville, where tens of thousands had gathered."

Bernard knew the Préfecture de Police was a symbol of the Gaullist resistance, while the Hôtel de Ville was the "house of the people"—the city hall where the Third Republic was proclaimed in 1870. As news of Paris's liberation spread throughout the city, a dense mass of Parisians had packed the historic square, waiting for an appearance from whoever was in authority.

"When he stepped to the balcony, the crowd went crazy, chanting, 'De *Gaulle*, de *Gaulle*, de *Gaulle*.' Declaring 'Vive la France,' the general said that more than ever, national unity was a necessity. Not once did he mention the FTP or the other comrade groups in the Resistance. That's when I knew we were had." Colonel Rol swallowed hard, lowering his head.

Immediately, voices from every part of the room rose in protest. Bernard sat silently, absorbing the news, when suddenly everything became clear. The key event had been the seizure of the Préfecture de Police six days earlier by the Gaullists, who realized that the police formed the largest armed French group in the city. The Paris police knew they could be charged with collaboration during the Occupation, so there was incentive to side with the Resistance once the fighting began. But the police were equally aware that the Germans would respond brutally to any shift of allegiance, so timing was critical.

The Gaullists had providence on their side when the 2,000 policemen immediately sided with them and fought the arrival of German tanks and troops. Together, they were protected by a solidly built structure designed to resist mob violence or an armed counterattack. Once the German assault was blunted, a stalemate ensued and the Gaullist forces had a strong footing.

Colonel Rol raised his hands to quiet the room. "This last week, we took the fight to the streets while the Gaullists watched from the Préfecture de Police. We manned the barricades. We guarded the bridges that were set with explosives. We acted independently in Paris in challenging the German military garrison. And now, this insult is our thanks."

The Colonel wasn't finished.

"De Gaulle notified us that he would be making his 'official entry' into Paris tomorrow afternoon with a parade down the Champs Élysées from the Arc de Triomphe to the Notre Dame Cathedral. I don't have to remind you of the symbolism behind this march. This will be a blunt proclamation that he has the support of the people."

"Surely he's not going to walk alone in this parade!" A voice in the back of the room dripped with indignation.

"In essence, yes. We will march tomorrow, arm in arm with other chiefs of the Resistance like the CNR, CPL, and COMAC," Rol said. "But there will be an important distinction. We must walk two steps behind de Gaulle."

A clamor arose throughout the private room of the Brasserie Lipp. The significance of striding along the Champs Élysées in de Gaulle's shadow was not lost on Bernard.

"What can we do?" asked one of the lieutenants.

Colonel Rol sighed and rubbed his temples. "At this time, nothing. But opportunities will present themselves. With emotions running so high, the people need a hero they can rally around. De Gaulle happens to be at the right place, at the right time, but if his qualifications during this volatile time can be discredited, sentiment can easily swing against him, and we in the Communist movement could assume a more active leadership role. We must wait and be patient."

The French Communist leader stood, signaling the meeting was over. "We are to assemble tomorrow at fourteen hundred hours at the Arc de Triomphe, where de Gaulle will lay a wreath at the tomb of the Unknown Soldier. À demain." *Until tomorrow.*

Flanked by two armed guards, Colonel Rol beckoned Bernard to follow. When they stepped onto the Boulevard Saint-Germain, he turned back to him.

"How did it go last night? Were you able to convince Colette of your loyalty?"

"I think so." Bernard paused. "I'm not much of an actor."

"Did you present her the locket?" he asked.

"Yes," Bernard replied. "Thanks for giving it to me. It was a good distraction. She sensed that something was wrong."

"If there's one thing I've learned during the Occupation, it's that you can't trust anyone. Keep me informed. I hope the gift was enough. She knows more than she is letting on and may prove to be a valuable source of information, but only if she trusts you."

Bernard nodded, but inwardly he was torn. He loved Colette, there was no question, but he was in a fight for something far more important than his emotions.

Angry voices rising on the boulevard distracted his thoughts. He turned to investigate the sound of rage.

A menacing crowd followed three women—stripped to the waist, their heads shaved. As the distraught women drew closer, he could see that someone had painted black swastikas on their breasts. The mob followed the half-naked women, filling the air with taunts for having been "mattresses" for the Germans. Others spat on them. The helpless three, bound together by rope, wept and hung their heads in shame. One wore a sign that read "I whored with *les boches*." It was a pitiful scene.

Rol raised a pistol into the air and fired twice, sending most of the crowd scurrying for cover. "That's enough!" he yelled, commanding respect. "Is this what the French people will be known for—this cruelty?"

Bernard knew about the "horizontal collaborators." Some were prostitutes who made a good living in the busy brothels frequented by Nazi officers with money to burn, while others were foolish teenagers who associated with German soldiers out of bravado or boredom. All too many, however, were young mothers whose husbands were locked up in prisoner-of-war camps. With no means of supporting themselves or feeding their children, they accepted sexual liaisons in exchange for food.

A half dozen of Colonel Rol's lieutenants raced from the brasserie upon hearing the shots.

"Get some blankets!" Rol ordered.

Then turning to Bernard, his eyes flashed anger. He pointed a finger into the air. "I want posters by tomorrow warning of reprisals against those abusing women collaborators. We will knock a few heads if we must, but it is time to restore order and respect to France."

Antoine Celeste loosened his grip on the rope binding the three whores. He looked toward the source of the gunshots, and it figured: they came from that moralist Colonel Rol.

The tall man with dark hair standing next to the Colonel

attracted his attention. Why did that face stir such emotion within?

Celeste dropped the rope as he moved for a better look.

Then a jolt of clarity surfaced. He had only a brief glimpse, but Celeste was certain that this was the same man.

Two years had passed since he had witnessed his brother's execution, helpless to intervene. But standing a few meters away was the man responsible for Philippe's needless death at the hands of the Nazis. All the emotions associated with that loss—shock, sadness, and anger—came back with a rush.

For two years he'd kept his eyes open and his ears to the ground. There were rumors about who'd stopped the train, but every lead had come up empty. Now the pieces were fitting together at the Brasserie Lipp, known as the unofficial headquarters of the Communist factions of the Resistance.

Had this young man risen in the ranks since the tragedy at the Pantin rail yard? Why else would Colonel Rol be whispering something to him, taking him in confidence? The famous freedom fighter was undoubtedly issuing instructions on what to do with the three sluts he and several men had picked up loitering near a bar.

It made no sense to stop him and his Gaullist friends from making an example of the traitors who bedded down with the Nazis, just as it made no sense to stop an attack on a train bearing such a rich target—Reichsmarschall Hermann Göring. The course of the war could have changed.

Now he knew where to find the fifth columnist, who, like the whores, had sold out his allegiance to France.

There was a score to settle.

13

Moonlight drifted through the bedroom window, carrying the music and laughter of a free people. Gabi moved around the twin-sized mattress, attempting to fit the bottom sheet around the second corner. The sheet smelled of soap and sunshine. Madame Beaumont insisted on helping.

"Please, Madame Beaumont. I can make my own bed."

"I will hear nothing of the sort," the matronly woman said. "You are our guest, as is Colette."

Colette made eye contact with Gabi. "You better listen to her. She gets her way around here."

"Not tonight," Gabi said lightly as she quickly finished tucking in the last corner. She lay the duvet on the bed and smoothed the covering.

With a soft giggle, Colette leaned over to level her duvet. As she did, the locket slipped from beneath her blouse, catching Madame Beaumont's eye. "My, what a beautiful locket. Is that new?"

"Yes, Bernard gave it to me this evening. Do you recognize it?"

Madame Beaumont straightened, stepping closer. "Let me have a look, dear."

"Bernard said it belonged to your mom."

"Really?" She took a closer look. "I don't recognize it, or at least, I never saw Mother wear it. But it's beautiful all the same."

There was an awkward silence.

"Maybe I misunderstood," Colette said.

"Perhaps so." Madame Beaumont fluffed Colette's pillow and set it on the bed. "I hope you can sleep with all the noise. I don't think the celebration will be ending soon."

Gabi noticed Colette's perplexed expression as she tucked the locket beneath her blouse. Then she looked toward the hoopla lifting up from the Beaumont courtyard. "I think you're right. I hope they're not expecting you to serve breakfast."

Madame Beaumont smiled. "Well, if they are, they're going to be disappointed. Sleep well, and I'll see you in the morning."

As soon as the bedroom door closed, Gabi traipsed into the bathroom for a long overdue bath. A half hour later, she emerged and placed her clothes on the back of a chair. There was a soft thud as the skirt she'd been wearing earlier that day bounced against the wooden base. Reaching down to investigate, Gabi felt the firm rectangular shape and then remembered the small black book in the pocket. It seemed like days had passed since she had opened the hidden compartment in the base of the small safe.

With the slim black leather book in hand, she slipped under the sheets, grateful for the bed and the bath. "That was awfully nice of Bernard's aunt to offer Eric and me a place to stay. I can't remember when a hot bath felt better. I certainly wasn't looking forward to another night in the car, but after such a long day, I could sleep standing up."

"We'll all sleep well tonight. That's for sure," Colette said.

Gabi peeled open the soft leather cover and found three columns of neatly printed accounting. A line item followed by two large numbers. Quickly paging through, she found about twenty-five pages of detailed entries. The German script seemed to be titles and artist's names . . . *Still Life with Sleeping Woman* by Matisse and *Reclining Nude with Cupid* by Jan Van Neck . . . followed by several columns of numbers, with the first always lower than the second. She did some quick mental calculations and noted they were all about 30 to 40 percent higher.

"So, you work for the Red Cross?" Colette broke in.

Gabi hesitated. "Uh, yes, I enjoy helping others." She propped herself up on a pillow, hoping she sounded convincing enough to avoid more questions.

"What do you have there?" Colette inquired. "Do you keep a journal?"

Gabi looked up with a blank expression. She realized that Colette was now staring at her.

"Oh, this?" Gabi raised the small book. "Actually, I forgot I'd put it in my pocket this morning."

"So what's in it?"

"I'm not sure. Seems like a listing of paintings."

Colette crossed the room and sat on the side of Gabi's bed. She looked over her shoulder, skimming the German text. After a few seconds, she caught her breath in surprise. "Where did you find this?"

Gabi paused. "It's a long story, but basically, it was in the bottom of a safe . . . there was a hidden compartment."

"The one downstairs in the corner of the dining room?"

"Yes, the one Bernard said he found at a German stronghold." Gabi studied the woman's face. "You seem to recognize these titles. What are they?"

"I should know. They are the names of paintings, many of which I appraised prior to their sale."

"Their sale? To whom?" Gabi pressed.

Colette looked up and shook her head. "A despicable German colonel. He worked for Reichsmarschall Göring, and his job was to purchase art for his collections."

"So this booklet contains a list of all the paintings, along with sale prices?"

Colette scanned a page again. "Looks like there are two columns here . . . one for the sale's price and the other for the invoice. The last column shows the difference."

"Which means . . ."

"Someone was padding the price, making a handsome profit . . . at Göring's expense."

"Interesting."

They paged through the hundreds of cataloged entries. At the bottom of each page, total amounts for each column were added up.

"If my suspicions are correct," Colette surmised, "I'll bet Colonel Heller has been defrauding Göring for years and has amassed a small fortune."

"Appears that way. So you know this colonel?"

Colette sighed. "Unfortunately, yes. He has made my life very difficult . . ." Her voice trailed off.

Gabi sensed by Colette's tone that she had struck a nerve. The woman was troubled by something deeper. Gabi didn't know her well enough to prod for more information, so she let it go, knowing full well that Colette wasn't telling her everything.

There was also that embarrassing moment with the gold locket. Why would Bernard tell her it was a family heirloom when the pendant clearly wasn't?

Gabi yawned but was still wide awake. There was more

to Colette—and to Bernard—than what she saw at face value.

Her mind was racing. Had she made a mistake . . . sharing the information in this book with a woman she barely knew?

14

The door swung open before Ernst Mueller had set foot onto the landing. Allen Dulles stood in the doorway, holding his pipe as smoke curled to the high ornate ceiling.

"You made great time." Dulles extended his hand and beckoned Ernst across the threshold.

Ernst studied the OSS director and noticed the furrowed eyebrows behind rimless glasses. As much as anyone, Ernst knew that Paris's liberation did not mean safety for his daughter, Gabi.

The chief directed him to the formal living room, where he took a seat.

"Can I pour you a cup of tea?"

Ernst leaned back in the nineteenth-century Charles II settee. "Certainly, Allen. And if you have any sugar, a teaspoon would be great."

"Tea, I have, but it seems sugar is worth its weight in gold these days." Dulles reached for a bone china tea service resting on a low French antique table. "I hope a dollop of Swiss honey will satisfy that sweet tooth of yours."

Ernst smiled. As an American married to a Swiss, he had worked as an undercover agent with Dulles's network for the last year and a half and had come to admire the unwavering civility of the "gentleman spy." The formal persona of this Ivy League patrician came together nicely inside his cut-stone apartment situated in the heart of Bern's medieval Altstadt. He watched the well-connected Dulles pour steaming tea through a fine-mesh stainless steel strainer and fill the Clarabelle-patterned cup.

The last forty-eight hours had been anxious ones for Ernst with the stunning news of Paris's liberation. When Dulles had rung him earlier this morning, Ernst hoped all was well. The director reassured him that Gabi was not in any immediate danger, and then he asked if they could meet in Bern. Dulles's guarded tone, as well as his unusual Saturday request to drive the ninety minutes from his home near Basel to Bern, alerted him that something important had come up.

Dulles poured a cup for himself and got right down to business. "The boys from Bletchley Park intercepted a message last night that you might find interesting."

Ernst, who had been glancing at the headlines of several Swiss newspapers strewn across a coffee table, perked up. It was uncanny how often the code breakers at the British Secret Service cracked the Nazi ciphers.

"What did they find?"

Dulles settled into his customary wingback chair covered in burgundy leather. "We believe the message came from a Colonel Heller, speaking on behalf of his commanding officer."

"And who would that be?"

Dulles adjusted his glasses. "A Reichsmarschall Göring."

Ernst inched farther forward. "To whom was this Colonel Heller sending the message?"

"Our friends Schaffner and Kaufman."

Ernst's mind was now on full alert. He had contacts within the Swiss counterintelligence community, and Hans Schaffner and Rolf Kaufman were German agents living in Switzerland since the fall of France. The scuttlebutt was that this pair would disappear for a while and then resurface—usually in a rowdy bar nestled inside Zurich's seedy Niederdorf, flush with cash.

Contacts believed Schaffner and Kaufman's main task was to launder money for the Nazis' ultra elite. The German operatives were also spotted entering and leaving numerous Swiss banks lining the Bahnhofstrasse.

Ernst took another sip of tea. "I'm not surprised. This further establishes the fact that Göring has people in Switzerland doing his bidding."

"Here's where it gets interesting." Dulles's eyebrows peaked as he explained that the German operatives were directed to drive to a chateau outside Annecy, where they were to take possession of the *Mona Lisa* and bring it back to Switzerland. The Dolder Bank would hold it for "safekeeping."

Throughout the telling, Ernst sat motionless, but anger pumped through his veins. The arrogance of Göring and the sheer audacity. He slowly shook his head. "Nothing should surprise us anymore."

"I've been thinking how to best approach this." Dulles took a draw from his pipe. "First, we have to get a message to your daughter and Eric and brief them. They need to get to the *Mona Lisa* before Schaffner and Kaufman, but that will take some time and planning. The painting is supposed to be in a chateau outside Annecy, but the exact location has not been confirmed, at least according to the intercept. Regarding Schaffner and Kaufman, you could loosen a few tongues in the Niederdorf. Talk to the streetwalkers and barkeeps, that sort of thing. From what I hear, these two Germans aren't the most discreet agents to walk the earth." Dulles produced a legal-sized envelope bulging with Swiss francs. "This should help you unearth some clues."

Ernst rifled through his memory of contacts in Zurich's red-light district. He smiled slightly, considering what the people in his congregation would think of the friendships he valued in such places.

"There was another message."

"Oh?"

"Anton Wessner was told by Colonel Heller to expect to hear from Schaffner and Kaufman and to give them his full cooperation. Carte blanche, the message said."

"Anton Wessner—the president of Dolder Bank?"

"One and the same. Are you surprised that a Swiss banker is in bed with the Nazis?"

Ernst paused. "No, not that a banker is collaborating, but Wessner is well-respected in Zurich."

Dulles reached for his cup of tea, but before he took a sip, his eyes bore into the agent. "It's up to us to stop them. The *Mona Lisa* cannot fall into Göring's hands. I don't know what our adversary is up to, but whatever his scheme, the fragile French psyche can't afford to lose their national treasure, not after Libération."

"Agreed. If I can borrow your transmitter, I'll contact Eric right away."

"You'll find it in the back bedroom. Interesting, though, how history repeats itself."

"How's that, Allen?"

This time, Dulles allowed himself a long drink of tea before answering. "The *Mona Lisa* was stolen right under French noses before the last war—1911, if memory serves me correctly. It was two years before they found the painting. Terribly traumatic for the French back then. I'm sure this distraction would be the last thing de Gaulle needs right now."

Gabi raised the window shade and looked into the empty Beaumont courtyard. Paper trash littered the ground, and broken glass created a mosaic on pockets of cobblestones. The boisterous revelers were undoubtedly sleeping off their celebration, leaving behind an eerie calm for the late morning hour.

A form stirred in one of the twin beds. "What's it like out there?" a voice moaned as she pulled the duvet back over her head.

"A bright sunshiny day," Gabi replied to her new acquaintance. Her voice sounded cheerier than she felt. The Ost soldiers had haunted her dreams, and a heavy presence weighed on her shoulders.

Colette turned over in the bed. "What time is it?"

Gabi found her watch on her nightstand. "Later than I thought. Just about 10:30."

Colette came out of hibernation and stretched her arms. She covered her mouth, stifling a large yawn. "When did the party stop?"

Gabi, who had been gathering her clothes to get dressed in the bathroom, stopped in her tracks. "I think the accordion player collapsed shortly after 4 a.m. At least, that's when I last looked at my watch."

A knock on the door caused both young women to look up.

Colette spoke in a whisper. "Probably Bernard's aunt, wondering when we're coming down for breakfast." She raised her voice. "Who is it?"

"Eric. Is Gabi there?"

"I'm here. Be there in a moment," Gabi said.

There was a pause. "A message from the Red Cross came over the transmitter," Eric's voice was urgent.

"Okay."

Gabi stepped into the bathroom and set her clothes on the edge of a rattan hamper. *Another message from Mr. Dulles?* She wondered why the OSS chief was contacting them again, especially after they just spoke last night. It didn't sound good.

If the events of the last twenty-four hours were any indication, today would be another day of surprises.

———

Eric had copied the letters of Morse code streaming through his headset onto a yellow pad. Then he used a codebook to decipher the message. He committed the contents to memory before burning the piece of paper in the bedroom fireplace:

Information from London indicates that the Mona Lisa painting is in harm's way in southern France. The painting is thought to be near Annecy, but waiting to confirm exact location. Begin planning departure for Annecy. The Mona Lisa must be protected at all costs.

—E

The *Mona Lisa*? Eric had many important missions before, but this . . . he couldn't put it into words. The *Mona*

Lisa was the world's most well-known painting, France's greatest treasure. He did not wonder why the Nazis wanted it . . . but how could he and Gabi stop them?

When she arrived in the dining room, Eric whispered the explosive contents to Gabi. Her eyes widened slightly as her mind took in his words. She nodded and smiled, and Eric let out a slow breath. He admired how she maintained her calm.

"We must find petrol, which will not be an easy task—"

The sound of footsteps bounding down the wooden staircase caused him to pause. He glanced up to see Colette and then turned back to Gabi.

Gabi gave Eric a knowing look. They'd resume the conversation later.

As Colette entered the dining area, Madame Beaumont stepped out of the kitchen, wiping her hands on a faded red apron. She shooed Eric, Gabi, and Colette toward the dinner table.

"Our hens must have known that Paris was liberated yesterday," she said gaily. "There were plenty of eggs this morning. I even have a little Comté that I can mix in some scrambled eggs," she said and then stepped back into the kitchen.

Eric missed his daily fix of animal protein. "That would be very kind of you, Madame Beaumont, especially at this late hour," he called to her.

He looked through the open kitchen door and saw Madame Beaumont crack a half-dozen eggs into a small bowl and then beat them with a silver fork before pouring them into the saucepan. She sprinkled dabs of creamy yellow cheese onto the foamy mixture.

The smell of cooking eggs *avec fromage* filled the living quarters, and Eric's stomach rumbled.

Five minutes later, Madame Beaumont walked out with scrambled eggs heaped upon a china platter. Steam rose into the air, spreading a delightful scent through the room.

"Did you rob a farm?" Colette asked.

"No, just happy chickens. Please, eat up."

"You're sitting down with us," Colette insisted.

Madame Beaumont declined. "I had something earlier—"

Colette turned to Gabi and Eric. "Madame Beaumont is as good at stretching a meal as she is at stretching the truth." With laughter in her voice, she turned back to Madame Beaumont. "You've eaten nothing but rutabaga and turnips all summer. We're certainly not going to enjoy these delicious eggs without you."

"Well, if you insist." Madame Beaumont returned to the kitchen to fetch another plate and place setting.

As they settled into their breakfast of eggs and ersatz tea, Madame Beaumont proudly expounded on the latest gossip circulating the neighborhood. Thousands of Germans had surrendered, and those paraded through the streets were cursed by jeering mobs. Some German soldiers were tackled and strangled with bare hands; others put a pistol to their temples rather than face the vengeful crowds.

"Then I heard on the radio this morning that the Free French and the Allied forces are dealing with stray snipers. Perhaps they didn't get the message that German forces had surrendered." Madame Beaumont shook her head.

Colette sighed. "Or they want to have the last word—or last shot—on the way out."

"Good point." Madame Beaumont clapped her hands together. "The other big news report was that General de Gaulle will be leading the big parade this afternoon on the Champs Élysées."

Eric set down his fork and knife. "I would imagine that Bernard will be marching."

"Maybe. I don't really know," Colette said.

"He didn't say anything when he left the party last night. I would imagine that's why he's busy this morning."

"How long have you known that he was with the Resistance?" Gabi asked.

"I had my suspicions all along, but one thing we learned quickly under Nazi rule is that you dare not raise such a topic with anyone, sometimes even with your boyfriend. Bernard is passionate about his political views, and it was obvious that he wouldn't be a passive observer throughout the Occupation, but we never discussed specifics. I think a tank parked in the courtyard is evidence enough."

Madame Beaumont stood up and began clearing dishes. "Mademoiselle Colette is correct. We all lived in fear of being turned in to the Gestapo. Thank goodness that era is over. Listen, I'll clean up and let you visit."

The matron stacked the plates with silver forks and knives and returned to the kitchen, closing the door behind her.

Eric could tell something bothered Colette. "Are you supposed to go in to the Louvre today?" he asked.

"No, my supervisor told me to return on Monday. Since I've been there, we've worked under German control. I can't wait to see how things will change. I would imagine the first thing we'll do is bring back the priceless art from their hiding places."

Eric and Gabi looked at each other askance.

"I always wondered what happened to your most famous pieces, like the *Mona Lisa* and Venus de Milo," Gabi said.

Colette shrugged her shoulders. "I guess it's no big secret

now. The most valuable pieces in the Louvre collection were moved out for safekeeping shortly after Hitler invaded Poland. Many were originally taken to various chateaus in the Loire Valley, but when Germany conquered France, the most famous pieces were trucked even further south into the Unoccupied Zone. The last convoy crossed the Loire River just hours before the bridges were blown."

"But didn't the Nazis want to get their hands on priceless works of art like the *Mona Lisa*?"

Colette sighed, as if she was measuring her words. "We had to stay one step ahead of them."

"That couldn't have been easy to do," Eric said. "We've heard rumors of how the Nazis deposited their plunder in Swiss banks."

"Most likely true. Especially if the paintings happened to be owned by Jews. While German art museums and, uh"—Colette hesitated for a moment—"private collectors augmented their collections by confiscations of art from what they called 'enemy aliens,' they also embarked on a purchasing program of gigantic proportions."

"You mean they bought the art they wanted?" Eric asked.

"Yes . . . there's no use hiding what they've done. The Nazis were fueled by unlimited funds made available from the economies of the countries they conquered. But many of our works at the Louvre weren't available at any price, and the Germans knew that. It turns out there were treasures that they could not steal."

Eric listened intently, fascinated by what he was hearing. "You seem to know a lot," he offered, baiting his hook, waiting for her response.

A guarded look crossed over Colette's face, and she hesitated a moment before replying. "Large museum. Small staff," she declared simply.

"I could imagine that you were put into some delicate situations."

Eric dared to press her further. "You mentioned last night that you were a curator. Can I ask who is in charge of the *Mona Lisa*?"

Colette paused and looked suspiciously toward Gabi, then back to Eric.

"C'est moi," she said. *It's me.*

15

The heavy scent of coffee and cigarettes filled the air.

Hans Schaffner was surveying the café when a woman seated at a front table caught his eye. Even though she tended to a baby in a pram, he noticed she met and held his gaze. He didn't mind keeping company with housewives whose husbands were away, but this potential liaison would have to wait. He cast her a warm smile, then with a sigh of reluctance, he brushed past.

Needing to keep his mind focused, he cradled a copy of the *Neue Zürcher Zeitung* and found an empty table in the back of the café, away from the other customers. What he read soured his *Kaffee crème*.

Zurich's newspaper of record, customarily with a gray visage, was one of the most austere in Europe. Uncharacteristically on this Saturday morning, however, three rectangular photos were splashed above the front-page fold: a half-dozen French infantrymen aboard a Sherman tank that motored past adoring crowds on Avenue Victor Hugo; an older woman in a pleated summer dress running up to General de Gaulle to plant a grateful kiss on his cheek;

and untidy rows of Wehrmacht prisoners—hands raised—parading past vengeful crowds.

"Nazis Driven Out of Paris," blared the headline in seventy-two-point type—another rarity for the stolid Swiss newspaper. "Parisians Celebrate Hour of Reckoning," stated the second deck.

Schaffner knew his fortunes rose and fell on the advances and retreat of the German front lines. For the last two years, the territory of the Third Reich had shrunk considerably—and so had the "jobs" he and his partner, Rolf Kaufman, performed on the behest of Colonel Heller. Sadly, most of the money wired into his bank account had been squandered on loose women, cheap wine, and mediocre card skills at the *jass* table. A chill of desperation passed through him as he reached for another sip of coffee. Their next job had to succeed. His lifestyle depended on it.

The door to the pastry shop opened, jangling the small bell affixed to the jamb. Schaffner unemotionally peered above the print to see Rolf Kaufman. Kaufman's eyes scanned the half-full restaurant, populated with coffee-klatch housewives taking a Saturday morning shopping break.

Schaffner silently stood to shake hands and offered his partner a seat. Then he turned the Zurich newspaper for his partner to see.

"Yeah, I caught it at the kiosk," Kaufman replied. "Not great news."

"Well, I have some better news. We're back in business."

"Oh?"

"A message from Heller last night. He has a job."

Kaufman rapped his knuckles against the wooden tabletop. "Does anybody get hurt?"

Fair question, Schaffner thought, especially for their

line of work. "There is always that possibility, but I don't know yet."

Schaffner took a sip from his coffee, then motioned for Kaufman to lean in. He lowered his voice. "He wants us to steal a painting—a very special one."

His accomplice regarded him with a quizzical expression. Kaufman looked a bit like a rat with his pointy nose and narrow-set eyes.

"Ja, und . . . ?"

"The *Mona Lisa*," Schaffner whispered.

Kaufman's eyes widened.

"I received a follow-up transmission this morning. Heller said, upon reflection, he realized that his request places us in a, shall we say, very delicate position. That's why he's authorized Wessner to pay us five times our usual fee and half the money up front." Schaffner's chest tightened at the idea of that much money, but he tried not to let it show.

Kaufman whistled under his breath and rubbed his fingers back and forth, as if he was already holding the money. "I could use the cash. So where's the *Mona Lisa*? I hope Heller's not expecting us to go to Paris."

"We're in luck. The painting is at a chateau fifty kilometers from Geneva. He'll send the exact location in the next transmission, but he wants us to discuss logistics with Anton Wessner before we leave the country."

"Wessner? The Dolder Bank president? Why would he get his hands dirty?"

Schaffner shrugged, fingering the spoon he'd used to stir his coffee. "I'd guess for the same reason we're going to steal the most famous painting in the world—money. We need to hand the painting off to him so he can store it in the vault underneath the Bahnhofstrasse, for which he'll be paid handsomely I'm certain. Once he takes possession of the *Mona Lisa*, Swiss banking laws will protect everyone, including Heller."

"You mean Göring."

"I suppose they're one and the same. Although, the way Heller has been skimming cream off the top, it's a toss-up who has more loot stashed away in Zurich. At least, that's what Wessner implied after one too many schnapps." He softly smiled to himself, proud that he knew how to loosen the lips even of bank presidents.

Kaufman held up his hand. "I'm not surprised, especially with the way the war is going. Everyone is storing up something for the long winter ahead. Nonetheless, the colonel won't be long for this world if Göring finds out. They'll be able to write a new chapter in the *Gestapo Torture Manual* after Göring's finished with him, but that's his problem." Kaufman slid his finger across his neck, mimicking a knife. "So when do we start?"

"As soon as we get the name of the chateau, we're on our way. First we'll have to find Wessner. I called his home, but there was no answer. He's probably at his chalet outside Lucerne. He seems to go there every weekend in the summer. But no answer there, either."

Kaufman crossed his arms and looked directly at Schaffner. "You're saying the painting is at a private residence, with no police protection, one hour from the border, and all of France has a hangover? This sounds too easy." He chuckled under his breath.

"I agree, but timing is everything."

Kaufman's eyes narrowed, and a smirk peaked the corners of his lips. "Say, Hansi, maybe we should keep the painting for ourselves. Work has been scarce."

"The thought crossed my mind," Schaffner shot back. "But I'll give you two reasons why we shouldn't. First, we couldn't fence the *Mona Lisa*, not even for a fraction of its value. Second, the thought of the Gestapo stringing us up with piano wire is most unappealing."

Schaffner sensed that this would be his last big score. But a question nagged at his thoughts: What would the Reichsmarschall do with a painting that was beyond priceless?

———

Colonel Heller, with flushed face, felt his blood pressure rising from frustration. The pounding pulse filled his ears as he strangled the phone receiver.

"I called Paris yesterday," he bellowed. "What do you mean—the telephone lines are down? Von Choltitz surrendered without firing a shot!"

"But sir," the operator interrupted, "we've had sporadic success all morning—wait, the line just connected. I'll ring you through."

"Bonjour, Musée du Louvre."

Heller took a long breath to steady himself, then slipped into French. He was careful to tone down his German accent.

"Are you open today?"

"For visitors, *non*, we are closed," replied the female voice.

"I thought maybe with Libération, everyone would be at the Louvre celebrating." Heller forced a lilt. The pretense of delight with events of the last twenty-four hours grated his nerves.

"No, we are closed today, except for a minimal staff. We expect to reopen in a week, monsieur."

"Actually, I was looking for someone, one of your curators, Mademoiselle Perriard."

"She's not in today, sir. I suggest you call back Monday."

The call clicked, and the operator was back on the line.

"I want you to try another number." Heller looked back

at his file and then dictated the phone number to Colette Perriard's apartment. A voice answered, although it didn't sound like Colette.

"I'm looking for Colette Perriard. Is she there?"

"No, I'm sorry, monsieur," said a female voice. "I haven't seen her since yesterday morning. I believe she is with her boyfriend."

Heller thought for a moment. "Is there a phone number? It is urgent that I speak with her."

"Let me see . . . yes, she left it."

Heller noted the number and thanked the roommate with flowery language.

He hung up and dialed the operator again, hoping that the lines stayed open.

This time, his luck had run out. Slamming the phone down, he took a deep breath and ordered himself to remain calm.

The German colonel opened a small notebook and turned to a dog-eared page. There were several entries lined through; the last one was the name of a chateau and a village.

If he didn't reach Colette by tomorrow, then Schaffner and Kaufman would have to go with this one.

Good thing the parade doesn't start until 2 p.m., Bernard thought. After celebrating "the greatest night the world has ever known"—as one Radio France commentator breathlessly described it—the champagne-filled citizens of Paris were understandably taking their time getting started the morning after.

With throbbing headaches, liberated Paris was still not entirely at peace. Bernard touched his fingers to his temples, noting his own migraine as he considered how the city hadn't been cleared of German snipers, trapped in their sequestered perches, either out of touch with the news or wary to be seen in uniform.

There also were reports that a combat team from the French 2nd Armored was on their way to the Le Bourget airport, where a body of German troops threatened to counterattack. None of the celebrating citizens wanted to think the Germans would try to reclaim the city, but Bernard hadn't pushed the worry completely from his mind.

After spending the night at Dubois' flat in the 8th arrondissement, he had gone for a walk and witnessed sights that brought mixed emotion. At the Place de la Madeleine, a little girl asked an American GI for "another ball."

In her small hands, she gripped an orange for the first time.

The sight caused his heart to ache. These small children had only known the Occupation. Then he witnessed a young woman Colette's age stop an American GI and ask in halting English, "May I wash your uniform?" He was caked in mud from his helmet to the tips of his combat boots, his face so filthy that Bernard was uncertain if he wore a beard. He watched as she led the soldier into the family apartment to get him cleaned up.

Making his way toward the Place de la Concorde, he passed the five-star Hôtel de Crillon, where doormen wearing dinner jackets blocked casual visitors from entering.

Plus ça change, plus c'est la même chose. The more things change, the more they stay the same.

He shook his head in disgust: the Hôtel de Crillon—gilded, crested, tasseled, and ornate—symbolized the bourgeoisie excesses that he and his fellow French Communists vowed to change. Marx's credo—"From each according to his ability, to each according to his need"—came to his thoughts. For France to become a nation where every person contributed to society according to the best of his or her ability and consumed from society in proportion to his or her needs—that was the utopia he sought and fought for. Now, more than ever, that dream was attainable.

As he made his way up the Champs Élysées toward the Arc de Triomphe, hundreds of VIVE DE GAULLE banners were being hung from second- and third-story windows and hundreds more were already pasted against regal buildings fronting the grandest boulevard in the world. Dubois had told him that printing presses had been running until dawn, and all morning long the radio had been heralding "de Gaulle's march" down the Champs Élysées.

The muscles in his neck tightened and his footsteps grew heavier. He wished he could stomp out de Gaulle's name. The synergy of frustration and pent-up anger built with the unfurling of each new banner.

Where was de Gaulle when blood from the Resistance had flowed? No doubt living in England in far more comfort than his fellow countrymen. He and his comrades were the ones who had done the heavy lifting. His shoulders slumped, considering he was just one among many countless and nameless fighters shunted to the sidelines by a general who seemed oblivious to their sacrifice.

This was de Gaulle's rendezvous with history, the radio commentators said, the culmination of his four-year crusade, the unofficial referendum in which he would establish his authority and silence political rivals. Millions were expected to line the parade route from the Arc de Triomphe to the Notre Dame, where de Gaulle and local dignitaries would witness a *Te Deum* Mass of thanksgiving inside the famous cathedral.

Spotting a VIVE DE GAULLE poster on the sidewalk of the Champs, he swooped down to pick it up, studied it pensively, and then crumpled the paper into a ball. With a flick of the wrist, Bernard discarded it into the gutter.

In many ways, he and the French Communists had been tossed aside by an imperious and opportune general who thought he knew what was best for the French people.

Vive de Gaulle? Not if he and his comrades had a say.

———————

From their vantage point at the Place de la Concorde, Gabi looked up the Champs Élysées, its thick borders black with cheering crowds. Young boys had climbed trees and lampposts overlooking the route. Women, children, and men lifted their faces, hoping for a glimpse of their national hero.

It was a few minutes before two o'clock, and everywhere she looked—from balconies, rooftops, windows, and curbs—hundreds of thousands of Parisians readied themselves to officially welcome Charles de Gaulle and the victorious Allies into Paris. This was their chance to formally embrace freedoms not felt in four years.

She, along with Eric and Colette, were scrunched behind a chain of police and firemen, who, with arms linked, attempted to hold back the encroaching crowd from the plaza. They were losing ground. Bodies pressed around them, and Gabi longed for a breath of fresh air.

"I've never seen anything like this." Colette placed a hand over her heart. "The radio said two million people might be on the parade route."

"Here, stand in front of me." Eric stepped back and created a pocket for Gabi behind the arm-linked guards. "You'll get a better view."

Gabi welcomed the sheltered vantage. The parade was about to begin. Eric wrapped his arms around her, and a smile filled her face.

Vive la France.

Bernard, positioned alongside his leader, Colonel Rol, took a deep breath and exhaled. The anger and frustration was slowly being replaced by a sense of excitement. It was impossible to be surrounded by hundreds of thousands of his cheering countrymen without being buoyed by their mood. Besides, it was clear this would be the only public recognition his branch of the Resistance would be given for putting their lives on the line for four long years. His mind flashed back to those who'd died. If he'd walk straight and tall for anyone, he'd do it for his comrades.

The grand Arc de Triomphe stood over them, casting a shadow over those who'd survived. Bernard looked up into the deep recesses of the Arc, then to the varied commanders and back again to the cheering throngs. Someday he would tell his grandchildren about this moment.

General Charles de Gaulle, tall and poised, stood erect before France's Tomb of the Unknown Soldier, where he laid a wreath of red carnations on the massive granite slab. Then, with a symbolic gesture, de Gaulle extended a torch and relit the grave's eternal flame, the first Frenchman to perform this solemn duty since June 1940.

The crowds hushed in a moment of silence, giving Bernard an opportunity to clear his mind. He moved his gaze to watch de Gaulle—with the eyes of Paris upon him—turn and inspect Leclerc's tanks and armored vehicles that ringed the Étoile. General de Gaulle's regal air and measured steps spoke volumes about the political power that he expected France to bestow.

Police cars led the procession—one with a loudspeaker announcing that de Gaulle was "confiding his well-being to the people of Paris"—followed by four tanks from the

2nd Armored. Bernard had never experienced this type of gathering before, and he understood the worry of the police. Enemies could still lurk among them. To eliminate de Gaulle would be a small but significant victory for the Germans, even in retreat with tails between their legs. The emotional crowds, surging forward on both flanks, were held back by members of the Free French Resistance as well as policemen.

As promised, de Gaulle made sure he was front and center, towering a head taller than his companions, at the parade start. "Messieurs, remember to stay behind me," he said as the march began down the Champs Élysées to nearly hysterical chants of "Merci!" and "Vive de Gaulle!"

The thunderous acclaim of a nation had begun.

From a distance of more than one and a half kilometers, Eric could feel the excitement surge among the mass of humanity ringing the Place de la Concorde with its giant Egyptian obelisk.

From Eric's view, the procession of police cars and tanks was orderly enough, but the rest of the parade flowing down the Champs Élysées resembled a disorganized mess. Minutes passed as the advancing parade moved at a slow but steady pace. Thirty minutes later, as de Gaulle neared their position, a kindergarten-age girl slipped through adult legs and handed the general a bouquet of flowers. He accepted with a smile and lofted her high before setting the girl down and pointing her toward her parents. De Gaulle then turned and handed the bouquet to—Bernard Rousseau!

Eric rubbed his eyes, making sure he was seeing correctly, but it was indeed the Frenchman.

"Salut, Bernard!" Colette yelled.

Bernard looked up at the familiar voice. He smiled and moved toward them, but as he took a step forward a rifle shot split the square.

At the crack of gunfire, thousands of onlookers fell to the pavement. Eric pulled both Gabi and Colette down under outstretched arms as screams of panic waved through the crowd. Eric crouched down, but not before he looked up to witness a sentinel moment. As thousands cowered, including Resistance members marching alongside, de Gaulle maintained his ramrod posture and moved indifferently forward, fully ignoring the chaos and panic.

He maintained his methodical gait as the parade made the bend onto the Rue de Rivoli—as if now invincible. The surrounding throng seemed to be bowing.

As his steps continued forward, panic turned into applause; first a ripple, then swelling into a tidal wave. The crowd was now delirious with adoration. De Gaulle had summited the peak into the pantheons of French immortality. The impromptu coronation was complete, christened with peals of "Vive de Gaulle!"

A brave man, Eric thought. *He never flinched.*

Bernard worked his way to Colette and wrapped his arms around her.

"Are you all right?" he asked.

"I'm fine," Colette replied over the din. "It doesn't seem as though anyone was hurt."

"I have to go," Bernard said. "I'll meet you at the Brassiere Lipp after the parade."

"Wait!" Colette reached toward her boyfriend, but he was already lost in a sea of humanity closing in behind the procession.

From the pedestal of the Obelisk of Luxor, Antoine Celeste scanned the front of the parade through binoculars, checking to see if anyone had been hit. He saw a man leave the route for a moment, then return alongside Colonel Rol.

Recognizing the face, he seethed. His brother's untimely death would not be forgotten.

Celeste's revenge would be unexpected and painful.

16

The party had never stopped at the Brasserie Lipp.

Gabi and Eric followed Bernard and Colette past the crowded tables toward the back of the restaurant where a red velvet curtain separated the main floor from a private room. Eric's hand protectively held Gabi's, and she noticed his eyes scanning the room as they walked.

Even during the victory celebrations pulsating through Paris, Eric was alert to any danger. She appreciated that about him, knowing his vigilance had protected her. She knew that he would continue to watch out for her well-being.

Gabi moved slowly, since the Brasserie Lipp was jammed following de Gaulle's parade. Outside, two dozen people waited for the opportunity to order from its menu of renowned Alsatian cuisine, although she imagined the selection had been limited in recent years.

Making it to the private room, Gabi counted twenty or thirty people, mostly men wearing berets, locked in conversations inside this section of the restaurant reserved for Resistance heroes. Small groups huddled with hand-rolled smokes and glasses of Chardonnay.

Bernard touched her arm. "Come meet some of my

friends." He led her and Eric toward a bareheaded older gentleman with a dimpled chin. His engaging smile reminded her of Roland Mueller, her grandfather.

"Gabi and Eric, I present to you Marcel Bertille, the mastermind of the Resistance."

His colleague deflected the characterization. "Bernard, you sell yourself short. You were always the one thinking one step ahead of the *boches*."

Bertille stepped closer to Gabi and Eric. "Did he ever tell you about the time he single-handedly stopped a train bound for Berlin?"

Gabi shook her head and noticed Eric doing the same.

Bernard held up a hand. "*Mon ami*, let's not bore our guests. That happened a long time ago."

"I'd like to hear the story." Colette smiled at her boyfriend.

"Today is not a day to tell stories from the past."

Gabi's interest was piqued as well, but she could see that Bernard wasn't in the mood for storytelling. She looked around and saw Resistance members milling about, cigarettes burning in cupped hands. From the body language, they were having intense conversations, and she noted an undercurrent of tension circulating within the room. Maybe Bernard knew something she didn't—or Libération wasn't what it seemed to be.

"Please, take our table." Bertille called a waiter over to dump the ashtray and remove the empty beer glasses. "There are others I need to talk with. Would you excuse me? You'd think with the Nazis gone, our job would be done, but so far that hasn't been true."

Gabi stepped back, giving Bertille room to slip past. *He has no idea*, she mused. *If they only knew about Göring's plan to steal the Mona Lisa.*

Bernard thanked Bertille, and the two couples pulled chairs around the scarred wooden table. A waiter scurried to wipe the surface with a dirty dishtowel.

"Anyone hungry?" Bernard asked.

Gabi's stomach rumbled. "I'm famished."

The Frenchman spoke to the waiter. "Could we see a menu, *s'il vous plaît?*"

"I'm afraid the kitchen is out of everything except for the *Pied de Porc Farci*, monsieur."

Eric turned to Gabi and spoke in Swiss-German. "Did he say stuffed pig's feet?"

Gabi nodded and laughed, then translated for Bernard and Colette. "I think Eric wants a double portion."

Eric grinned as laughter circled the table. "Surely the chef must have something else," he said to the waiter.

Five minutes later, the waiter returned with half a loaf of rye bread with *pâté de campagne*—country-style pork pâté—and bowls of the soup du jour, a tomato bisque.

Gabi turned toward Bernard. "On a day of celebration and thanksgiving, I can't help but notice that some of your colleagues don't have the same *joie de vivre*. Their smiles seem to be missing. Is something wrong?"

"Very perceptive, Mademoiselle Mueller." Bernard slipped into a formal elocution. "They're talking about the sniper attack on de Gaulle at the Notre Dame."

"Don't you mean at the Place de la Concorde?" Eric asked.

"No, there was a second attack." Bernard set his piece of bread with a dab of pâté back on his plate. "You noticed that a bullet fired in de Gaulle's direction didn't faze him. Well, there appeared to be another assassination attempt at the Notre Dame, but with more shots fired. I saw it. So did my colleagues." He tipped his head toward the men gathered in the private section.

"What happened?" A look of concern crossed Colette's face.

Bernard leaned in. "We were marching into the plaza in front of the Notre Dame when I looked up toward the tower on the left. I saw the tips of three rifles extend between the openings of one of the pylons. Before I could warn anyone, shots swept across the square. French soldiers weren't sure where the bullets were coming from, so they raked the rooftops. You can imagine the panic as people screamed and scrambled for cover, even though there was no place to hide.

"Once again, de Gaulle was indifferent to the bullets aimed in his direction. He strode into the cathedral as if it was Christmas morning. The pews inside the Notre Dame were full, but when I arrived, everyone had ducked for cover."

"Did the thanksgiving service go on?" Gabi asked.

Bernard nodded. "De Gaulle walked up the center aisle while we could still hear shooting from the plaza. He took his place of honor at the front of the main aisle, and then he and the priest recited the Magnificat together. When they finished, I think they both realized it was folly to continue, so de Gaulle departed with the same steady pace. I watched the expressions of everyone. They looked at him like he was walking on water. When news gets out about what happened at the Notre Dame, de Gaulle will have France resting in the palm of his hand."

As Gabi listened, everything made sense. The Resistance in Paris had been dominated by Communist-led cells and organizations, but it was de Gaulle who was winning the hearts of the people at just the right moment in history. No wonder these Resistance members at the Brasserie Lipp were dismayed.

"Colonel Rol thinks the Free French were taking the potshots," Bernard continued. "That it was a setup orchestrated

to make de Gaulle's arrival look like the Second Coming."
He cursed under his breath.

Gabi looked at Eric, but they both were silent. She
was beginning to understand the war was far from over.
It was obvious the French Communist leadership was an-
gered by the apparent checkmate from their rival, Charles
de Gaulle.

She wondered what their next move would be.

Eric also noted the tension in the room, and even at the
table. But now was the time for him to make his move—to
get the help he needed—or France would lose much more
than they already had.

"Colette, there's something we want to tell you," Eric
lowered his voice so only she and Bernard could hear. "Gabi
and I are part of an underground as well, although our work
for the Allies has been from the Swiss side of the border."

"Really?" Colette said. "Are you some sort of spies?"

"Not a term we use." Gabi remained composed. "But we
help where we can, which is why we drove to Paris yesterday
with the medicines and supplies on behalf of the Red Cross."

"So why are you telling me this?" Colette eyed them skeptically.

"Because we need your help."

"With . . . ?"

"The *Mona Lisa*."

Eric registered the looks of shock and distanced determination at the mention of their national treasure.

"Hear me out," he encouraged, seeing Colette pull away.
"We have solid information that German operatives are
preparing to steal her."

"What?" Colette's eyebrows knitted with incredulity.

"How could you know this? And why would they want to take *La Joconde* now?"

Bernard's face hardened. "The painting could never be sold to another collector. It's priceless. Even if it was sold, they would be found out."

"Which makes the painting the ultimate bargaining chip," Gabi chimed in. "This is pure speculation, but we think a Nazi bigwig might want to use the painting to save himself from the hangman's noose when the war's over."

"Any ideas on who that could be?" Bernard asked.

"We have a strong assumption that a Colonel Heller is involved," Eric replied smoothly.

Colette's chin quivered, and tears rimmed her lower eyelids. Eric could see she was distraught by the news—and even more so by the mention of Heller's name.

Eric fixed his eyes on the beautiful curator. "Does Heller's name mean something to you?"

Colette reached into her small purse and pulled out a handkerchief and dabbed her damp eyes. "Sorry. I feared something like this during the Occupation, but not . . ."

The curator stopped herself. "What I mean is, I don't think I—or France—could bear the news that the Germans have the *Mona Lisa* in their possession. It would be devastating for all of us. Unthinkable, especially now that we've been liberated."

"What do you know about Heller?" Eric persisted.

Bernard's gaze bore down on Colette as she gathered herself.

"This is complicated . . ." Colette looked pained.

Bernard placed his hand on top of hers. "But you know this *boche*, correct?"

"Unfortunately, yes, I know the colonel all too well," she began. "He has been a painful thorn in my side since I took my position at the Louvre. I believe he's working for Göring and serves as a buyer of art—I'm talking about massive quantities—on his behalf." She paused and looked around the table. "Colonel Heller is a shrewd and determined man. One not to be underestimated."

The sudden revelation left the table silent, absorbed in thought. All eyes remained transfixed on Colette.

"Do you think Heller really knows where *La Joconde* is hidden?" Bernard was staring hard at Colette. "After all, isn't this a carefully guarded secret?"

Colette, with upturned palms, said, "But of course. She's been moved several times since the war began. So who knows if Heller has this information? He's a ruthless man. I wouldn't put anything past him, including extortion and murder."

Gabi motioned to speak. "We don't want anything to happen to the *Mona Lisa*. We can help you bring her back."

"You're sure your intelligence is reliable," Colette said.

"Quite sure."

"Then we have to do everything we can to bring her home. If Heller gets to her first, she'll be gone for good."

Eric turned to Bernard. "Could you come along? We don't know who or what we'll find, but you have a lot of field experience."

Bernard smiled. "But of course. Anything to save our national treasure."

"Good. First, we'll need some fuel." Eric was eager to get started.

Bernard frowned. "Petrol has yet to trickle into Paris. From what I hear, they're saying Monday. Plus, I imagine the line would stretch the length of the Champs Élysées."

"I might know someone who can help," Eric said.

If Dulles could get to the right people, their car would be the first to fill up in Paris.

Evening had dropped like a curtain over the City of Light.

As the group stood to leave the Brasserie, Bernard told the others to go ahead. "There's someone I need to talk to."

After the trio had departed, Bernard caught Bertille's eye and waved him over to the table.

He got right to the point. "We need to meet with Colonel Rol."

"Something happen?"

"Yes." Pulling him aside, Bernard shared the startling new development. What he left unsaid was how the German operatives even knew *where* the *Mona Lisa* was being hidden at this moment. He feared that Colette had relayed that information but hoped that wasn't true.

Bertille tugged on his right earlobe, lost in thought. "I know what the Colonel would say."

"What?"

"Nous faisons d'une pierre deux coups." *We hit twice with the same stone.*

"I don't quite understand—"

"You secure the *Mona Lisa*, which solves one problem. Then at the right moment, we deliver *La Joconde* with maximum public attention, which will solve another."

Bernard frowned. "It sounds like you're asking me to steal the *Mona Lisa* before the Germans do."

"Exactly, comrade. If we have possession of *La Joconde* under de Gaulle's watch, we undermine confidence in his leadership. We can go to the people and say, 'Look, de Gaulle is in charge for one week, and the first thing that happens is that the Nazis steal our crown jewel! This wouldn't have happened under a democratic socialist government.' Then we deliver the *Mona Lisa*, saving the day, just as we have during the entire Occupation while de Gaulle sipped tea in England."

Bernard saw the merit in Bertille's thinking. The public *would* blame the Gaullists if the painting fell into German hands—and create a perfect public relations nightmare. Colonel Rol could disseminate a story about how the *Mona Lisa* was stolen, and then at the most advantageous time, they would "recover" the celebrated artwork and reap a windfall of goodwill—and support for the Communist Party.

But that meant taking possession of the *Mona Lisa* from Colette. What would happen to her? He rationalized that as an informant, no matter the outcome, she had it coming, but things would be worse if the painting was lost. Either way, all fingers would point to his girlfriend's loose lips. He would do what he could to protect her, of course, but one thing was certain: it would cost him their relationship.

Bernard's heart ached. His emotions felt torn between Colette and the future of France. Then again, what if she was part of it? She seemed saddened and anxious by the news . . . maybe her fearful eyes were due to the fact she'd been found out. There was so much he didn't know, and Colette herself admitted her help in selling their country's priceless artwork to Heller. How could he trust her?

He couldn't bear to see his political cause lose out due to his affections for a traitorous woman. If forced to decide between Colette and the political direction of France under Communist rule . . . well, that decision would be easy.

Seated at the end of the bar, sipping a glass of beer, Antoine Celeste watched Rousseau and Bertille walk to the front of the restaurant to use the telephone. The two men huddled near the entry as Bertille made the call, probably to their leader Colonel Rol.

With his hat pulled low to conceal his eyes in the shadow of its brim, he saw that Rousseau—with his back to him—concentrated on his colleague's phone call.

This was his chance. He rapidly closed the distance between them with his hand buried in the pocket of his jacket, fingers tightly wrapped around a handle securing the tang of a wide six-inch blade. His dying brother's face filled his vision.

Then, just as he neared his mark, a waiter carrying a tray of empty beer glasses high above his head squeezed in between, stopping Celeste's advance.

The waiter passed by with a swish of his apron. Celeste looked up to find himself face-to-face with Rousseau. The element of surprise had vanished. He froze for an uncomfortable moment. Rousseau made an awkward nod of greeting, and instinctively, Celeste nodded in return, then slipped out the front door.

Standing on the curb, Celeste steadied his trembling right hand. He lit a cigarette to calm his nerves and think through what had just happened. He'd almost snuffed out the quisling, but the opportune moment was gone. He could have skewered Rousseau and slipped back into the crowd, lost in the commotion.

Revenge would have to wait.

17

Hans Schaffner paced the Bahnhofstrasse—leading to Zurich's fashionable business district—with purpose. Rolf Kaufman strode by his side. It was good to be back in business, even if the assignment to steal the *Mona Lisa* was so audacious.

Schaffner knew that neither Göring nor Heller would ever take physical possession of the *Mona Lisa*. The priceless painting was to be delivered to the banker Anton Wessner for safekeeping. From there . . . well, who knew? All he cared about was his fee and the freedom it would provide.

They had an appointment to meet with Wessner on this quiet Sunday afternoon. Three or four years ago, Germans like him would have been invited to the bank to meet in an expansive office or over a sumptuous meal at the Alt Züri, one of Zurich's finest restaurants. But when the tide of the war changed—especially after the Allies gained a foothold in Normandy—Germans became persona non grata. The Swiss might blather on about their sacrosanct neutrality, but they knew how to choose sides when the outcome was no longer in doubt.

It came as no surprise—Wessner didn't want to meet in a public place.

Department stores and shops along Zurich's famed Bahnhofstrasse were closed for the Sabbath. Only a few restaurants remained open, including the Zeughauskeller, packed with the after-church crowd enjoying a decent bratwurst and a half-liter of Klosterbrau.

The pair walked past the busy restaurant and turned left at the corner. Across the street, they saw an olive-green Mercedes 170V parked, facing away. Wessner watched them from his rearview mirror. With his left hand, he patted the door to get their attention.

They approached the car on the passenger side, and Wessner leaned across the seat and opened the door. Schaffner climbed into the front, and Kaufman took a seat in the back.

"Good afternoon, gentlemen." Wessner extended his hand. He was in his late forties with close-cropped black hair flecked with gray. The smile appeared genuine but his manner was abrupt.

"Shall we get right down to business? Let's start with your plan to obtain the painting." Wessner turned at a forty-five-degree angle to face both men.

Schaffner looked to Kaufman, who nodded his head, indicating he wanted his partner to take the lead.

"Procuring enough petrol will be difficult, even with bribes," he began. "I don't see how we can get out of Zurich before mid-morning, at the earliest."

"Perhaps I can help—" Wessner stopped himself. "No, sorry. On second thought, it's better that you solve this problem. I suppose our mutual acquaintance anticipated this since I have been authorized to give you a sizable advance."

"I figured as much." Schaffner had never known a banker to get his hands dirty. "Speaking of money . . ."

"Everything you need is under your seat."

Schaffner leaned forward and looked underneath the bench seat, spotting a dark leather attaché case.

"You'll find fifty thousand Swiss francs inside, various denominations," Wessner said. "That should get you started. Another fifty thousand francs will be divided in half and deposited into your private accounts upon delivery of the painting."

Schaffner nodded. Over their four-year association, Wessner had never missed a payment, large or small, and fifty thousand francs was a lot of money—enough to buy ten houses in Switzerland. Once the job was complete, he and Kaufman would be set for life. The smallest hint of a smile formed on his lips as he tried to conceal his excitement.

"Did you get the address?" Wessner asked. "I was driving back from Lucerne and couldn't receive messages this morning."

"Yes and no," Schaffner replied. "Heller sent a message an hour ago saying he could not reach his contact in Paris, but last month he was told that the *Mona Lisa* was being kept at the Chateau de Dampierre, somewhere outside of Annecy. That's all he knows. He doesn't have an address, just the chateau's name."

"Chateau de Dampierre? Sounds like a winery."

Schaffner shrugged. "Could be. At any rate, we'll find it. May take us a little extra time, but castles tend to stick out. We plan on getting on the road once we receive confirmation from Heller."

"How's your French?" Wessner asked.

"Rusty. What about you, Rolf?"

"Better, but that's because I like the French girls." Kaufman flashed a lecherous grin.

Schaffner turned to Wessner. "We'll manage. If not, we'll let our Lugers do the talking."

"And after the *Mona Lisa* is in your possession?" Wessner's left hand drummed the steering wheel. The money said the banker trusted them to do the job, but his nervous twitches said otherwise.

"If the getaway is clean, we don't anticipate a problem at the border." Schaffner spoke with confidence, attempting to put Wessner at ease. The German had his own concerns, but he trusted his instincts. They'd always managed to get out of trouble before. This time would be no different.

Schaffner cocked his chin and continued. "We'll wait until late evening and pass through one of the back roads into Switzerland, probably near Annemasse. The border guards at these small outposts leave every evening at six o'clock, rain or shine. With a little luck, we should be standing inside your bank's underground vault five or six hours later. You might want to prepare for a night deposit."

"Excellent. But don't bring the *Mona Lisa* back to Zurich."

"Why's that?"

"I got a tip a few weeks ago from a fellow named Dieter Baumann. Do you know him?"

Schaffner's mind filed through his lists of contacts, but the name didn't sound familiar. Then again, just because he didn't know the name didn't mean he didn't know the man. Few revealed their true identities in his line of work. He slowly shook his head.

"He's a Swiss working for the Americans, but he likes to work both sides of the street, if you catch my drift." Wessner let the subtlety sink in before continuing. "He told me that American operatives were keeping our bank under surveillance, although he would not elaborate. If true, it would be foolish to walk into the Dolder Bank carrying the *Mona Lisa*—even in the wee hours of the morning."

Finally, in Schaffner's mind's eye, a face filled in. Handsome, but ruthless. "Oh yes, I remember now. I have met Baumann. I didn't trust him. He would sell out his mother. I assume this tip was not gratis."

"Correct. I gladly paid."

The Swiss banker sat straighter in his seat. "Here's what I want you to do. Come to my mountain chalet outside Lucerne instead. I'll send for an armored truck to pick up the painting. My chalet is fairly remote, so if someone is sniffing around, we'll know about it."

Gabi leaned into Eric's embrace and wrapped her arm around him, tucking herself close to his side. For the past hour, they'd been walking along the Seine River, discussing what they could do to foil the Germans intent on stealing the *Mona Lisa*. Both were frustrated that they couldn't get on the road today but understood that there wasn't any petrol to be had in battle-fatigued Paris. They had done what little was needed to prepare for their early departure. After helping Madame Beaumont clean the courtyard and tidy up from the party, there was nothing to do but wait. Getting out of the house for some fresh air was just a way to maintain their sanity.

"I'm concerned that Heller's agents will get to Annecy before we do. What if they are on their way right now?" she asked.

Eric stopped and turned toward her. "Nothing we can

do, but Dulles said in his transmission that London hadn't intercepted any more messages from Schaffner or Heller, so we have to assume they haven't left Zurich. The chief knows we need petrol before we can leave, and we'll get it—but not before the morning. Hopefully, Colette can get through to the Count or Countess by phone and warn them."

Gabi sighed, and they continued a little farther. When they came to a stone wall overlooking the Seine, they took in the Sunday afternoon traffic on the peaceful waterway. The Bateaux Mouches were still moored to the docks, no doubt because of the fuel shortage. Only a handful of rowboats glided across the glassy surface.

"Let's walk across the Pont Neuf." Eric steered her onto the gilded span and led her toward a wrought-iron railing above one of the bridge's medieval arches, affording them a view of the placid river and the teardrop-shaped Île Saint-Louis. "Funny how they call it the Pont Neuf—or New Bridge—even though it's the oldest bridge in Paris. A few days ago, if Hitler had his way, this bridge would have been reduced to a heap of rubble. What a shame that would have been."

Gabi switched to English. "Yup. That would have been in-Seine," she smirked.

Eric shook his head. "Nice one."

Gabi tucked herself closer to his side. "When are we due for dinner?"

"We're supposed to meet Bernard and Colette at the Brasserie Lipp at 7 p.m. But Bernard says he wants to take us to another restaurant."

"Good. I was hoping for someplace other than the Brasserie. In a city known for great food, there has to be more than one place to enjoy a nice meal."

"There's a small sidewalk café across the street from the Brasserie. Why don't we have a cappuccino and wait there?"

Gabi gave him a squeeze. "Sounds perfect."

———

The call girl at La Boîte à Bonbons, or the Candy Box, knew her customers well and was a magnet for information. Ernst Mueller was most appreciative and passed her five large denomination banknotes.

Her directions led him to an alley just past the Zeughauskeller, where Mueller had a clear view from his Peugeot as Schaffner and Kaufman crossed the street and stepped into a green sedan. They had never seen their tail.

Fifteen minutes later, he watched the two Germans exit the vehicle and noted Schaffner carrying a small satchel. They looked both ways and then headed back in the direction they'd come. He couldn't see the driver's face, but the vehicle matched the description of Anton Wessner's car from the profile Dulles had given him.

Assuming the satchel didn't contain the bank's annual meeting notes, Ernst surmised that the cash advance had been made.

He watched the green sedan pull away and then turn left at the next corner. Immediately, Ernst eased his car from the alley and pulled up near the next cross street in time to see Schaffner and Kaufman enter the Zeughauskeller. From their languid manner, they didn't appear to be in any hurry—which could only mean that they weren't leaving today for Annecy. Most likely tomorrow.

When Ernst departed Dulles's Bern apartment, the OSS director had said the code breakers at Bletchley Park were sifting through transmission traffic, watching for more communications between the conspirators. Nothing had surfaced. Ernst hoped it meant the two German agents were still waiting to receive confirmation of where to go. From their confident body language, the two had the look of cocksure thieves who believed they were about to steal the most famous painting in the world.

He wished he could stop them dead in their tracks, but there were too many witnesses, plus his congregation might not understand why their church pastor was arrested for gunning down two men in front of a crowded restaurant. He parked near the corner with a clear view of the entry.

An hour later, they still hadn't emerged from the Zeughauskeller. Growing impatient, Ernst decided to go inside to investigate. The after-church crowd had thinned a little, but he was unable to spot his marks as he surveyed the room. Stopping one of the waiters, he offered a brief description and asked if he'd seen them.

"They left five minutes ago," the waiter replied, "but they headed toward the back, to the men's room."

After checking the restroom and finding it vacant, Ernst rushed outside.

They were gone.

Eric and Gabi arrived a half hour before their dinnertime rendezvous and found a table for two at the sidewalk café. The sun cast long shadows across Boulevard Saint-Germain, where more couples strolled in the shade on an undemanding late afternoon. A general feeling of relief was the mood du jour.

Eric flagged down a passing waiter. "Two cappuccinos, please."

Gabi settled into her rattan chair, surveying the early evening patrons. She knew as an agent that she should never let down her guard, but as she looked around—and gazed across the table to Eric—she felt herself relax. "This is something I wanted to do before we left Paris—sit at an outdoor café and watch the world pass by."

"It's hard to believe how much has happened since we left Switzerland." Eric paused. "Actually, it's been quite a month."

Gabi nodded in silent agreement. Her thoughts raced back to the events, just a few weeks ago, that preceded their drive to Paris. "I wonder how Captain Palmer is doing? That American was quite a pilot. If it hadn't been for his flying prowess, I wouldn't be here. I'm guessing he's in a Swiss theater watching his favorite Bogart movie."

"He sure loved spouting lines from *Casablanca*." Eric chuckled.

"I think he had memorized the entire movie after seeing it so many times in Davos with the other interned Allied pilots. But I know what you're going to say."

Eric switched from Swiss-German to English. "Darling, we'll always have Paris," he said in a nasal-like imitation of Humphrey Bogart.

Gabi made a show of setting her napkin on the table. "If Bogey had been a redheaded Swiss dairyman, that still would have been an awful impersonation!"

Her smile slowly disappeared as she focused on something across the street. Eric swiveled in his seat to see what had attracted her attention.

"Take a look at that guy—the one with the scruffy beard, leaning against the building. He looks agitated, and his eyes keep darting back and forth like he's searching for someone."

"The one in the tan shirt?"

"Uh-huh."

"Seems intent on something," Eric said.

"He's been there ever since we sat down."

"Anything else look amiss?"

Gabi's eyes scoured the wide sidewalks fronting Boulevard Saint-Germain as well as the entrance to the Brasserie Lipp, which was directly across the broad avenue. "No, I don't see anything else—ooh, wait a minute. There's Bernard and Colette."

Gabi caught Colette's attention and waved them over. They pulled a couple of chairs over from a nearby table and greeted their friends.

After they'd taken their seats, Gabi glanced back across the street. The man was still there and staring right at them. "Do you know that man?" Gabi asked.

Bernard and Colette looked in the direction of Gabi's line of sight.

As soon as the stranger noticed they were looking in his direction, he turned and walked around the corner.

"I saw him last night. He bumped into me at the Brasserie."

Bernard shared the story of their awkward moment. "I didn't recognize him, as I do most of the patrons of the Lipp. He probably mistook me for someone else, or he was admiring my good looks."

"More likely, our beautiful companions." Eric raised his cup toward Gabi, then Colette. "Would you like to join us for a cappuccino?"

"Sounds good," Colette replied. Gabi noticed Colette's strained look. She definitely wasn't the same playful girl who had been teasing Madame Beaumont as she made the bed this morning.

Eric must have noticed too. He held up two fingers to signal the waiter, then turned to Colette. "How did it go today at the Louvre?"

"I must have tried twenty times to reach the Chateau. Apparently, the phone lines between Paris and Annecy are down. It's anyone's guess how long it will take to get them repaired. I want to go into the office tomorrow morning and try one last time."

"No problem. Once we get our fuel, Bernard and I will pick you up at the Louvre."

"I also need to see Monsieur Rambouillet before we go. He oversaw the delivery of the *Mona Lisa* to the Chateau de Dampierre last spring, so he can confirm the directions."

"Speaking of confirming things, I made reservations at a small bistro near my aunt's home," Bernard said. "It's called the Café de Flore. The *Poulet à la Montrache* is their calling card. You'll love it."

Eric turned to Gabi. "Sounds like a great meal to celebrate our night out in Paris."

———

As Bernard promised, Colette found Café de Flore's house specialty—pan-fried chicken immersed in a mushroom and cream sauce—to be delicious.

She offered the last of her roasted potatoes to Bernard, who cut them in half and used each piece to mop up what little sauce remained on his plate. Colette assessed his clean dish and wished there was more. French cuisine was uniformly excellent, but the portions were *trop petit*.

The four shared a pear tart with a small dollop of whipped cream for dessert, but Colette had only a bite. An infectious yawn circled the table, and she was eager to call it a day. She couldn't sit this close to Bernard without feeling tension radiate off him like heat from a wood-burning stove.

Colette stood quietly by Bernard's side as Eric paid the

check. Just as they reached the door, Gabi announced that she wanted to buy some things to eat on the trip.

"Maybe the chef will part with a few provisions—or an extra tart," she said with a smile.

Eric patted Bernard's shoulder. "Feel free to go on ahead. We'll catch up."

Colette followed Bernard as they made their way onto the sidewalk, welcomed by the cool evening air.

Bernard's aunt and uncle lived only a few blocks away off the Boulevard Saint-Michel. Turning in that direction, Bernard folded her arm into his, and they headed down the dimly lit street, enjoying the chance to let their dinner settle.

Colette had been worried Bernard would hound her, wanting to know information about Heller, so she was pleasantly surprised he said nothing, asked nothing. How could she explain what she had done?

As they passed a small alley next to the restaurant, Colette noticed the smell of cigarette smoke drifting from the darkness. Crossing the alley's entrance, she detected the sound of someone coming from behind.

Turning first, she saw the flash of polished steel as a man emerged from the alley, running toward Bernard. Her voice caught in her throat and she forced it out.

"Bernard, look out!" she cried.

The blade rose just as Bernard turned. Instinctively, she pushed Bernard to the side as the sharp blade came slashing down. The razor-sharp edge caught on the sleeve of her jacket. She cried out as she felt herself losing her balance. Her feet stumbled, and she crashed to the sidewalk. Her shoulder hit first, then her cheek. Pain radiated down her arm.

Colette recoiled, expecting a second blow. As the attacker

lunged again at Bernard, she recognized him as the person lurking outside the Brasserie Lipp.

"Stop!" Colette cried out.

Bernard jumped away from the man's reach just as the blade slashed down. She watched helplessly as they warily circled each other. The bearded man again lifted the wide serrated knife, ready to strike.

"Who are you?" Bernard shouted.

"You don't know me, but you should remember killing my brother!"

Had Bernard done such a thing? Colette covered her mouth with her hand and wondered if she should run for help. Instead, fear planted her to the ground.

"You've mistaken me for someone else!"

The assailant slashed the blade across Bernard's chest, slicing his khaki shirt as he leaned away.

Colette scurried to her feet. The agitated man looked like he only wanted one thing—to avenge his brother's death. He again whipped the air with his knife and advanced on the Frenchman.

"The Pantin rail yard. Two years ago. You stopped that train."

Bernard backed up. "Yes, and saved dozens of French lives!"

"But not my brother's!"

The crazed man lunged, making another attempt to thrust the blade toward his chest. Bernard sidestepped the advance and caught the wrist of his attacker. The momentum of the assailant's driving force knocked Bernard back, causing both to plummet to the concrete sidewalk. Colette stepped back and then stood by helplessly, wondering if she should try to jump in and separate them as they rolled, arms flailing.

"Colette! Bernard!" It was Eric's voice down the street as he sprinted toward them.

"Hurry!" The exclamation came out in a desperate gasp as she watched each man trying to gain the upper hand. Then, with a thud, the two tumbled off the curb and into the street.

Neither moved.

Eric neared, rushing to grab the back of the assailant's shirt. With amazing strength, Eric yanked him off Bernard.

Colette's knees grew weak, and tears filled her eyes as she saw a large red stain already forming on the front of Bernard's shirt.

Colette rushed to his side. "You're hurt!"

Bernard gulped for air, a wild look in his eyes. A small gasp followed, then another. Finally, Bernard shook his head. He still searched for air when Colette helped him scramble to his knees.

The attacker groaned but lay motionless as Eric turned him onto his back. A black handle was all that could be seen of the knife protruding from just below his armpit.

Bernard crawled toward the assailant and shook the wounded man's shoulders. "Why were you trying to kill me? It wasn't my fault!"

"You . . . Nazi traitor!" the attacker seethed through clenched teeth. Short gasps were punctuated with feeble coughs.

"When you stopped . . . the train . . . you killed . . . my . . . Philippe. He want . . . he wanted Göring."

"But Göring wasn't on the train!"

The wounded man looked momentarily confused. Then his eyes rolled upward as his head fell backward, smacking the pavement hard.

His quest for revenge was over.

18

The deadly attack shattered the fragile peace ushered in with Libération. Two days after the German Army pulled out of Paris was too early to let your guard down.

Despite the warm August night, Gabi shivered while she and the others patiently answered questions from a police detective following his arrival by bicycle. The *inspecteur* scribbled their statements into a notebook as he attempted to sort out what happened or what prompted the assassination attempt on Bernard.

The detective knew the attacker. Said his name was Antoine Celeste. Well-known member of the Free French. A hero of the Resistance, but also emotionally unstable following his brother's brutal execution at the hands of the Nazis two years ago.

"Ça suffit." *That's enough.* The detective quietly shut his notebook. "Since there were no other eyewitnesses to the events at the Pantin rail yard, I chalk this up to Celeste's inability to deal with his grief."

Another tragedy of this war, Gabi thought.

She watched Eric pull Bernard aside as a horse-drawn team from the morgue carted off Celeste's body.

"You doing okay?"

The tired Frenchman sighed. "It was him or me, and I didn't want to be the one to go."

Gabi watched Bernard's eyes move to where Colette sat on a nearby stoop. Her arms were crossed, and she pulled them tight against her. With head lowered and shoulders slumped, she was clearly shaken. Colette's reaction was understandable. She'd thought—momentarily—her boyfriend was dead.

What Gabi didn't understand was Bernard's reaction. As he looked at Colette, Gabi didn't see worry or sadness. She saw regret on his face.

What does he regret? That he put her in danger? Gabi wondered.

Bernard pressed a hand to his forehead and then walked toward Colette with determination.

He cares, Gabi thought to herself. *I can see he loves her. He never wanted to put the woman he loves in that type of situation.*

——————

With grim faces, the two couples stepped into the Maison Beaumont, where Irene Beaumont prepared a pot of tea upon learning of the attack. Eric and the others gathered around the dining room table and described their side of the story to the Beaumonts' friends who had stopped by to visit.

The appropriate remarks of outrage were made, and one by one, Eric noticed that the Beaumont friends drifted away, leaving them alone.

Eric was thankful that neither Bernard nor Colette were hurt. He needed them. As much as he believed in Gabi— and his own resources—they couldn't save the *Mona Lisa* by themselves.

The phone rang, and Madame Beaumont answered. She called Bernard over, who listened and didn't say much until he thanked the caller and hung up. He turned silent for a moment, as if he was replaying the conversation in his mind, trying to believe what he'd just heard.

"Did you find some fuel?" Eric asked.

"More like the fuel found us," Bernard replied with a confused look. "Looks like we can drive over to the 2nd Armored depot at the École Militaire first thing in the morning. A Colonel Tollet will be expecting us. Apparently, he received a message from London telling him to give us as much petrol as we need, no questions asked. But who . . . how . . . did they know to call here?"

He was completely flummoxed. "Who did you say you worked for?"

"I didn't . . . so how early can we go? I'm worried about beating the Germans to Annecy."

"I was told not before 7 a.m."

"That'll work. Once we get going, how long do you expect us to be on the road?"

"Let's see." Bernard unfolded a fraying road map of France and spread it across the table. "I've heard it's nine or ten hours . . ." He measured the distance of one hundred kilometers on the scale bar with his thumb and forefinger and "walked" that measurement from Paris across France in a southeasterly direction.

"*Et voilà*. Right around five hundred kilometers. If we can average fifty or sixty kilometers an hour, we should get there between six and seven o'clock, provided we leave Paris by 9 a.m. How many jerry cans do you have?"

"Two," Eric replied. "That was enough to get us here from Bern and should be more than enough to get us to Annecy."

"Did you hear anything about the road conditions?" Gabi asked. "The Germans are in retreat . . ."

"They took off due east for the Fatherland"—Bernard nearly spit out the words—"but we're going south. Still, we have to stay alert."

"We can't be delayed," Colette said. "If those two German agents get there first, we'll lose the *Mona Lisa*—perhaps forever."

"We'll get there as fast as we can." Bernard leaned forward, elbows on the table. "Eric said he wants to be a race car driver after the war, so now's his chance for some practice."

Gabi looked at Eric in mock surprise, the first light moment of the evening.

Eric smiled. "Bernard's kidding. But if the roads are in good shape, I'm flooring it. Of course, some roads could be torn up from bombs or blocked by disabled vehicles. We just don't know."

He scanned the map, thankful for Bernard's expertise. "So show me . . . which route are we taking?"

"Certainly. We'll leave Paris through the Porte d'Italie, and then take the Route de Fontainebleau in a southerly direction."

Eric followed Bernard's finger, which took them through Rozay-en-Brie. He didn't say anything, and a quick glance at Gabi's poker face meant that she wasn't going to bring up the incident with the Ost soldiers again.

For the next ten minutes, Bernard carefully explained the entire route they would follow. Eric could tell that he was thorough in his approach, as well as his calculations.

"Colette, tell us what you know about the family," Bernard said.

"A count and countess live at the chateau," Colette answered. "I've corresponded frequently with Countess Ariane

Valois. Up until last week, we spoke together by telephone every fortnight when service was available. But I've never met her or her husband."

"It's a shame you couldn't reach them," Gabi said.

"I tried several times. I'm worried about the safety of the Countess and *La Joconde*. All we can do is hope for the best."

"Is the plan to drive back to Paris the following morning?" Eric asked.

"Depending on what we find there, the answer is yes."

Gabi looked from the map to Colette. "If we're spending the night, where are we going to stay?"

Colette grinned for the first time in hours. "Apparently, this 'little' chateau has fifteen bedrooms. I would imagine the Countess will extend hospitality, given the unusual circumstances."

Bernard folded the map as everyone stood up to go off to bed.

Things were shaping up nicely, although the more he learned about Eric and Gabi, and their connections, the more his guard went up. They were not to be trifled with, especially if things got sticky with the *Mona Lisa*.

He mentally reviewed some items he needed to pack in his satchel, such as a pistol, ammunition, knife, blackjack, and handcuffs.

Preparation was key. He would bide his time until the right moment, and then he would strike.

There was a knock on the bedroom door.

Colette sat up in bed. She knew it wasn't Gabi since her

friend was taking a bath. She pulled her blanket closer to her neck.

"Entrée," Colette said.

Madame Beaumont stepped inside. "I know it's terribly late, but there's a monsieur on the phone who insists on speaking with you."

"Who could be calling at eleven o'clock?" Colette's tone was foreboding.

"I don't know, but he said there was a pressing matter regarding the Louvre."

Colette rose and slipped on a robe, her heart pounding. She rushed past Madame Beaumont and hurried downstairs. Knowing who it could be . . . but not wanting to believe it.

Cupping the black handset to her ear, she felt her pulse race and a queasy feeling sweep through her body.

"Oui?"

"Mademoiselle, you are a difficult one to reach these days."

"How did you get this number?" she snapped.

"I still have a few reliable contacts in Paris. Our military may have departed your beloved city, but there are assets willing to help, for a price."

"I am no longer one of your 'assets.' Now that Paris is free, there is no need for you to contact me again. I wish you a pleasant evening." Colette started to hang up the phone, but something caused her to pause. If Heller knew how to reach her by phone, he no doubt could send his "reliable contacts" after her—and after them.

"I am concerned for Madame Beaumont's safety," Heller continued in a cool tone. "These are uncertain times."

Fear stiffened Colette. She could hear the older woman humming as she cleaned the kitchen. If Heller had the ability to track her down in the middle of the night, he still had the clout to follow through on his threats.

"What do you want?"

"Just confirmation that the *Mona Lisa* has not been removed from the location that you gave me a month ago."

Colette inhaled sharply and paused. She released the breath slowly, hoping her next words would sound convincing. "Actually, she is en route back to the Louvre as we speak." Her voice rose in mock confidence.

"I see. That is most unfortunate. Well . . . c'est la vie. I would hope that you haven't tried to mislead me, my dear Colette. It would be such a tragedy to make Madame Beaumont suffer needlessly, in addition to your brave boyfriend." The line went dead.

Colette stood motionless. Her hands trembled as she pushed open the door into the dining room. Replaying the conversation, she hoped she was persuasive. The problem was, he'd caught her off guard, and she knew that had the roles been reversed, she would have seen through the attempted deception.

Even though fear from tonight still had her on edge, it would take more than a phone call to scare her off.

She would not let Heller win.

Not this time.

A thousand kilometers to the east, Colonel Heller had his answer. A broad, odious grin slowly emerged across his face. Colette's breathing pattern and fractional pause had given away her bluff. The painting was still outside of Annecy; she was in Paris. Certainly, transporting such an important archive would have been supervised by the curator herself.

Heller, no stranger to torture and interrogation, prided himself on being a master at reading the emotions of others, especially when intimidated. He could detect a lie, and this had the classic markings of one. As he relived the moment, he became certain of his instincts. With a bit of luck, Schaffner and Kaufman would get to the chateau before Colette, but the race would be close.

Lifting the receiver again, he told the operator he needed to send an urgent message to Hans Schaffner.

19

"I see them."

Bernard pointed toward the double doors leading out from the Sully Wing. Colette, clutching a file to her chest, walked their direction. Gabi was at her side.

He and Eric sat in the Red Cross vehicle, parked at the Louvre's Cour Carrée shortly after eight in the morning. Three days after Libération, a dozen workers in blue over-alls were scattered across the vast courtyard, cleaning up and performing odd jobs in preparation for reopening the grand museum. Workmen had waved their car into the plaza after recognizing one of their own—Bernard Rousseau.

The Frenchman stepped out of the vehicle, followed by Eric.

"Any luck?" Bernard asked as Colette approached.

She frowned. "I wasn't able to speak with Countess Valois—or the authorities in Annecy. The phone lines are still down. Monsieur Rambouillet said he'd keep trying. I hoped I could tell her to call the local police and ask for protection."

Gabi spoke up. "Too bad you couldn't get through. We received a transmission this morning saying that he hadn't heard anything regarding the whereabouts of the Germans, so no help there, either. All we can do is make good time."

Colette nodded in silent agreement and took a deep breath, debating whether she should share the phone call from Heller last night.

She couldn't.

From the backseat of the Red Cross Mercedes, Gabi looked back for one last glimpse of the Eiffel Tower, but the nineteenth-century ironwork that defined the Paris skyline had slipped beneath the horizon. A feeling of wistfulness fell over her as the awe-inspiring city gave way to pastoral farmlands outside the Porte d'Italie, the southern gateway of Paris.

A somber mood was pervasive following the harrowing attack on Bernard. Nonetheless, after forty-five minutes of near silence, Gabi asked the question everyone wanted to know. "Bernard, what exactly happened at the Pantin rail yard?"

"Although most would think I'm some sort of hero, what happened that day was a tragedy." He shared the entire story, describing the crates of paintings being loaded on the train, the dash through Paris streets on his bike, and his split-second decision to stand in front of the Berlin Express.

Colette reached forward from the backseat and placed a hand on his shoulder. "It was a shame that a Frenchman died, but he was murdered by the Nazis, not you. Anyone who knows the facts would understand that you saved many innocent French lives. You also saved invaluable art. And for that, you *are* a hero!"

"The war is full of such unfortunate events." Eric took his eyes off the road for a brief moment to meet Bernard's. "Those in the Resistance knew they were putting their lives on the line every day."

The others agreed, and Bernard nodded slightly.

Gabi let out a sigh. "Just as today . . . we know the price we could pay for saving the *Mona Lisa*. It's for something bigger than ourselves, which is why I take comfort in knowing that ultimately we are in God's hands."

Colette echoed her agreement, then continued to stare at nothing in particular through the side window. The passing scenery became a blur as a contemplative mood enveloped them.

After several minutes, Gabi tapped Colette on the shoulder. "So tell me—why *is* the *Mona Lisa* the most famous painting in the world?"

Colette's eyes brightened. "The first time I saw her, I was a schoolgirl. My parents took me to the Louvre during a holiday, and I begged them to let me see the *Mona Lisa* first. The moment I laid eyes on her, I couldn't believe how beautiful the painting was. Her posture was perfect with straight shoulders and her hands folded across one another. She wore an unadorned dress, no jewelry, and not even a wedding ring. Her face was slightly pronounced at the cheekbones, high at the forehead, and pointed at the chin. Her nose was narrow, and her lips were turned up ever so slightly in that famous smile of hers."

"That smile baffles me," Gabi responded. "First, she is smiling, right? Then the smile fades, only to return. Why is that?"

"When the original subject sat for her portrait, da Vinci had someone amuse her with jests to keep her from making that look of melancholy so common in portraits. Somehow, the artist captured a faintly wistful smile on her face, something the Italians call *sfumato*. It means blurry, vague, and left up to the imagination. How da Vinci was able to convey this ambiguity through an oil painting makes the *Mona Lisa* a masterpiece. Especially when you know that the *Mona Lisa* was painted on poplar wood, not canvas."

Colette turned and met Gabi's eyes. "During that first visit to the Louvre, I felt like the *Mona Lisa*'s warm and self-assured brown eyes were only for me, even though there were always dozens of people gazing at her."

Gabi was moved by Colette's description. "Da Vinci was an Italian painter, so how did the *Mona Lisa* end up in France?"

"Another interesting story. We're fairly certain that da Vinci painted the *Mona Lisa* in Florence between 1503 and 1506, but he kept the portrait for himself because it was his favorite. Toward the end of his life, François I of France gave him a generous commission to come live at the Royal Chateau at Amboise, where the French king was often in residence."

"Amboise? Where's that?"

"The Charolais Brionnais area of central France. François I decided that the best way to glean the ideas of the Italian Renaissance was to import the greatest artist of his day to France, so for the last three years of his life, da Vinci puttered with his mechanical inventions and sipped tea with his royal patron. After da Vinci died in 1519 at the age of sixty-seven, François I purchased the painting from his heir for 4,000 gold florins—a ton of money back then—and hung it in his royal bath. From that moment on, the painting became part of the French monarchy's art collection. For several centuries, she was a showpiece at various palaces around France—Fontainebleau, Versailles, and the Tuileries."

Eric slowed the car to pass two dairy cows nibbling tall stalks of grass along the road's shoulder. When he accelerated, Colette resumed her story.

"During the chaos of the French Revolution in 1789, the *Mona Lisa* was hidden in a warehouse. Louis XVI went to the guillotine and his palaces and prized possessions became property of the newly formed state. When Napoleon came to power, the enigmatic lady was restored to a place of honor in the emperor's luxurious bedroom. After the Louvre Palace was turned into a public art museum, though, the *Mona Lisa* was installed inside the former palace, where she has resided ever since. Except for the time when she was stolen."

The juxtaposition of *Mona Lisa* and the word *stolen* startled Gabi and prompted Eric to join the conversation.

"Someone stole the *Mona Lisa*?" he exclaimed from the front seat. "When did that happen?"

"Back on August 21, 1911. It was the greatest art theft ever, although no one talks about it now."

"Since we're trying to prevent the *Mona Lisa* from being kidnapped, maybe we can learn something," Gabi suggested.

"I doubt it. Even today, the brazen theft seems unfathomable—like the Eiffel Tower falling over. But one Tuesday morning in 1911, a guard walked into the Salon Carré only to find the *Mona Lisa* missing from her place on the wall. All that remained were four iron hooks and a rectangular shape several shades deeper than the surrounding area. The guard thought the *Mona Lisa* had been taken away to be photographed. Photography was relatively new in those days, and there was a project at the Louvre to photograph the entire collection. The idea was that in case of damage, loss, or future restoration, the museum would have an accurate picture to work from.

"A few hours passed, and the *Mona Lisa* was still missing. Someone thought to check with the photography studio, where the guard was greeted with stares as blank as the Salon Carré wall. They had a problem."

Eric looked into his rearview mirror and locked eyes with Colette. "You mean security was so lax in 1911 that anyone could have walked into the Louvre and walked out with the *Mona Lisa*?"

"Apparently so. Art treasures were poorly guarded in those days. More than one hundred passkeys floated around the Louvre. The museum was closed the previous day, a Monday, so anybody could have been walking around. The most famous painting in the world wasn't even wired or bolted to the wall; it hung there on four simple hooks. Once the authorities at the Louvre discovered that the *Mona Lisa* had been stolen, all France went into a state of shock. Extra editions of Paris newspapers screamed, *MONA LISA A DISPARU!*

"The Louvre was closed until further notice while the Paris police started an investigation. They stopped cars on their way out of Paris. Trains were searched. Ships inspected. The borders of France sealed. The Louvre curators expected a swift recovery or a ransom demand, but that never materialized. Meanwhile, the story of her disappearance traveled around the world."

"Did they think it was an inside job?" Gabi asked.

"Initially, yes, but that's all the police had to go on in those early days. There was tremendous pressure to break the case and recover the painting. When the Louvre reopened a week after the *Mona Lisa* vanished, long lines of crowds filed through the Salon Carré to view the empty space on the wall, like mourners at a funeral. As the weeks and then months passed and denial turned into acceptance, everyone assumed she was lost forever."

"So the *Mona Lisa* wasn't found right away?" Gabi pictured the long line of mourners.

"Not at all. Fifteen months after her disappearance, France officially called off the search. Public sentiment had turned from shock to sorrow, from disgruntlement to disappointment. When the new Louvre catalog was published in January 1913, the *Mona Lisa* was not listed in the collection. It looked like the perfect crime, although there were numerous 'sightings' all over Europe—Belgium, Holland, and even your Switzerland. Still, the public sentiment was that she was gone for good."

Eric turned to Bernard. "You know this story, don't you?"

Bernard bobbed his head. "Yeah, it really is amazing how they found her. When Colette told me the story, I had trouble believing it."

"So . . . go on," Gabi prodded. "I'm dying to find out."

Colette leaned closer to the front seat. "Pure luck broke the case. An Italian antique dealer named Alfredo Geri placed a classified ad in several Italian newspapers that he was in the market to buy art objects at good prices. This happened in the fall of 1913. He received a letter from a fellow in Paris who called himself 'Leonardo.' He said he was in possession of the stolen *Mona Lisa*.

"The Italian art dealer didn't believe him. Geri wrote a return letter saying he would have to see the painting before he could offer a price. Could he bring it to Italy and show him? On December 10, 1913, an Italian man with a moustache showed up at Geri's office in Florence. He said his name was Leonardo Vincenzo and that he had the *Mona Lisa* back in his hotel room. He explained that he had stolen the painting to restore to Italy what had been stolen by France. Thus, he made a stipulation that the painting was to be hung at the Uffizi Gallery in Florence and never given back to France. He also wanted a half million lira for his trouble.

"Geri did some quick thinking. He said he needed to have the director of the Uffizi confirm that it really was the *Mona Lisa* before he handed over the money. They made arrangements to meet the next day. When they returned to his hotel room the following afternoon, Leonardo pulled out a wooden trunk. He opened it, tossed out a pair of underwear, an old shirt, a pair of shoes, and removed a false bottom. There lay the *Mona Lisa*!

"Geri and the museum director turned the painting over and noticed a seal from the Louvre. The museum director said he needed to compare the painting with other works by da Vinci, so he needed to take the painting with him. I have no idea why Leonardo agreed to this, but he said yes. Geri and the museum director carried the *Mona Lisa* out of the hotel and called the police. They stormed the room and arrested the man, whose real name was Vincenzo Peruggia."

"So the guy who stole the *Mona Lisa* was an Italian after all?" Gabi asked.

"Yes, he was born in Italy but had moved to Paris, where he had worked at the Louvre since 1908. All the guards knew him. Apparently, on that fateful Monday morning, when the Louvre was officially closed, he noticed that the Salon Carré was empty. He grabbed the *Mona Lisa*, dragged it over to the staircase, removed the painting from its frame, and walked out of the Louvre with her under a painter's smock. Can you believe he simply walked off with the world's most famous piece of art?"

"I would imagine the French were happy to learn of the discovery."

"Ecstatic! The public went wild. After being displayed throughout Italy, she was returned to France on December 30, 1913, to great fanfare."

"What happened to Peruggia?" Eric asked.

"He got fourteen months in jail, but he was hailed for his patriotism in Italy. A 'crime of passion' was how the heist was described in the press. He became an Italian folk hero."

"I don't think the French press will call Göring's attempt to steal the *Mona Lisa* a 'crime of passion,'" Gabi declared with rectitude. "A 'war crime' seems more apropos."

"I'm just hoping it's only an attempt," Colette replied.

Gabi remained pensive, nodding in agreement. "If the French people were that devastated during peacetime, can you imagine what the loss of the *Mona Lisa* would do to morale now? There has been so much pain already. A theft would be a crushing blow."

———

Bernard unfolded the map and scanned their route. "We are coming up on Rozay-en-Brie," he announced.

Gabi, who had been lost in thought, looked up with a grim expression.

"Bernard said this would be the fastest route to Annecy." Eric made eye contact through the rearview mirror. Gabi looked troubled, confirming his suspicion.

Gripping the wheel harder, he eased down on the accelerator and knew she was reliving their encounter with the Ost soldiers.

Gabi, her face drawn and pallid, averted her eyes.

Five minutes later, Eric recognized the Romanesque medieval church that dominated the small village. Everything was coming into focus again: the tall cornfields outside the hamlet with ears of corn waiting to be picked; the faded barns and dilapidated homesteads dotting the landscape; and the dirt road leading into town. This time around, Eric counted a half-dozen men working in the fields, no longer afraid of German patrols.

"Stop!" Gabi cried out.

Eric, startled, reflexively slammed on the brakes. The four wheels locked up as the car slid to a stop, slightly askew. A trailing cloud of dust enshrouded the car. All eyes turned toward Gabi, who was transfixed as she stared out the window. With a click, they heard the door latch give as she stepped out and moved to the side of the road. Then she slowly walked ahead of the car, inspecting the ditch.

Eric exited the car and quickly caught up with her. Gabi had paused. With arms crossed, she was looking down at something.

The bodies were gone, but there—staining the dirt on the left-hand side of the road—were imperfect circles of dried blood, the color of burnt sienna.

Gabi wrapped an arm around Eric and looked up at him with a faint smile. "I'm all right. For some reason, I needed to see it again." She let out a low sigh. "We were saved for a reason."

"I agree." Eric pulled her closer as they slowly walked together back to the car.

Colette watched with a concerned expression. Eric shook his head as if to say, *Don't ask. I'll explain later.*

"The Ost soldiers?" Bernard asked.

Gabi nodded and closed the door.

―――――――

Eric eased the sedan into Rozay-en-Brie's picturesque town square, where there were more signs of life this week. In the cobblestoned plaza, women slapped wet clothes against a washing stone while their young children played nearby. On the opposite side, two elderly men shared a bench, each with their hands resting on wooden canes. The setting was peaceful.

"Why don't we stop for a short break," Gabi said.

Eric swung the car next to a farmhouse dotted with colorful geranium boxes and parked behind an abandoned buggy. He stepped out of the car and looked in the direction of the old men sitting across the square. One tipped his hat, and Eric replied in kind. The others exited the vehicle and stretched their legs.

"Would you like a *petit pain*?" Colette asked. She reached into the small sack and pulled out a brown roll. "We also have some cheese, tomato, and mayonnaise from Madame Beaumont, if you feel like a sandwich."

Eric smiled. "Sure. Bernard and I only got some fruit for breakfast since we were in a hurry to get to the École Militaire."

Colette, using the hood of the car as a makeshift table, spread a small cloth and assembled the sandwiches with Gabi's assistance.

Eric came up next to her. "That was a fascinating story about how the *Mona Lisa* was stolen. Where did you learn all that?"

"I studied art history at the École des Beaux-Arts in Strasbourg, where I grew up."

"Strasbourg? Your city has volleyed back and forth between France and Germany for centuries."

"Well, we are on the border. Strasbourg reverted back to France following the Great War, and now it's under Nazi rule, but not for much longer I hope. I worry for my parents."

"Verstehen Sie Deutsch?" Eric asked. *Do you understand German?*

She hesitated to answer. Still speaking in French, she said, "We had to learn German in school, but mine isn't very good."

Eric could see that she didn't want to talk about Strasbourg and knew why she would be concerned about her parents. For the last year, Allied aircraft had bombarded the city.

He looked to Bernard. "So, *mon ami,* how much longer?"

Bernard took a long draw on his cigarette before answering. "I'd say another six or seven hours if we don't run into any problems. The tough part should be over. We're south and west of any German military—"

A steady mechanical hum was growing in the distance. Eric cocked his head toward a hazy sky filtered with blue.

"Hear that?" he asked.

"Look at them!" Colette pointed to the source of the droning noise.

Eric craned his neck in time to see several hundred B-24s and B-17s, heading east toward Germany, moving across the sky. Mustang fighters, which looked like gnats next to the big four-engine bombers, escorted the air armada.

The rows of bombers dotted the sky like a swarm of bees.

"Churchill calls it 'round the clock bombing,' " Eric said. "The United States Eighth sends its sorties by day, and the RAF gets the night shift. Some place in Germany is going to get hammered in about an hour—Munich, if I had to hazard a guess."

Colette shaded her eyes and looked skyward. "I hope one of those bombs has Heller's name on it."

20

With the folded-out map resting on his lap, Bernard's eyes followed the route between the Paris basin and the Rhône valley. He pointed his finger at Annecy, a medieval city nestled at the doorstep of the French Alps.

They still had some distance to go but were making good time. Pastoral landscape streaked past the dirty windshield. Farmlands were flanked by wooded foothills crowned with high-walled villages, many adorned with French flags. Looking up, Bernard spotted a regal castle with a red-white-and-blue *tricolore* affixed to a stone turret. "News travels fast," he said to no one in particular.

Suppressing a nagging sense of guilt, he focused on his current role of spoiler. If he could return to Paris in possession of the *Mona Lisa*, he and the French Communists would orchestrate *une affaire* that would make the Italian's theft of the *Mona Lisa* look like a warm-up act at the Folies Bergère.

When the people hold de Gaulle's feet to the fire, we'll see how he responds. The general's grip on the country will be slippery at best.

He knew that Colette wouldn't understand why he had to

take temporary possession of the *Mona Lisa*. She belonged to the insular world of art, which made her a puppet of the bourgeoisie. Like millions of clueless French, she didn't realize that they were being swept along by a tidal surge that began in 1917 when Vladimir Lenin introduced communism to combat Russia's economic problems brought on by civil war. France would be the next great Communist country, a worker's paradise where property and money would be equally shared. She would come around to his point of view when a new dawn arose in France.

He checked the map again to verify their location. Eric was burning up the kilometers since they pulled out of Rozay-en-Brie an hour ago, steering the heavy Mercedes around potholes like a Swiss skier negotiating a slalom course. If they didn't run into any road closures, they would arrive in Annecy sometime around 7 p.m., matching his pre-trip estimate.

What happened when they arrived would change the direction of postwar France.

Colette closed her eyes and pretended to sleep, missing the tableaux of sunflower fields and lavender meadows. The scenery didn't interest her at the moment. Her focus was singular, driven by the oppressive responsibility entrusted to her. Failure would be a crushing blow to national morale and would decimate her professional reputation. She loathed Heller for his coercion, forcing her to decide between her love for Bernard and her professional obligation to secrecy.

At this point, nothing could be done to speed up their trip. Only the anticipation of arriving at the Chateau de Dampierre and taking possession of the *Mona Lisa* would ease her breathing.

Eric's question about whether she spoke German un-nerved her. If Bernard knew she was fluent, he would ask questions—uncomfortable ones. Soon, when the time was right, she would tell him the truth about Colonel Heller and how she had traded information in exchange for his life. But not yet.

Bernard sat within a few feet of her, but it was as if a canyon spread between them. They'd turned to each other during the dark days of war; at the present time, it didn't seem right that freedom would put this gaping hole between them. She ached knowing he lied to her about the locket. Even more than that, at the aloofness she saw in his eyes. She pushed those thoughts aside. Bernard was not her main concern now.

"Where are we?" Gabi questioned. "This wasn't part of our route when we left Bern."

"This is a faster way," Eric said.

Bernard consulted his *carte*. "We just passed Vincelles, and the next town is . . . Cravant, probably three kilome-ters. Just before we drive through, we'll cross a bridge at the L'Yonne River. My parents used to take my brother and me to this part of France every summer."

Ever since they'd left the Left Bank, Eric noted that Ber-nard had been a nonstop tour guide and political commen-tator, offering sophistry on the future of France. One thing was certain: Bernard and his Communist comrades wouldn't be settling their political differences with de Gaulle and his loyalists over a glass of Beaujolais.

While Bernard rambled on about the difficulties de Gaulle was sure to face in coming weeks, Eric cracked open his window to increase airflow and help drone out the stuffy commentary. He diverted his eyes from the road, which was straight as an arrow for as far as he could see. They passed through thick apple orchards, laden with fruit, on both sides of the two-lane road. Checking his petrol gauge, he noted they would need to refuel with one of their jerry cans in the next hour. Then something in the sky caught his attention.

A trail of brown smoke followed a P-51 that was losing altitude . . . fast! The canary yellow nose with matching tail markings identified the United States fighter plane. No more than three hundred meters off the ground, the P-51 fluttered across Eric's horizon, moving from his left to right. The fighter's wings dipped from side to side, a clear indication that the pilot was fighting to stay aloft.

"He must have gotten hit by flak over Germany," Eric said. "He's going down."

"Where will he end up?" Bernard leaned forward in his seat to track the crippled fighter. "Hopefully, he can find a grassy field, but I don't see anything around here. Unless . . ."

What happened next froze Eric's hands to the steering wheel. The injured fighter banked hard right and lined up in their direction.

"He's coming our way!" Bernard shouted. "He's going to land on our road!"

The women in the back were silent, hunching forward to catch a glimpse of the plummeting aircraft. Eric willed himself to think through his options.

"He's going to hit us!" Colette cried out.

She was right. The P-51 pilot had lined up his crippled plane for a landing on the road, and he was coming right at them. Eric quickly looked left, then right, but driving off the dirt road wasn't an option because of deep drainage ditches.

The P-51 was closing in faster than he expected. In a split

second, Eric made his decision and stood on the brakes, grinding the tires to a halt.

"I'm getting out of here!" Bernard grabbed at his door, but Eric yanked his shirt.

"Hang on!" He threw the car into reverse and floored the accelerator. The Mercedes responded with a jerk to the sudden increase in speed.

"Are you crazy?" Bernard shouted. "Let me out—"

Eric ignored him as he turned to view the road through the rear window. The transmission wound up to a high pitch as Eric held his line and focused on the road. No need to look back toward the oncoming plane. This was his only option.

The speedometer passed forty, then fifty kilometers an hour. He could see from the expression on Gabi and Colette's faces that the plane was gaining on them.

The crippled fighter would be forced to land any second. A loss in momentum would introduce the hood of the Mercedes and the four occupants to the churning four-bladed propeller of the P-51 Mustang.

"Gabi, what's happening? I can't turn around."

———————

"Go faster! He's about to land!"

Gabi's eyes were locked on the P-51, wheels down, fluttering like a butterfly in a breeze. With full flaps gathering as many air molecules under the wings as possible, the pilot was pulling up the plane's yellow nose, trying to keep the Mustang in the air and give their car more time to clear his active runway. Hovering ten meters off the deck and four hundred meters away, the plane's distinctive engine and wing-mounted .50 caliber machine guns were closing in fast.

She saw Eric press down even harder on the accelerator, but it was already floored. The transmission screamed for mercy as the speedometer remained pegged at 60 kilometers per hour.

The plane was just one hundred meters from their retreating chrome grill when the heavy fighter dropped awkwardly onto the road and bounced from one wheel to another, sending up plumes of dust as rubber met the road. She saw Eric's grimace as the roar of the P-51's engine overpowered the shrill scream from the German transmission.

Gabi dug her fingernails into the leather seat. "You can do this. He has to slow down soon."

She counted out the distance to help Eric as he gritted his teeth and concentrated on keeping the speeding Mercedes on the road. "One hundred meters . . . fifty meters . . . twenty-five meters . . . he's slowing down . . . ten meters. . . ."

The plane was centered on the distinctive Mercedes star. "God, please save us," she whispered.

With just a few meters separating them and the plane still gaining, an earsplitting explosion erupted. Gabi and Colette shrieked in unison as all six midwing Browning machine guns came to life with white-hot muzzle flash. The lead fusillade and tracers blistered the air.

Is he trying to kill us? Doesn't he know we're on his side?

Gabi ducked in fright, fearing they would all be killed by American fire. She glanced behind her, following the stream of bullets. Several hundred meters down the road, the heavy caliber bullets tore into the orchard, splintering heavy limbs into toothpicks and vaporizing fruit. The explosive recoil from the six cannons instantly slowed the plane with a jolt, and their car pulled away.

"The plane's stopping!" Gabi yelled.

Eric eased up on the accelerator as the drone of the Mustang diminished, then coughed and backfired into submission.

Eric eased down on the brake, subduing the high-pitched whine as the gears gratefully wound down. Coming to a complete stop, the four of them fell back into their seats. The miasma of dust, exhaust, and spent gunpowder—mixed with shock—left them all speechless.

"What happened?" Gabi asked, breaking the silence.

Eric shook his head. "The kickback from the machine guns must have slowed the plane. I doubt they teach that in flight school."

Dust settled around the now-silent Mustang and idling Red Cross sedan. The two vehicles eerily sat facing one another, like two gladiators in a ring, agreeing not to fight. Then the canopy of the smoking Mustang slid open. Gabi watched the aviator step onto the wing and jump to the ground, flight cap and goggles still in place. He made his way toward their car.

With two arms, he motioned for Eric to back up farther. Smoke around the stricken plane was starting to thicken. Eric obeyed without hesitation, retreating another twenty meters. He looked up to see the pilot running in their direction. A small surge of flames flashed upward from the belly of the aircraft.

Then the road and plane disappeared into a ballooning orange fireball. The explosion and shock wave rocked the car, filling it with a searing heat wave. The blast blew the advancing pilot off his feet, skidding forward with outstretched arms.

"He's on fire!" Eric jumped from the car and raced to his side, quickly extinguishing the flames from the pilot's pants leg with hands full of roadside dirt. Bernard was in hot pursuit. Eric leaned over the fallen pilot, protecting him from the shrapnel of hot metal.

With a groan from the stricken pilot, Eric and Bernard

helped him to his feet. They moved him behind the open car door, shielding them from the heat.

"That was close." The pilot caught his breath, then extended his hand. "I'm Lieutenant T. J. Rawlings. But you probably don't understand a word I'm saying."

"Actually, I do." Gabi stepped out of the car. "You've got a burn there."

"Just a scratch, ma'am," Rawlings replied with a shy grin as he looked toward the torrid blaze. "Coulda been worse."

"Let me take a look at that leg." It wasn't a request. Gabi led him to the backseat, where he removed his leather aviator cap and goggles and allowed himself a grimace from the pain. Colette offered him a sip of water from a canteen.

After Eric handed her a first aid kit from the trunk, Gabi cut a vent up the side of his flight suit, exposing a calf that had already formed a cluster of blisters. She applied an ointment and wrapped his lower leg with a sterile gauze. "You're in pretty good shape, but we need to get you to a doctor. Burns can get easily infected. If all goes well, you'll be flying again in no time."

"That's good news, ma'am, cuz we're swatting those Nazis out of the air like flies with these new Mustangs. They're one heckuva fighter!"

"Great to hear. Now if you don't mind, T.J., we're going to get you to the closest doctor."

"You're the boss." The pilot then looked to either side at his seatmates. "I'm feeling better already."

Eric swiftly maneuvered the car around the twisted metal skeleton engulfed in flames. Even through closed windows, intense heat radiated into the car. The explosion had pushed the plane's main fuselage off the road—giving them just enough room to pass by.

The American pilot had a somber expression as he

watched the conflagration consume his plane. "So long, Sally. You were one sweet ride," T.J. whispered.

After a moment, he turned back and patted Eric on the shoulder. "That was a slick bit of driving back there. You some kind of race car driver?"

Eric and Gabi laughed as Bernard and Colette looked on with a quizzical expression, waiting for the translation.

"There's been talk of a new career after the war," Gabi replied.

"Well, if there's a race that's run backwards, I'd put my money on you," T.J. deadpanned, then broke into a wide smile.

Ten minutes later, they rolled into Cravant and located the town doctor. The group accompanied T.J. into the office, and Gabi described the pilot's wounds to the doctor. She felt compelled to stay and translate, but by the time T.J. got settled to wait his turn, she could see that everyone was anxious to get back on the road.

"We're losing too much time. We have to get to Annecy as soon as we can," Colette fumed. "Surely you understand . . ."

Gabi forced herself to hold back her words. "You're right. I just want to be sure the doctor doesn't have any more questions for Lieutenant Rawlings."

"Ma'am, is something wrong?" T.J. pushed up from his chair and limped over to Gabi's side. "I heard my name mentioned, but I didn't understand what else was said."

"It's just that we're supposed to be somewhere today . . ."

"Then go. I'll manage just fine. Believe me, I'd be in a world of hurt if Sally and I hadn't limped back into French airspace."

The weight of caring for him slipped off Gabi's shoulders. "Are you sure?"

The pilot nodded. "Go."

"Thank you for understanding."

Once back in the Red Cross car, the urgency of the mission returned. They needed to keep moving.

After departing the village of Cravant, Gabi nudged Colette. "If the plane had hit us . . ."

"Yeah, we would have lost our chance." Colette didn't say any more.

Gabi knew they were the only ones standing between a Nazi megalomaniac and a country's national treasure. Somewhere out there, another team was trying to reach *La Joconde*. Colette had been right—the American pilot could handle things for himself.

Gabi's fingers tightened around the door handle. She hoped she hadn't cost them their chance at saving the painting.

= 21

Colette shuffled through the *La Joconde* file twice before finding the correct piece of paper.

"We won't be going all the way into Annecy," she said. "We need to be looking for Saint-Martin-Bellevue. Once there, Chateau de Dampierre is four kilometers off the Route d'Annecy, according to these instructions."

"Got it," Eric said from the front seat.

Colette took a deep breath and exhaled slowly. She leaned forward to flip through her notes, feeling the back of her dress—wet with perspiration—pull away from the leather seat. It had been a long, sticky day. Even though the trip had been harrowing, nothing compared to the tension building in her gut like a coiled spring, ready to explode.

Anticipating their arrival, she had no idea what they would find—but someone would be at the chateau, whether it was Countess Valois or the majordomo. When the family took custody of the *Mona Lisa*, one of the stipulations was that there would always be a "person of authority" on the estate grounds.

"I'm supposed to keep my eye out for a big castle with serfs working in the fields, right?" Bernard's sly smile belied his resentment of the class difference between the landed gentry and the proletariat.

"As castles go, I don't believe the Chateau de Dampierre is anything ostentatious," Colette said, ignoring the bite in his words. Chateaux in this part of France were large-scale manor houses or country homes of nobility—not the spectacular royal palaces pictured in history books. Colette wasn't sure what to expect since there wasn't a photo in her file.

While Eric followed the twisting road past alfalfa fields lined with hedgerows, Colette noted several properties on a grand scale. She was looking at the right side of the road when a Renaissance-era castle of exquisite proportions arose into view above a massive stone wall. Two stories tall, the stately citadel was constructed of beige stone with a blue slate mansard roof accented with dormer windows. Round towers with conical tips finished all corners and bracketed the wide terraces adorned with vine-entwined balustrades.

"Nice place." The irony in Bernard's voice was clear.

Eric turned right into a private drive covered with fine crushed granite. A sizable wrought-iron gate flanked by stone pillars protected the Chateau de Dampierre.

"A buzzer should be on the left side," Colette said.

"Found it." Eric left the car idling in neutral and approached the stone pillar on his left.

Seconds after pressing the button, the sounds of barking dogs erupted from a wooded barn on the property. A workman wiping his hands on a towel soon appeared, walking their way.

"I'll take care of this." Colette stepped out of the car with her file in hand. She showed him several papers, and the hired hand nodded. The gate opened, leading them to a long circular driveway, frontage to the regal entrance. Intricately designed wooden doors with iron rivets were recessed just beyond a stone alcove.

"Amazing," Eric commented. "Only thing missing is the moat and drawbridge." He followed the salmon-colored driveway past a sparkling stone fountain and came to a stop in front of the stately entrance, cutting the engine.

Colette shivered as she scanned the windows for movement. Just then, an oversized door opened. Out stepped Countess Ariane Valois, holding the hand of a young girl who looked to be about ten years old. The Countess was dressed in a soft, feminine white blouse and a gathered A-line ankle-length mauve skirt, a look that balanced sophistication and simplicity.

Colette hurried from the car and mounted three steps. "Bonjour, Countess Valois. I'm Colette Perriard from the Louvre."

"Quelle surprise!" The Countess threw open her arms in greeting.

Colette accepted the hug with a lift of her eyebrow. She'd expected a more constrained demeanor from nobility, especially with commoners.

"I certainly know you from our correspondence. Welcome to the Chateau de Dampierre!"

"Thank you very much."

"When I heard we had visitors, I wasn't sure who would be arriving in a Red Cross car."

Colette looked back toward the dirty vehicle, where Gabi, Eric, and Bernard were standing. She motioned for them to join her on the landing.

"The car belongs to two friends, Gabi Mueller and Eric Hofstadler, and this is my . . . colleague from the Louvre, Bernard Rousseau."

"A pleasure to meet you," the Countess said. "And this is my daughter, Kristina."

After the four of them shook Kristina's hand, the Countess looked toward her daughter. "Do you know why we have visitors today?"

The young girl shook her head.

"Because they've come to take your friend with them back to Paris."

"But Mommy, I don't want her to go." Sadness suddenly filled her eyes.

The Countess patted her daughter's cheek. "Remember? We've been praying that this day would come. It means France is again a free country."

Kristina put her arm around her mother's waist and buried her farouche expression. Smiling, the Countess turned back to her guests. "So tell us, what's happening in Paris? We've heard the great news about Libération."

Bernard beamed. "The *boches*—I mean, the Germans—have run like sewer rats back into their holes. Paris is overwhelmed with joy. We can again live in freedom."

"I can only imagine the celebration along the Champs Élysées." The Countess smiled and ran a hand down her daughter's silky dark hair. "I listened to Radio France on Saturday, and the description of General de Gaulle laying the wreath on the tomb of the Unknown Soldier moved me."

Colette noticed Bernard's complexion redden. She knew he detested the general, and hoped he'd soon come to his senses. To her, French politics was a waste of time. They had control of their country back. What more could they desire? Effort should be put into bringing health and pride back to their country—not in fighting within their borders.

"We were there," Bernard said in a matter-of-fact manner. "The general was reserved, which he should have been for such a solemn moment."

"Bernard is being modest," Eric interjected. "Sure, we

were all there, but he was part of the official ceremony at the Arc de Triomphe. Our friend walked with the Resistance leadership down the Champs Élysées, all the way to the Notre Dame."

"You were with the Resistance?" the Countess asked. "Then we have a real hero in our midst."

A smile returned to Bernard's face. "I answered the call to duty, Countess. Nothing more, nothing less."

"I'm sure you're being far too modest. Please, come in."

They stepped into the chateau's entrance foyer, and it took several seconds for Colette's eyes to adjust to the darker surroundings. The foyer was magnificent: quarter-sawn oak floors in a herringbone pattern, a sweeping staircase leading to the living quarters on the second floor, a formal receiving room with a wood-paneled library, and four sets of French doors showing the way to an expansive terrace at the rear of the chateau.

The Countess led them toward the formal living room. "It's a shame that my husband isn't here. He's in Sainte Foy-la-Grande tending to business."

The Countess stopped. "Have you had dinner? I prepared a beef bourguignon this afternoon. We have plenty."

Colette looked to the others. "We've been in a rush to get here, so we haven't eaten. Did Monsieur Rambouillet reach you today?"

"No, phone service has been sporadic. Is something wrong?"

"Actually, there is." For the next couple of minutes, Colette outlined the threat against the *Mona Lisa*.

"Thank you for telling me the situation," the Countess said. "Then we will have to hurry. I'll get dinner ready. I only need a few minutes."

"We would be most grateful." Colette felt that she

couldn't say no to the Countess's offer of hospitality, but they couldn't linger.

Kristina suddenly pulled on her mother's skirt. "Mommy, can I show them?"

"Show them what?" she teased.

"You know—"

With that, the girl beckoned for her mother to lean over so she could whisper something into her ear.

Colette's heart warmed from the cute interplay between mother and child.

"What do you want to show us?" She teased Kristina with a puzzled expression.

Kristina reached out and grabbed Colette's hand, and the rest fell in behind as she led them up the long staircase.

"Come back down in five minutes," the Countess called out. "Dinner will be on the table." She then retreated to the kitchen.

———

Gabi's excitement level rose with each step. Knowing that she was so close to the *Mona Lisa*, to actually see her for the first time, was electrifying.

The long hallway that led to the young girl's bedroom was tastefully adorned with a variety of artwork, including canvas paintings, many of the trompe l'oeil technique.

Kristina dropped Colette's hand and ran the last ten steps, placing both hands on the doorknob.

"Are you ready?"

Gabi nodded but didn't say a word. She followed Colette into the bedroom, and there, on a wall behind her four-poster bed, was *La Joconde*.

Gabi stopped breathing. Da Vinci's painting was so exquisite, so perfect—so emotional. She reminded herself to inhale.

Slowly moving into the room as if on hallowed ground, the group assembled at the foot of Kristina's bed. All eyes fixed on the mesmerizing masterpiece. For a minute, no one spoke.

Awestruck, heat rose to Gabi's cheeks as Eric slipped an arm around her waist.

"Everything that people have said about the *Mona Lisa* is right," she whispered. "Her smile is mesmerizing."

Bernard folded his arms across his chest. "I can see why no other painting has captured the world's imagination like this one."

"She is exquisite."

All heads turned to the voice from the doorway. Countess Ariane stepped to the side of the bed. "She's kept watch over Kristina every night since her arrival in February. *La Joconde* has become her friend."

"I don't want her to go, Mommy."

"Listen, *mon petit chou*, the *Mona Lisa* doesn't belong to us. She belongs to all of France, and it's time for her to go home . . . and for us to head downstairs and eat."

"Can we visit her in Paris?"

Gabi watched Colette step closer and bend her knees until she was at eye level with the young girl. "I'll make sure you have a private audience with her every time you visit. You can even stay with her after closing. My promise."

The Paquis neighborhood was Hans Schaffner's kind of place.

This part of Geneva was a melting pot of thieves, pickpockets, and hustlers—the type of place where prostitutes openly gathered on street corners while they waited for approaching customers from the Rive Droite.

Inside a tawdry bar on the Rue de Berne, Schaffner and Kaufman took a table among the lowlifes. The congenial waitress who took their order immediately switched to a passable German after hearing their fumbling French. Schaffner got the feeling that they weren't the first Germans to find themselves in Geneva's red-light district.

They had driven into the border city at dusk, arriving as lights illuminated the Jet d'Eau, a water fountain shooting a plume of lake water high above the majestic buildings along the southeastern bank. They were running right on schedule, thanks to their German resilience in overcoming the travel setbacks.

A dinner break in Geneva would give them time to regroup and go over their plans again. Schaffner told his partner that he was actually expecting more trouble finding the chateau than snatching the *Mona Lisa*.

"The good news is that the moon will be bright, so you'd think a big place like that will stick out like a sore thumb," Schaffner said. "Let's take a look at that map again."

The Chateau de Dampierre was on the way into Annecy, a small city and Alpine pearl he had visited before the war. No more than thirty-five kilometers, less than an hour from the border.

"Seven kilometers before Annecy, we take this turnoff . . . looks straightforward to me."

The borders between Switzerland and France and Germany had been sealed since 1939, but Schaffner had done some checking and found a country road in Thônex, a small town outside of Geneva, where patrols were sparse and the customs booth on both sides of the border closed at 6 p.m. Once they slipped into France, they would have a clear shot toward Annecy.

"Have you ever seen the *Mona Lisa*?" Schaffner asked.

His partner shook his head. "Only pictures."

"I don't understand what the fuss is all about. She looks like she has constipation, you know?"

Kaufman grinned and unloaded his fork. "Do you think we'll find any resistance?" He half mumbled his words past the food.

"Heller doesn't think so. The Count is apparently out of town, checking on one of his wineries in the Bourgogne. There should only be the Countess, their young daughter, and a few farmhands on the estate. Maybe we'll see a *paysan* with a pitchfork. I don't know. But I can tell you this: nothing is going to keep me from collecting the second half of our fee."

22

"This is the first beef I've had in a year, and it was worth the wait."

Colette savored the rich and tender bite of beef bourgui-gnonne. It was a heavenly preparation made by the Countess herself. She was a great *cuisinère* and an elegant hostess, so when seconds were offered, she and the others could hardly refuse.

Yet even as Colette enjoyed the meal, tension was build-ing again. Every little noise drew her attention, and when Kristina dropped a piece of silverware, she thought she'd jump out of her skin. This dinner was taking too long.

Countess Ariane set her silver fork on her plate. "We read of your deprivations in Paris, and I'm pleased the braised beef is raising your spirits."

"May I raise my spirits a third time?" Bernard held up his plate, which elicited light laughs around the long table set in the formal dining room. If he had been seated closer, Colette would have elbowed his ribs. Didn't he understand that they'd come to Chateau de Dampierre on a serious mission . . . and not to indulge?

The Countess's eyes lit up. "Hand over that plate, young man. You have a long night ahead." The Countess scooped another generous helping from the enameled casserole dish.

Every minute that passed, the Germans were potentially that much closer. Colette set her fork down harder than intended and saw that all eyes had moved to her. "As much as we'd like to stay, we must get back on the road to Paris—as soon as possible."

Colette turned to Kristina, who sat next to her. "I'm sorry, sweetheart, but we have to pack up *La Joconde*. I hope this news doesn't upset you."

Kristina made a brave face but was near tears. "Does she really have to go?"

"Yes, dear." Colette wrapped an arm around her shoulders.

"I would imagine that you have to be very careful when transporting a priceless painting," Gabi interjected, attempting to change the subject.

"You should have been here when she arrived," the Countess said, warming to the memory. "The *Mona Lisa* was in her protective crate, and when the truck pulled up to the front door, four men carried her in like Cleopatra on the Nile. It was quite a production."

"Where have you stored the crate they used to transport her?" Colette asked the Countess.

"You'll find it under Kristina's bed."

While Bernard finished mopping up the last drops of brown sauce from his plate, Colette forced a smile and worked the napkin in her hands.

She rose, unable to contain herself any longer. She needed to begin packing the *Mona Lisa* in the protective transportation crate—now.

"We really have to get moving. Countess, is there any

way Kristina can give you a hand in the kitchen while we get started?"

The Countess smiled in understanding. "She can help me clean up the dishes, but I know Kristina will be heartbroken if she doesn't say goodbye."

"Very well. When you're done, come on up. But this should only take us fifteen or twenty minutes to get her ready."

Colette, followed by Bernard, mounted the limestone staircase to Kristina's bedroom, where her eyes were again drawn to that hypnotic smile. Taking a deep breath, she cleared her mind and ran through the packing process. She was thankful that the *Mona Lisa* was not set behind glass since that would have posed special challenges during transportation. Slivers of broken glass with razor-sharp edges and fragile centuries-old oils . . . not a good mix.

"Bernard, can you offer your handyman's opinion?" She motioned toward the floor under the bed. "I want to insure the integrity of the original box used to transport the *Mona Lisa*. One can't be too careful."

She'd heard stories about things going wrong when moving a work of art—scratches, chipped paint, even tears in the canvas. That would not happen on her watch. The Florentine lady had to be fully protected at all times.

Bernard dropped to his knees and lifted the heavy floor-length bedspread and folded the lightweight comforter back atop the four-poster bed. He reached underneath and pulled out a rectangular wooden box that was covered with white linen. A light layer of dust coated the sheet, but the box looked like new.

The Frenchman looked up when Eric entered the room, holding the handle of a small gray toolbox. Gabi was right behind him.

"Where would you like this?" Eric asked.

"Set it over there." Colette pointed to the window over-looking the circular driveway. She turned her attention back to the wooden box set before her. Six cross-slotted flat head screws around the perimeter secured the lid.

"Here, allow me." Bernard reached for the metal tool box. After finding the Phillips head screwdriver, he began loosening the screws.

"Careful." Colette knew she was hovering like a mother hen, but she didn't want Bernard to damage the crate.

Within a few minutes, the six screws lay in a neat pile, allowing Bernard to lift off the top section.

Inside the custom-made box was a precisely fitted cavity lined with royal purple velvet. The recessed interior matched the exact proportions of the framed *Mona Lisa*. Lying at the bottom of the box was a folded purple slipcover with a drawstring, to place over the painting. There were also two wooden braces wrapped with velvet to secure the painting inside the crate.

"Everything looks in order to me," Colette said. "What do you think?"

Bernard ran his fingers over the velvet lining and inspected the crate for cracks. "I don't see any problems."

"Excellent." Colette clapped her hands together. "Bernard, Eric—would you bring the *Mona Lisa* over here? You'll need to lift straight up to release her from the four supporting hooks."

The two eyed each other, and Colette saw looks of resolve.

"We better move the bed first," Eric said.

"Good idea, but be careful not to bump the frame."

Bernard nodded his agreement as he and Eric positioned themselves midway on either side of the bed. They lifted simultaneously. Then with controlled steps, they moved the heavy bed away from the wall, giving them ample room.

Colette held her concerned expression. "You gents think you can handle her?"

"She's not heavy, is she?" Bernard asked.

"My notes say that the painting and frame weigh ten kilos because she was painted on a wood panel. That's not very heavy but perhaps more than you'd expect from a traditional painting on canvas."

"We'll be very careful," Eric reassured.

Colette placed her hand over her heart as they carefully lifted the *Mona Lisa* up several centimeters so she was no longer tethered to the wall.

"Got it?" Bernard asked.

"Got it."

They took mincing steps as they carried the painting toward the wooden crate.

"Ready to turn?"

"Ready."

The two men turned the *Mona Lisa* on her back and slowly descended to the floor, where they carefully set the painting into the wooden crate.

"So far, so good." Colette snapped the purple slipcover to get rid of any dust. She then reached down into the velvet pouch to ensure that nothing abrasive could come in contact with the delicate paint.

At that moment, the Countess and Kristina appeared in the doorway, holding hands. "Are we too soon?" the Countess asked.

"Perfect timing." Colette waved the girl over. "Ready to tell your friend goodbye?" she asked.

Kristina knelt at the base of the crate next to Colette. She ran her fingers across the polished frame and then blew a kiss. "I'll come visit you soon," she whispered.

The young girl then stood next to her mother, wrapped

her arms around her waist, and watched as the men tilted up the base of the painting while Colette gently eased the slipcover over the frame. Halfway up, they placed the base back in the crate and tilted the top up. The cover slipped into place like a satin glove. After the silk-braided drawstring was cinched down, the painting was placed in the recessed velvet cradle. Kristina inched forward for a closer look as Bernard secured the two wooden crossbars horizontally across the velvet covering.

Eric sidled up next to the Countess. "As you now know, there's an imminent threat by German operatives to steal the *Mona Lisa*, so Bernard and I will have a look around before we leave."

The Countess nodded. "I wondered if there would be such a threat during the Occupation. Frankly, I'm not surprised, other than it's coming now, after Libération."

"Do you have someplace that you can go tonight? I think it would be safer . . ." Eric's voice trailed off.

"We can stay with my sister, who has a villa less than five kilometers from here. I'll let her know we're coming. I wouldn't want Kristina to be in any danger. Thank you for suggesting this."

Colette saw Eric and the Countess step closer just as Bernard sealed the lid with six screws. "That should do it," she said, showing some signs of relief.

"Come, darling." The Countess took hold of Kristina's hand. "Let's make some sandwiches, and then I have a surprise."

"Sandwiches? But we just had dinner."

"Not for us, dear. For our new friends. Remember, they're leaving for Paris right away, and they need food for the long drive back. Then we're going to spend the night at Aunt Louise's. You'll be able to play with your cousins."

Kristina beamed with approval, then looked back to the wooden box lying next to her bed. "Au revoir, *La Joconde*." Then the two disappeared down the hall.

Seconds later, the Countess reappeared. "I nearly forgot. There are several cans of petrol in the garage. If you need them, please help yourself."

Then with a brief smile, she hurried down the hall.

"Give me a hand with the bed." Eric bent down to move the queen-sized bed back into position.

"Colette and I will get that," Gabi said. "Why don't you take care of the petrol? Take Bernard with you. Those Germans could be out there."

"You're right. Let's get moving."

For Eric, a sense of urgency returned as uncertainty of the Germans' whereabouts underscored the fact that they could be close. Until they were back on the road, there was real danger in being a stationary target.

The pair departed through the front door and jumped into the waiting Mercedes. Eric pulled around to the large four-car garage on the north side of the chateau. They found the cans of petrol neatly placed against an empty wall in a garage that housed a black Rolls Royce with silver trim and a polished red Mercedes coupe. They took turns ferrying the full cans and emptying them into their gas tank. After topping off, they filled an empty jerry can as their reserve supply.

"Nice to be royalty," Bernard quipped.

"So it would seem," Eric replied. "But you know, the Countess was so down-to-earth and hospitable, I almost forgot about it."

"She was nice. I'll have to give her that. And she even cleaned up in the kitchen."

Eric closed the garage door, glad to breathe fresh evening air after inhaling gasoline fumes for the last ten minutes. He took a deep breath and hopped into the filthy Mercedes sedan for the short drive back to the chateau's front entrance.

After cutting the engine, he turned to Bernard. "I think we should look around before we go back in. Make sure everything is buttoned up."

The two walked around the chateau. Not finding anything amiss, they returned to the gravel driveway and headed toward the wrought iron gated entrance. Illuminated by a nearly full moon, a stone wall two meters in height outlined the estate.

"Too bad we don't have a key to open the gate," Bernard said.

"I saw the hired hand reach here." Eric approached the guardhouse next to the stone pillars framing the entrance. He reached above the doorjamb and found the key.

They stepped out onto a deserted dirt road. Eric looked right, then left—when he spotted a car parked fifty meters away.

"See it?" he asked Bernard.

The Frenchman strained his eyes in the moonlight. "Let's go check it out."

Within ten steps, Eric recognized the model of the car—a BMW 320, probably five or six years old. Alarm bells went off in his head, and he broke into a sprint.

"Look at the license plate—from Zurich!" The white plate said ZH 499.

Bernard was already racing back to the chateau.

They hurried for the chateau's formidable entrance, weapons drawn.

The massive front door stood ajar, causing the hair on the back of Eric's neck to bristle. He had no idea where the Germans were—upstairs or downstairs.

Together, they listened through the gaping entrance for any sort of noise.

Hearing none, Eric waved his hand, and together they both slipped silently into the darkened passage. Staying close to the alcove wall, they headed to the left and passed through the dining room. Bernard held up a hand—then a muffled noise came from the kitchen.

They carefully stepped through the dining room, but the suppressed sounds stopped. Eric willed himself to remain calm, but he feared what was beyond the kitchen door.

He crept closer, followed by Bernard, but then he hit a spot on the wooden floor that caused a loud squeak.

Eric stopped and held his breath.

"Kommen Sie herein und Hände hoch!" said a graveled voice. "Oder wir töten unsere erste Geisel." *Come in here and hands in the air! Or we kill our first hostage.*

Eric whispered the translation to Bernard, who responded with panic in his eyes. "We have to believe them," Eric said.

"We're coming," Eric called out in German. He dropped his pistol into his pants pocket and mimed for Bernard to do the same.

They pushed through the swinging door with arms raised. One swarthy German held a gun to the temple of the shivering Countess. A thin sliver of blood trickled down her forehead. A thick rope bound her to a kitchen chair.

The other assailant, with close-set eyes and a fiendish grin, stood behind another chair, pointing his gun at Kristina. The young girl was blindfolded and seated, her cheeks wet with tears.

On the floor, Gabi and Colette were fettered with rope

around their hands and feet. They leaned against kitchen cabinets. At their feet, the makings of sandwiches—sliced bread, lettuce, and tomatoes—were strewn across the parquet floor.

"Two more to add to our collection," the heavier German said. "Very interesting. You know what we are here for, right?"

Eric glared back in silence.

"First, your guns."

Eric bluffed and kept his arms raised. *If one approaches to disarm me, that'll give me an opening . . .*

The Germans didn't fall for it. Instead, the one holding the Countess pressed his revolver against her temple. A sob escaped her lips.

"My daughter . . . please release my daughter," the woman pleaded.

The German ignored her words. His eyes remained fixed on Eric.

"She means nothing to me, so if you don't drop your weapons now, she'll be the first to go."

Eric translated for Bernard's benefit, and the two reached into their pockets. They dropped their guns to the floor and kicked them in the direction of the Germans.

"We are in a bit of a hurry, so bring us the *Mona Lisa* . . . *schnell!*"

Eric's brow furrowed as he weighed his options.

The second German snatched the wrist of blindfolded Kristina, who let out an ear-piercing shriek. He yanked her arm and placed her hand on the kitchen counter to a cacophony of more bloodcurdling screams. With his free hand, he reached into his pocket and produced a large switchblade. With a flash and metallic click, the released blade locked into place.

"You have sixty seconds to return with the painting. If you are tardy, the girl will lose one finger. Be gone two minutes, and she loses a second finger. Do you understand?"

"No, no, please, please—!" the Countess begged.

The beady-eyed German ignored her. He maliciously pressed the girl's wrist to the cutting block and placed the blade's sharp end against her pinky.

"You now have *less* than one minute. Then Rolf starts cutting," the taller German said with satisfaction.

Eric bolted for the kitchen door, with Bernard in hot pursuit.

———

The screams of the young girl reverberated through the spacious chateau. Eric and Bernard raced for Kristina's room, where they found the wooden crate on the floor in the same place they had left it.

Eric took one end of the crate as they hustled down the staircase sidewise, step by step, in record time. Then it was a race through the dining room. When they burst through the kitchen door, the German was counting down the time.

"Acht, sieben . . ." The German glanced up from his watch. "Just in time. I would have hated for the Countess to witness this." He motioned for them to set down the wooden crate and raise their hands. They obliged.

"Now let her go," Eric said with gritted teeth. "You've got your painting."

The second German relaxed his grip, and the young girl pulled off the blindfold and ran to her mother. Kristina wrapped her arms around her mother's waist and sobbed.

The German in command then turned toward Eric and Bernard, whose arms were still raised high. "Rolf, tie them up."

He kept his pistol trained on Eric and Bernard as his partner bound their hands and feet. Then he pushed them to the kitchen floor, where they landed in a heap with Gabi and Colette.

The heavier German then waved his pistol toward the Countess. "I need a screwdriver," he announced.

Gabi translated the question, then the Countess's answer. "Top drawer . . . right side."

The German began pulling out kitchen drawers. One near the pantry had the tool he needed. He returned to the crate and placed it on the counter.

Eric watched helplessly as the heavier German loosened the screws for the cover, then quickly moved to the screws holding the wooden braces inside the crate. When finished, he tilted up the painting and pulled back the velvet covering.

The famous face looked back, unconcerned with the deteriorating situation.

"Unglaublich." *Unbelievable.* "It really is the *Mona Lisa.*"

The German covered the painting and reset the framed portrait inside the transportation crate. He secured the crate and replaced the screws. He moved quickly, the effort causing sweat to bead up on his forehead.

Wiping his brow, the German set the screwdriver down on the kitchen table while his partner kept a gun trained on the hostages.

"If you attempt to follow us or if we feel a police dragnet has been set, we will kill the girl."

Gabi spoke first, her voice flaring with indignation. "You're taking Kristina hostage?"

"You heard me. When the *Mona Lisa* is safely delivered, she will be released."

Pandemonium swept the kitchen as Gabi and Eric shared the news with the others. A gunshot split the air as the heavier German fired his pistol into the ceiling. Plaster dust filtered down amid the silenced voices. The Countess's soft weeping was the only sound.

With a slight nod to his partner, the second German roughly pinned Kristina's hands behind her back and bound her wrists together with thin white rope and replaced the blindfold. The girl, hysterical with fear and unable to see, resisted until the restraints were set. She whimpered while the German gagged her with a strip of cloth.

"Remember what I said. Otherwise, the girl dies."

With that parting directive, the heavier German hoisted the wooden crate into his arms. His partner held on tightly to the frightened young girl, and together the three disappeared through the kitchen door. The silence was deafening.

A panic-stricken Countess Ariane strained against the ropes that held her back. With unbridled fury, she twisted against the restraints that tore into her wrists and ankles. The force of her efforts caused the chair to tip over.

As she lay writhing against her bonds, Eric saw the ferocity in her eyes that could only come from a mother trying to protect her child.

23

The scramble to free themselves started the moment the Germans left the chateau.

Gabi tugged against the restraints, her fingers fighting to untie the ropes around her ankles. She knew every second counted if they were to catch the kidnappers.

"Eric, swing your legs around. Maybe I can reach your knife."

He did as she asked and with her teeth she pulled up his pants leg. Then she turned and freed the blade from its sheath with her bound hands. She turned the knife upside down, holding the handle, then pressed with the weight of her body and pinned the tip into the floor. Eric spun around and positioned his roped wrists against its razor-sharp edge. Then he slowly worked the restraints against the blade.

As Eric cut through his ropes, Bernard brought himself to his feet and hopped to the kitchen counter. "Which drawer for the knives?"

The Countess, who was desperately trying to work herself free, directed him. "A little farther . . . yes, that one."

With his back to the counter, Bernard used his bound hands to pull out a drawer. He fumbled for a blade until his hands grasped the handle of a carving knife. He dropped to his knees, leaned back, and commenced to cut through the rope binding his ankles.

Eric's hands were freed first. He quickly cut the ropes from Gabi's hands. She then untied her feet and began helping Colette. Eric was already untying the Countess. Three minutes later, everyone was free and dashed out of the kitchen.

The Countess raced through the dining room and out the front door, calling out Kristina's name. The rest of them followed. Her cries were emotionally wrenching.

The Countess didn't stop running until she reached the front gate, which lay open, just as Bernard and Eric had left it.

"We saw their car over there—along the wall," Eric said. The BMW sedan was gone, and the night was eerily still.

The Countess reached into her pocket for a handkerchief while Gabi squeezed her shoulders. "I don't think they'll harm Kristina. She's worth far more as a hostage. At least we know the direction they're heading . . . and their destination. Once they're in Switzerland, Kristina's situation improves because we have more resources that can be put into play."

"But we *have* to chase them—now." Bernard rested his hands on his hips. Anger flashed across his face. The edge in his voice bordered on desperation.

Gabi understood. Not only had the *Mona Lisa* slipped from their grasp, a young girl's life was on the line. "Shouldn't we call the authorities first—before they get to the border?" she asked.

"I agree," Eric said. "We need to call the local police, and I can contact our colleagues in Bern. Perhaps they can get word to the border checkpoints. The Germans can be caught, but it has to be done in a way that won't harm Kristina. I'll call right now and tell them the situation."

The Countess looked relieved that action was being taken. "Let me take you to the telephone in my husband's study." She dabbed the handkerchief on her eyes as she hurried forward.

As they walked back, Gabi momentarily glanced at Colette, who appeared to be thinking about a different young woman, albeit four centuries older. Her faraway eyes and poker face conveyed the idea that as much as she did not want to elevate a Renaissance portrait to the life of an innocent young girl, she was having a hard time separating the two.

They were approaching the chateau's front entrance when Gabi noticed their Red Cross automobile leaning at an awkward angle.

"Uh-oh. I think they punctured our tires." Gabi rounded the sedan to examine the right side of their vehicle. She'd guessed correctly.

"Use my car." The Countess pointed toward the garage. "You have to save my little girl."

"We will, Countess, as soon as we make those phone calls."

"The line is dead!"

Eric cupped the handset to his ear again, but all he heard was a slight hum.

"What happened?" Countess Ariane's face melted into grief.

"They must have cut the telephone wires," Eric replied.

"How far is your nearest neighbor?" Gabi asked.

The Countess composed herself. "A–a few hundred meters, maybe half a kilometer. Take our Rolls Royce. It's gassed up and ready to go."

Eric quickly headed toward the door. "I'll get the car. Keys?"

"In the ignition," the Countess replied.

Eric moved toward the front entrance. Bernard and Gabi followed.

"Eric!" Colette's voice caused him to pause.

He glanced back.

"I'm staying with the Countess. She can't be alone at a time like this." Colette took the woman's left hand into her own. "I know—I know you three will do all you can to find—" Her voice faltered.

Eric nodded, and his respect for the woman grew. Staying behind with the Countess spoke volumes. Eric glanced at Bernard and noticed the shocked expression on his face. A new thought emerged. *Maybe they could accomplish more if they split up.*

"Gabi, you go with Bernard to call the local authorities. I'll use the transmitter to reach our contact in Switzerland. We'll leave as soon as you get back."

The Countess scribbled a phone number on a piece of paper. "Can you also call my husband? Tell him about the dire situation and that he needs to come back home immediately."

"Of course," Gabi replied. She and Bernard hustled toward the garage while Eric approached the Red Cross sedan, now sitting lopsided. He popped the trunk, pulled out the transmitter, and ran back up the front steps.

Back in the study, Eric plugged in the transmitter while the Countess and Colette looked on.

"Should warm up in a minute. I'm hoping we can get a message relayed to the checkpoints heading into Switzerland."

Eric heard the heavy Rolls crunch gravel as the car headed

out the driveway. He glanced out the study's window in time to see a pair of taillights disappear. He then turned back to the portable Mark II Morse code transmitter and checked the frequency, which was already dialed in to the receiver in Dulles's apartment. Thinking through what he wanted to communicate to the American director, his fingers tapped in frenzy for five minutes.

When the transmitter sat in silence, Eric turned to the Countess. "All we can do is pray that the message gets forwarded to the Swiss border guards before the Germans reach Geneva."

Eric busied himself with packing up the transmitter. Then he heard the engine of the Rolls Royce entering the grounds of the Chateau de Dampierre and slow to a stop. The distinctive round headlamps illuminated the driveway, and Gabi jumped out, running toward the front entrance with everything in her.

The BMW 320 with Zurich license plates encountered little to no traffic in its race for the Swiss border.

Hans Schaffner made eye contact with his partner sitting in the passenger's seat.

"She doing okay?"

"I haven't heard her make a peep."

Schaffner thumped the steering wheel. "I'm talking about the *Mona Lisa*, not the twerp in the trunk."

"The painting is doing fine." Kaufman reached into the backseat and rapped the wooden box with his knuckles. "But we're still going to need the girl."

Sometimes Kaufman made sense, and in his dim-witted way, he was right. The Countess's daughter was a nice pawn to have on the chessboard.

He figured they had a fifteen-to-twenty-minute head start on the others—even if those fancy cars in the garage had gas.

They were just minutes from the border, so it was unlikely that the ineffectual French police—or whoever was officially in charge of this part of France—could stop them now.

As for the two Swiss he found at the chateau, that was unexpected. How did they get involved? Or why? Schaffner had a feeling that the drive through Switzerland was about to get more complicated. He had a contingency plan for that as well. Of one thing he was certain: Kaufman had cut the phone lines, so that would buy some time.

Figuring out how they'd reenter Switzerland had been the tricky part. There was no way they could hide a wooden crate—and now a bound-and-gagged school-age girl—from the border guards. To keep their border secure during this war, the Swiss also relied on regular patrols along their common border.

Coming *into* France on their way to the chateau, they had exited Swiss territory via a country road in Thônex, a placid village outside of Geneva that backed up to the French town of Annemasse. The border gate was unmanned—by both countries—when they'd passed by after dinnertime.

A half hour after their rapid departure from the chateau, Schaffner exited the principal route between Annecy and Geneva onto a secondary road. He was happy to get off the main drag. A car with Swiss tags—even in the dark of night—might as well have been lit up like a cinema marquee on a Saturday night.

Ten minutes later, he pulled off to the side of the road at a rural intersection. Schaffner reached into the glove compartment for binoculars.

He lifted the high-powered Zeiss lenses to his eyes, and what he saw didn't surprise him. The French border crossing was dark—the frogs still didn't have their act together—but two well-lit Swiss guards with shouldered rifles stood next to each other, rocking back and forth in their boots.

A black sedan rolled to the checkpoint. The Swiss border guards sniffed around, and then ordered the driver to open the trunk. His papers were closely inspected before he was allowed to proceed.

"There's our answer." Schaffner set the binoculars in his lap.

"Someone got the word out?" Kaufman asked.

"That would be my guess. Probably used a neighbor's phone to call the authorities. They would know we were coming."

Gabi pulled Eric to the side just within the front door.

"The family down the road let me use their phone. No one answered at the police station. They must be closed for the night. So I called home and got through to my father. He said he knows Heller's henchmen."

"Really?" Eric waited to hear the rest.

"Apparently, Hans Schaffner and Rolf Kaufman have been living in Switzerland since 1940 at Heller's beck and call. He believes they've stashed a lot of cash and valuables, including paintings, inside Swiss bank vaults."

"Does he know where they're going?" Eric asked.

"Dad saw the pair meet yesterday afternoon in Zurich with Anton Wessner, the Dolder Bank president. He thinks the two Germans are taking the painting directly to the bank branch on the Bahnhofstrasse."

"Good. We'll have a welcoming party ready for them."

"That's if they get there. Their car should be easy pickings for the Swiss police. Dad said before the hour is out, there'll be an all-points bulletin for a black BMW sedan with a ZH 499 license plate. Even if they slipped through the border, the Geneva authorities will find them before they pass the Jet d'Eau."

"What about the Count? Were you able to reach him?"

"Yes. He's rushing home and will return late tonight."

———

Bernard left Gabi and Eric at the entryway and hurried into the kitchen. He arrived to find Colette sitting with the Countess, who still worked a handkerchief in her hands.

When Colette looked up, he could see that she had been crying as well. "I have some good news." An ache clawed within, and he looked away from Colette and turned to the aristocratic woman instead. "Countess, Gabi was able to talk to your husband—"

Without a word, Colette rose and dashed through the kitchen door and out to the backyard garden.

Bernard watched her leave. Part of him told him to follow, but he needed to speak to the Countess first. He could only handle one distraught woman at a time.

"Your husband," he continued, "is heading back home now. We also now know the identity of the kidnappers, and their destination. If they make it past the border, we will get them in Zurich. There are already men waiting."

"Thank you." The Countess nodded. "I know you are doing all you can."

Bernard excused himself, then headed out the back door after Colette. The moonlight gave the back gardens a soft glow. He spotted her standing by a maze of hedges and rosebushes.

"Colette!"

She turned and faced him under the moonlight. Bernard

couldn't wait any longer. He couldn't pretend that everything was all right. He hated to think that Colette had any part of this, yet deep down he wondered why she wasn't willing to chase the Germans and preferred to stay with the Countess. Was it because she was feeling guilty for allowing this to happen?

"We're in a real jam right now," he began.

"Don't you think I know that?" Tears had given way to anger, meekness had transformed to defiance.

"Why are you mad at me?" Bernard questioned. "This whole mess is all your fault."

Colette gasped. "What are you talking about?"

"An innocent girl has been kidnapped. The *Mona Lisa* is missing. All because you informed Heller where the painting was."

A look of shock registered on Colette's face. Her eyes widened and her mouth opened. "What—what are you saying?"

"Don't act so innocent with me. I know the truth. Last week, we found a safe from the German stronghold at the Luxembourg Gardens. Inside were files, including a list of those who were cooperating with the *boches*. Your name was on the list!"

Colette's face flushed. "So that's why you've been acting different."

"What was I supposed to think?"

"You obviously decided I was a collaborator—or maybe worse."

Bernard shrugged. "Call it what you like, but it doesn't change the fact that you helped the Nazis. I didn't want to believe that you were an informant, but when I saw your name—"

"Did you ever consider I was blackmailed?" She stepped closer to him.

"Blackmailed?"

"Heller told me that if I didn't tell him what he wanted to know, he would have the Gestapo arrest and torture you."

"Arrest and torture me?"

"Yes, he explained how he'd do it, in graphic detail. He told me how you stopped the train at Pantin. He was the *boche* who aimed a gun at your head. Then he let you go, even though he knew you were part of the Resistance."

Bernard fumbled for words. He had misjudged his girl.

"I'm . . . I'm sorry. I never believed for a moment that you would collaborate with the *boches*. But I saw too many of my comrades betray others. I had friends who were tortured, lined up against an alley wall—"

"Listen to yourself, Bernard. You just contradicted yourself. One second you accuse me, the next you deny doubting me. You wouldn't know the truth if it hit you in the face like a sledgehammer. I thought you were smarter than this. But you deceived me and lied to me as well, including your stupid little game with this locket."

She reached for the golden ornamental case and yanked it off her neck. "Here, it's yours. We both know it never belonged to your grandmother."

She threw the jewelry at his feet, and with that, she hurried back to the chateau.

Gabi and Eric paced the study lined with dark mahogany bookshelves. High-back chairs and couches decorated the oversized room that smelled of leather and cigars.

"We have to get going," she said. "There's no need for Bernard to go with us to Zurich anyway—"

"Let's get in the car," Eric moved to the door. "If Bernard doesn't show up in one minute, we'll leave without him."

They headed to the awaiting Rolls Royce Wraith, black with silver trim. Eric turned the ignition key. The giant engine sprang to life. He shifted the vehicle into gear just as a flustered-looking Bernard emerged from the entry and bounded down the steps, followed by the Countess. But no Colette.

Gabi stepped out of the car. "What took you so long?" she asked.

Bernard ran his hands through his black hair. "Colette is upset with me, and that's an understatement. I had no idea she cooperated with the *boches* to save my skin. How can I convince her of that?"

"That's your problem." Gabi barely glanced at the Frenchman. "Eric and I are leaving now. We'll drive back to Switzerland and join in the race for Zurich. It's our turf, and we'll move quicker with just the two of us."

"You're going without me?" Bernard threw up his hands in disgust.

"Gabi's right," Eric interjected. "There's nothing you can do in Zurich. Besides, you don't speak German. You should stay here, at least until the Count arrives home."

"*C'est impossible*. Someone representing France needs to be there when *La Joconde* is freed from their clutches. Otherwise, there will be an international incident, especially if something happens to her. No, this I cannot accept. I will accompany you. The matter is closed."

Gabi looked at Bernard, and her eyes followed him as he got into the backseat. "As you wish."

Eric got out with Gabi to meet the Countess hurrying down the entrance steps to say goodbye.

"Countess . . . I want you to know that we'll do everything we can to bring your daughter back home safely." Gabi leaned forward and bussed her on both cheeks.

Eric repeated the same farewell. "As soon as we hear anything, you'll be the first to know."

"Thank you. And I have something for you." The Countess handed Eric a cigar box.

"My husband's revolver. Take it with you, just in case."

"Thank you, Countess. If I have to use it to save your daughter, I will."

────────

Schaffner fired up the engine, and the BMW lurched into gear. Instead of driving toward the Swiss customs point, he steered the car onto a desolate road running parallel to Switzerland's border.

The German driver looked up into his rearview mirror. Kaufman, wisely, had been watching to see if they were being followed. They weren't. Only faintly lit farmland and fruit orchards beyond the thin dust cloud settling back on the hardpan.

They drove for ten minutes until they saw a sign announcing a left turn toward La Louvière in Switzerland. Yet another pipsqueak border crossing, but they couldn't risk driving through. He continued past the turnoff.

The dirt road veered closer to the border as the two-lane route continued to run parallel to the *frontière* between France and Switzerland. He was looking for the right spot . . . and there, in the dim light, he could make out the outline of a barn—the same one he'd spotted two hours ago. The cowshed rested just on the other side of the Swiss border. Only a fence of barbed wire blocked them from crossing.

Schaffner downshifted and parked the BMW beside a towering oak. "Let's make this quick."

"I need you to unlock the trunk," Kaufman said.

"Of course."

Hopping from the driver's seat, Schaffner lifted the lid to the sight of a bound and blindfolded girl, shivering in a fetal position.

"Allez." Schaffner knew that was about the extent of his French.

Kaufman herded the girl while Schaffner opened the back door to retrieve the wooden crate.

She whimpered softly, but thankfully she had stopped crying. He was glad. Children's cries grated on his nerves.

They crossed the deserted road with Schaffner carrying the *Mona Lisa*. Kaufman yanked on the girl's left arm to steer her. She stumbled and then righted herself again.

Only one hundred meters of grassy farm separated them from the Swiss border, delineated by a barbwire fence.

Schaffner's eyes and ears were tuned to any Swiss border patrols in the area, but the only sounds came from their own leather boots as they flattened stalks of alfalfa grass.

When they arrived at the barbwire fence, Schaffner set the wooden crate on the ground. His arms were tired from the exertion, but thoughts of their reward drove him on.

"You have the wire cutters?"

"In my jacket." His partner nodded while maintaining a grip on the girl.

Kaufman reached into his pocket with his free hand and handed the cutters to Schaffner. He set to work, aggressively cutting his way through three lines of heavy barbwire. The fencing filament spun to the ground, creating a large opening.

The trio resumed their march. This time, they veered in the direction of the ramshackle barn. The blindfolded girl had stopped whining and seemed resigned to her fate. When they arrived, Schaffner pulled away a barn door—and there was the Citroën Traction Avant.

"I couldn't believe the bartender let us borrow his car," Kaufman scoffed.

"Wouldn't you have done the same if someone paid you twice as much as it's worth?" Schaffner congratulated himself for coming up with a brilliant plan. The Swiss would be looking for a BMW two-door, which they had stolen yesterday. There was no way the vehicle could be traced to them. Besides, in twenty-four hours they'd be rich and could disappear for the foreseeable future.

Schaffner doubted anyone would report finding the '38 BMW anytime soon. He left an inducement behind: the keys were in the ignition—and there was more than a half tank of gas.

He kicked the front tire of the Citroën. "She may not look like much, but she's our ticket to freedom."

24

The Citroën progressed along the Quai de Cologny, past watch stores and private banks that fronted the western bank of Lake Geneva.

The image Schaffner wanted to project to prying eyes was that they were a couple of guys out on the town, meeting their friends at their favorite bar.

They followed the quai and passed the Jardin Anglais—English Garden—where Schaffner recognized the local landmark, a manicured flower clock. Then a more disturbing sight caught his attention—several policemen stationed at the streetlights leading to the Pont du Mont Blanc, the bridge spanning the Rhone River.

"Don't make eye contact," he said to Kaufman.

They were in luck. The lights remained green, and they didn't have to stop.

From the corner of his eye, though, Schaffner saw that no one was paying attention to the Citroën. A BMW coupe, however, was parked at the side of the road, and the driver was being questioned by a cop.

They drove along the lake to Lausanne, then took a less-traveled route through vineyards as they followed road signs toward Neuchâtel, heralded as the wine- and watch-making capital of Switzerland.

Traveling out of their way on minor roads would add extra hours, but for a job like this, the extra caution was justified.

———————

After Countess Ariane alerted the caretaker and his family to the tragic events, she sat down with Colette in the breakfast nook.

The young curator wiped away tears. "I'm so sorry, Countess, that Kristina has been kidnapped and there is nothing I can do to help."

The Countess refilled her cup of tea. "Don't blame yourself for this, Colette. We always knew there was a risk, and yet . . . we did what little we could to help France, even if it was only to protect her art. This isn't your fault, and Bernard should have known that you would have never betrayed your country, even with your name on the list. Perhaps there was a misunderstanding—"

"There was no misunderstanding! Bernard should have known that I would only cooperate with the *boches* under extreme duress. I didn't have any bargaining power. How was I to know that something like this would happen—that your daughter would be kidnapped? I'm wracked with guilt. I feel horrible." Colette blew her nose and looked glumly into the distance.

The Countess laid her hand gently on Colette's arm, a forced smile belying the fear that numbed her. Somewhere in Switzerland, her daughter was in the clutches of two men who'd probably kill her once her usefulness ended.

———————

West-to-east traffic in Switzerland never took this route.

They were certainly taking the long way to Lucerne, traveling along Lake Neuchâtel, the largest lake within Switzerland. The kitschy cuckoo clock shops, elegant watch stores, and inviting pastry shops were buttoned up for the evening.

Even though it was past midnight, Schaffner had no problem remaining alert. The adrenaline coursing through his veins fueled his charge through the canton of Neuchâtel.

Kaufman, who had been dozing, stirred with a question. "Where are we?"

"We've passed Neuchâtel, and soon we'll hit another long lake on our way to Biel/Bienne. Or is it Bienne/Biel?"

Kaufman perked up. "Biel/Bienne is on the border between the French- and German-speaking parts of Switzerland."

"I hope we don't have to show a passport," Schaffner said dryly.

The remark elicited a grunt from Kaufman. "No language border check. But it will be good to be back on the German side of Switzerland. So which route are we taking to Lucerne?"

"There are lots of small roads. I'm thinking we'll go to Solothurn and then cut down to Hutwil. A couple of mountain passes will slow us down, but that'll get us to Lucerne. We'll probably get there in the early morning."

―――――――

"I can't believe we're in this situation. My heart breaks for Kristina."

Eric's ears perked up at the sound of Gabi's words coming from the passenger seat of the plush Rolls Royce.

Bernard stirred from the rear. "All is not lost. We'll find these mongrels. If we don't, at least we'll know where the *Mona Lisa* is being kept. France will apply pressure on the

Swiss government to have the painting released from her prison inside a Swiss bank vault."

The Geneva border check rolled into view. The flash of Eric's red Swiss passport from a black Rolls Royce was enough for them to be waved through by the night shift.

The four-door luxury sedan rolled smoothly through the dark and deserted streets of Geneva, staying on frontage roads to the lake. Eric looked again into the rearview mirror, but Bernard wasn't there. He was lying down, alone with his thoughts.

Gabi's head rested against the thick glass window. The smooth Swiss highway and gentle ride of the luxury sedan had lulled her to sleep. Eric reviewed what had transpired the last couple of hours. It was a forlorn sight when he had last looked in his rearview mirror and saw the Countess offering a weak wave. But he was pleased to know that the hired hand's family was there to offer moral as well as physical support.

Now their destination was Allen Dulles's apartment in Bern, where they would regroup. Pressing down on the accelerator, the in-line six-cylinder engine with 4,257 cubic centimeters of finely tuned power responded instantly.

They would make it to Bern in record time.

25

The Citroën balked at the gain in elevation, and they were inching along in first gear at fifteen kilometers per hour. Cirro-cumulus clouds billowed in an azure sky, and a pair of white paddle steamers sliced through the crystal blue waters of Lake Lucerne. To the south, the jagged crags of Mount Pilatus loomed dramatically over the medieval city.

"We shouldn't be much longer. Another ten minutes is what I'm figuring."

Schaffner had visited Anton Wessner's mountain chalet on several occasions, purely social. Now that he was thinking about it, neither he nor Kaufman had been invited back since the reversals began on the Eastern Front. He was confident the red carpet would be rolled out today, however.

The winding dirt road—one lane wide in most places—corkscrewed precipitously past postage-stamp plots where brown cows with golden cowbells munched on thick grass. They continued their ascent high above Lucerne until they were a thousand meters above the city's signature landmark—the Kapellbrücke, or Chapel Bridge, the oldest wooden covered bridge in Europe, spanning the Reuss River. This was William Tell country.

After a final hairpin turn, a long uphill driveway delivered them to Chalet Rigi. The outsized chalet was a veritable fortress in wood with walls consisting of barricaded tree trunks in tiers—one trunk on top of another and notched firmly together at the corners. The roof, covered with slabs of gray slate, protected against the lift of mountain gales. Boxes of pink geraniums lined the second-story balcony of the wide A-frame structure.

Schaffner looked up and saw Wessner standing on the veranda. A wide smile creased his face. He wondered if his countenance would change after he learned they had the girl.

The German operative parked the car next to an olive green Mercedes sedan just as Wessner stepped outside the chalet's front door, painted red to match the shutters. The handshake was formal. "Welcome to Chalet Rigi," Wessner said.

Schaffner was still pumping hands when he looked up to an unexpected sight. A severe-looking man dressed in a casual suit exited the front door.

"Colonel Heller?"

"Good to see you, Schaffner. Don't look so surprised. This is a momentous day for all of us, unless you were not able to—"

Schaffner exhaled. "I think you will be pleased, sir."

The German colonel visibly relaxed, and a warm smile formed on his lips. "So you really have her?"

"Yes, take a look in the back."

Kaufman opened the rear door where the wooden crate lay on the leather seat. Heller leaned in for a closer look when a thumping sound came from the trunk, gaining intensity with each pounding.

"What's that?" Heller pointed toward the trunk.

Schaffner reached for the keys in his pocket and opened the trunk. A young girl, bound, blindfolded, and gagged, struggled against her restraints.

Heller shrugged his shoulders. "The Countess's daughter, I presume."

"She was our ticket out of the chateau. Let's just say that the girl assured everyone's cooperation."

"You can tell me about it later. Herr Wessner, would you bring the girl inside and give her some food and water? Make sure she remains blindfolded, however." Heller clapped his hands. "Let's get the *Mona Lisa* inside. I want to see her with my own eyes."

Gabi had been to Dulles's apartment in Bern's Old Town several times before, always in the company of her father.

A sober-minded OSS director welcomed their group into his living room, and father and daughter hugged. For Dulles's benefit, the language was English; Gabi translated the introductions into French for Bernard and identified Dulles as a liaison for the American Allied effort.

Dulles cleared his throat. "I'm afraid that Schaffner and Kaufman slipped into the country with the painting."

"But wasn't every BMW between here and Geneva stopped and inspected?" Gabi asked.

"Their car was found and searched, all right—in France," Dulles said. "We learned an hour ago that their BMW was abandoned not far from the La Louvière border crossing."

"Was Kristina with the car?" Gabi asked.

Dulles remained grim. "No, which concerns me. She will complicate things when we make our move."

"So they must have had another car waiting for them

across the border. It's easy enough to walk across a field these days."

"The Nazis," Eric said, "have put us in another tough spot—retrieving the *Mona Lisa* and saving Kristina. I believe we can accomplish both objectives."

"I share that sentiment, Eric." Dulles played with his unlit pipe. "But we have a 'good news, bad news' situation on our hands. The bad news is that the *Mona Lisa* is apparently in Switzerland, but not in Zurich as we had anticipated. The good news is that we know where the painting is."

Gabi thought she didn't hear right. "I thought their plan was to take the painting to Zurich—the Dolder Bank. So what happened?"

"We're playing catch-up," Dulles said. "They must have figured we'd put two and two together with the relationship between Anton Wessner and Heller's knucklehead agents. But there's been a curveball—"

Ernst Mueller interrupted. "The Swiss don't play much baseball, Allen."

"Sorry, Ernst. What I mean is that Schaffner and Kaufman didn't drive to Zurich, as we expected. We believe they've delivered the *Mona Lisa* to Wessner's chalet above Lucerne . . . Chalet Rigi."

"This is all new information. How did you find out?" Gabi remained focused.

"The code breakers at Bletchley Park picked up traffic late last night between Wessner and Heller. The first message, from Wessner, notified him that the painting was coming to Location RG. Heller replied that he was on his way and would be taking a Luftwaffe flight to Freiburg and then a train to Basel, where he wanted to be picked up."

"How did he pass through customs?"

"On a German diplomatic passport. I informed my

contacts in the Swiss intelligence community, so they knew he was coming. We let him through, knowing he would lead us to the *Mona Lisa*, since we weren't absolutely sure where the alternate rendezvous was located. A driver picked him up on the Swiss side of the Badischer Bahnhof. Several tails followed him through Basel's Altstadt, and then one by one they dropped off as they drove the highway between Basel and Lucerne. The last tail, however, had to let him go just as the car left Lucerne and started to ascend into the mountains."

"So how did you find Chalet Rigi?" Gabi asked.

"Because I've been there."

The voice was new to the conversation, but one she recognized.

From the library, Dieter Baumann strode into Dulles's living room.

"What are you doing here?" Disgust rose in Gabi's voice. The last time she and Baumann had been in the same vicinity, she had barely escaped with her life.

Before Baumann could answer, Gabi's father spoke. "For the last few days, Herr Baumann has been cooperating fully with our investigation. He's provided us with useful information that has been independently corroborated, including his dealings with Anton Wessner. Herr Baumann has also helped determine the alternate location. He's been to the banker's chalet, knows the lay of the land, and is offering to help by giving us details of the property."

Gabi looked to Eric, wondering what he thought. At one time, Dieter was one of Dulles's go-to operatives. The Swiss, a handsome man in his late twenties, had been put in charge of the Basel office of the OSS, and Gabi had worked for him in the translation department. He had feigned a more-than-professional interest for her, but it turned out to be a ruse to use her safe-cracking abilities to line his pockets.

"I know what Gabi's thinking," Eric said. "The Dieter we know was always working an angle. Looking out for himself first. So what's in it for him?"

Dulles stepped into the discussion. "A more than fair question. Mr. Baumann developed a network of contacts on both sides of the fence that he exploited—er, maintained—over the years. Now he wants to make sure he's on the right side of history. Ernst and I cannot divulge why we're confident that we have Mr. Baumann's full allegiance, but he's on our side."

Gabi turned to Dieter. She was repulsed, but if her father and Dulles trusted the man, she had no choice but to listen to what he had to say. "Okay, let's hear it."

Baumann pursed his lips. "First, let's turn our attention to Anton Wessner. He's a vain man running a private bank as his personal fiefdom. He accepted dirty money and an assortment of valuables long before Hitler's troops invaded Poland, much of the stash arriving by courier to his Alpine chalet because many of his clients demanded secrecy and discretion. In other words, they refused to walk through his bank's front door on the Bahnhofstrasse carrying a purloined painting in their arms. That's why deliveries of a sensitive nature were brought to his chalet, away from prying eyes. In those situations, Wessner sends for an armored truck to make the pickup."

Baumann stopped and opened a thick folder and began spreading the contents across the table. "Here's what I think you should know."

For the next ten minutes, Baumann used a map of the access roads, photographs of the property, and sketches of Chalet Rigi's floor plan to help formulate a plan.

After all of the options were assessed and discussed, Dulles took the floor. "Excellent presentation, Mr. Baumann." He tamped his pipe in preparation for his first smoke of the day while Dulles's secretary escorted Baumann from the room. After the door closed, he continued.

"Of course, Gabi, we don't trust Mr. Baumann any further than we can throw him, but he has found himself in a . . . shall we say . . . difficult situation. I believe he has been honest regarding his assessment of Chalet Rigi, which will be beneficial for you to gain entry, undetected. We will keep him detained here until your mission is completed to avoid the risk of any leaks."

"There's something else we need to discuss," Gabi said.

"And what would that be?"

"An interesting item that I found in a safe stolen from a Nazi stronghold in Paris." Gabi produced the black notebook and handed the slim volume over to Dulles.

"We have good reason to believe that this belongs to Colonel Heller. Inside, you will find documentation of the paintings he purchased on Reichsmarschall Hermann Göring's behalf. You will notice separate columns showing the sales price, the invoice amount, and the generous cut he took for himself. The Louvre curator, Colette Perriard, oversaw many of these sales and has verified the actual sale prices. As you will see, the colonel has given himself a substantial commission for all the transactions. I estimate at least three million Reichsmarks since the start of the war. Not bad for a military officer."

Dulles studied the notebook intently for several minutes and then passed it over to Ernst Mueller to examine.

"I wouldn't want to be Colonel Heller or be standing anywhere near him when Göring finds out about this," said her father.

"Take your time, gentlemen."

Heller expressed caution as Schaffner and Kaufman carried the *Mona Lisa* in her wooden crate to Wessner's oversized desk, positioned at the far side of the living room on the second floor.

He watched Wessner place a woolen blanket across the surface to protect the glassy finish from the crate. A screwdriver was produced.

"May I?" Schaffner asked, looking in Heller's direction.

The German colonel nodded his approval. He had become a bit blasé over the years since it was his job to purchase the finest of fine art for his benefactor, but the *Mona Lisa* was in a league of her own. He had never seen that fascinating smile—described as an expression of "sweet perfidy, androgynous beauty, and desperate hope"—in person. Would he see the smirk of a kept woman who dined off her husband? Would she appear confident or reticent?

After removing the wooden braces, Schaffner and Kaufman stood up the framed painting, still encased in its royal purple covering. They loosened the drawstring and allowed the covering to fall.

It *was* her. The soft golden shade of her complexion was unmistakable.

The *Mona Lisa*, just as she had been portrayed in a million books and magazines, loomed larger than life. She had the colors of the Tuscan countryside and an ethereal, almost magical quality that made her face glow. She was seductive yet serenely contained, instantly recognizable yet elusive. Quite simply, the *Mona Lisa* was the most coveted woman in the world.

And now she was in his possession. The ultimate bargaining chip and their passage to another life.

"When is the armored truck arriving?" Heller asked.

Wessner consulted his watch. "Later this afternoon. The dispatcher apologized for not being more responsive, but with such late notice, that's the best he can do."

"So we have a few hours." Heller's face brightened. "Why don't we enjoy her until she starts gathering dust? I say we prop her up on a chair and break open a vintage from that wine cellar of yours."

Wessner considered the request. "Of course. As you wish, Oberst Heller." He returned a few minutes later with a silver tray, four lead crystal glasses, and a dusty bottle of Chateau Latour 1937.

"The Americans are looking for her arrival in Zurich." Wessner worked the corkscrew. "I just received a phone call that two additional cars are staked out on the Bahnhof-strasse. So, I have made arrangements to keep the painting at our branch office in the Limmatplatz for a few days. Then we'll transfer her to the Dolder Bank when it's safe."

"Aren't you concerned that the Americans are watching you?" Heller was uneasy with the revelation.

"Not in the least," the banker replied. "Swiss banking privacy laws date back to the Middle Ages, and client confidentiality protects me even from the Yanks."

26

For Colonel Heller, the view from a thousand meters above Lucerne—the gateway to central Switzerland—was an impressive panorama. Although the nearby mountainous peaks of the Pilatus, Rigi, and Stanserhorn had lost their crowns of snow, the appealing contrast between the bright green alpine landscape and the steel-blue Lake Lucerne was worthy of a two-franc postcard.

As impressive as the vista was from behind the series of two-meter-high plate glass windows, the view didn't hold a candle to the *Mona Lisa*, whose enigmatic smile teased him from Wessner's buffet hutch, where she leaned against a wall. He allowed his mind the luxury of thinking through how his life would change once he escaped from his role as Göring's minion.

The *Mona Lisa* had taken his breath away, not because of her towering stature in the art world, but what she meant to his future. The war would be over soon, and with the inevitable loss Germany was now facing, a sizable account at the Dolder Bank would be his only hope for a new identity and a new home far from the Fatherland.

The options were dizzying, especially from his current

lofty vantage at Chalet Rigi, but he didn't allow his mind to get ahead of himself. First, the painting must be secured. He could not rest easy until the armored truck arrived to chaperone the keystone of his future to the security of the bank vault.

He looked at his watch, an action noted by Anton Wessner.

"Oberst Heller, they are on their way. It won't be long now."

The German officer turned toward the Swiss bank president. "You don't know how much is riding—"

A phone call interrupted the Nazi colonel. Wessner walked across the generous living room and answered the phone. After listening intently for a few moments, he thanked the caller and said he would relay the message.

"Herr Colonel, that was the owner of the armored truck company. He was calling from Lucerne and said the truck would be here in twenty minutes. See? We can all breathe easy."

The perpetual frown on Heller's face turned to a faint smile.

His eyes inspected the main living quarters and were drawn to the single entry at the far end of the room. Next to it was a dining table made from dark polished wood. A rough-cut stone fireplace on the left dominated the room. Dark russet leather couches fronted the fireplace at ninety degrees with heavy end tables on either side. A heavily beamed ceiling created an air of openness in the large room, which included Wessner's study to his right with its picturesque view of the valley.

Perched at the end of the couch was the young French girl, hands and feet bound and with blindfold still in place. Heller wasn't thrilled that Schaffner and Kaufman brought her along; nonetheless, she was a bit player in the grand scheme of things. Perhaps she would return to her parents, but if not, the young girl would become another faceless casualty of war.

With a clap of hands, Wessner announced to Heller, Schaffner, and Kaufman that he would like to propose one last toast. With a swirl of the full-bodied Grand Cru, they raised rose-stemmed glasses to da Vinci's masterpiece and postwar prosperity.

"Time to get her ready for the next journey." Heller nodded in Schaffner and Kaufman's direction, and the pair set down their wine. Together, they carefully lifted the *Mona Lisa* from the hutch, slipped her back into the velvet pouch, and then inside the crate.

"Freeze! Keep your hands where we can see them!"

Eric leveled the Colt .45 and leaned out of the hallway door leading into Wessner's living room. Bernard, from the other side of the doorway, trained his semiautomatic handgun on the four men across the expansive room.

From his briefing with Dulles, Eric was told that Kaufman was the loosest cannon in the bunch and kept his focus locked on him. Sure enough, the German operative reached for a Luger tucked under his belt. Eric reacted first, firing twice. Bernard aimed his volleys, and three of the four heavy .45 caliber slugs found their mark in his torso. Kaufman's body stuttered with each impact as his arms flailed upward, loosening the Luger from his grip. The weapon fell to his left as his heavy frame crashed into a bookcase behind the desk. With a perplexed expression, Kaufman slid to the floor, staring back through unseeing eyes.

The other three scrambled for cover. Wessner and Schaffner took refuge behind the massive desk, where the *Mona*

Lisa lay in her crate, while Heller dove behind the nearby couch where Kristina sat.

"Get down, Kristina," Eric yelled in French. The girl responded immediately and dropped to her side.

He could see Schaffner's hunched back rise slightly and assumed he was pulling his weapon from his waistband. Eric couldn't get a clear shot. The German operative reached just above the desktop and got off three blind shots, which plugged into the rough-hewn crossbeams above Eric's head.

Eric wanted to return fire but didn't have a shot. Bernard kept his response in check as well. Suddenly, Schaffner—still hunched over—ducked from behind the side of the desk, giving Eric an opening.

Eric fired twice, striking him once in his shoulder and spinning him off balance. Bernard got off two more shots. The first missed high, just above Schaffner's head, and struck the large picture window.

The sound of splintering glass filled the air. Fragments tumbled to the floor, leaving a gaping hole in the center with jagged shards hanging precariously from the perimeter. Bernard's second shot had caught Schaffner just below his collar bone, knocking him back. He backpedaled to regain his balance.

Gabi, frantic to shield Kristina from the melee, darted between Eric and Bernard.

"Cover her!" Eric yelled as she dashed toward the fireplace.

He stepped from the doorway and fired at Schaffner again, squeezing off three shots. Bernard followed suit. Two of the big slugs caught Schaffner in the upper body, propelling him through the open glass. The thigh-high windowsill stopped his fall as shards impaled his lower back. Eric watched him flail his arms and legs to free himself like a beetle trapped on its back.

Movement to his right caught his eye, where Gabi—still bent at the waist—rolled across the floor and smashed into the side of the sofa next to where Kristina lay prone.

He glanced at his semiautomatic and saw the slide locked open. Pushing the magazine release with his thumb, he simultaneously reached for another, sliding it into place and locking the magazine with the heel of his left hand. Rousseau, also empty, did the same. The sound of the two mags hitting the floor must have been the moment Heller was waiting to hear.

In a flash, he reached over the sofa, holding Kaufman's Luger in one hand and grabbing Kristina by her ponytail with the other. Heller yanked her back into a sitting position, eliciting an ear-piercing scream. Using the girl as a shield, he stared down the barrel trained on Gabi's forehead.

"Drop your guns, or the Fräulein dies . . . now!"

"Don't shoot!" Eric yelled back.

He dropped his gun to the floor. "Drop your gun, Bernard. Do it, or he'll kill Gabi." Eric looked hard at Bernard, and the Frenchman's expression confirmed what he knew in his heart.

They had no choice but to surrender.

Bernard complied with a sign of defeat while memories of the Pantin rail yard flooded back. He had witnessed Heller execute a wounded and defenseless man in cold blood without the slightest hint of emotion.

"Everyone, hands up!" Heller demanded as he rose to his feet and wrapped an arm around Kristina's neck. She was sobbing, and tears saturated the blindfold.

"Let the girl go," Bernard pleaded. "She's an innocent victim."

Heller remained stone-faced and squinted his eyes. He switched to French: "I know you . . . oh, yes, the train at Pantin. Bernard Rousseau, isn't it? I never forget a face . . . or a name. I'm glad I didn't kill you back then. Your life, it seems, is quite valuable, especially to the lovely Miss Perriard. It took the threat of your arrest and Gestapo torture to coerce information from her lips."

So it was true, Bernard thought. Colette had been blackmailed and risked her career and a national treasure to save him. Now feeling weak and clammy, he couldn't deny that he'd been a fool, losing both Colette and the *Mona Lisa*.

"Herr Wessner, you can come out of hiding now. Gather their guns and bring them here," Heller ordered.

"Bernard is right," Gabi started. "She's done nothing wrong. Let the girl go."

"All in due time, Fräulein."

Bernard glanced out the side window as a silver armored truck labored into view.

"Ah, perfect timing." Heller exhaled. "Our ride has arrived."

"The painting will do you no good," Gabi continued. "You are a dead man unless you run now."

"Excuse me, mademoiselle, but I believe I'm the one in control here." Heller spoke in a sarcastic voice as Wessner returned with the weapons. "Pick up the painting, Anton, and we'll be on our way. Unfortunately, we'll need to take some insurance." He dragged Kristina backward by her neck from the couch.

Kristina's terror-filled whimpers escalated.

Bernard's legs quivered, and he realized they were running out of options.

The pitiful cries from Kristina broke Gabi's heart. With Heller's gun trained on her and the others, she felt helpless. Desperate.

"Hold on, Colonel. I have something you might trade the girl for. May I?"

Without waiting for an answer, she slowly reached into her pants pocket, keeping one arm raised. With her free hand, she produced a thin black book. After opening the journal, she began reading.

"On October 12, 1940, you authorized the purchase of van Gogh's *Portrait of Dr. Gachet*. You invoiced the German Cultural Ministry for 150,000 Reichsmarks on October 14 and made a payment of 110,000 RM on October 27. Matisse's *Pianist* was purchased on November 14, 1940. The invoice amount was—"

"Stop. Where did you get that?"

"Paris. The Resistance lifted a Bauche safe. I cracked the combination and found your black book inside a hidden compartment."

"Give it to me. If you don't, the girl dies!" Heller trained his gun on shivering Kristina.

"In exchange for the girl," Gabi demanded, stepping forward.

"It seems you are as stupid as you are beautiful," Heller fumed. "I could just kill you and take it."

"Killing me to get this book won't end your problems."

Gabi waved the black journal at Heller. "Göring knows all about the way you've diverted millions into your Swiss bank accounts here, or he will very shortly."

Gabi saw a slight sheen of sweat form on Heller's lip.

"Do you expect me to believe that you picked up the phone and spoke to the Reichsmarschall about your discovery?"

"Of course not," Gabi replied. "But the German consulate

to Switzerland, Rudolf Baumgartner, listened to what we had to say a few hours ago. He said he couldn't approach Himmler without proof, but we weren't about to give him this black book until the *Mona Lisa* and the girl were back in our hands. Ask Wessner if I'm telling the truth." Gabi motioned with her head toward the banker standing with the *Mona Lisa* tucked under his arm and a Colt in his other hand.

"Do you know anything about this, Wessner?"

Wessner remained silent.

"Anton?" Heller yelled.

Startled, the banker responded, "I'm afraid the woman is telling the truth . . . I received a call from the Consulate General's attaché before you arrived."

Gabi swallowed hard and then straightened her shoulders. "I can only imagine the 'reception' that the Gestapo is planning for you. We told Baumgartner that if we don't return, then you'll have the black book. But if you give us the girl and let us go, we can make this all go away. And you get to keep the painting."

Instead of a conciliatory gesture, Gabi saw the colonel's face redden with rage.

"You will pay for this with your life, but first, you will watch Kristina die because of your stupid ploy."

He pushed the girl to her knees and pressed the Luger to the back of her head.

"No . . . stop!" Gabi screamed.

The gunshot was deafening . . . Gabi saw Heller release his grip, and Kristina tumbled to the floor.

Transfixed, Wessner watched Heller slowly turn, eyes glazed with rage and hatred. Color drained from the colonel's pasty face. His lips parted to form a word, then quivered slightly as blood filled his mouth and spilled down his chin.

Anton Wessner looked down at his hand trembling in part from shock and in part from the powerful recoil of the Colt .45. He regarded the smoke curling from the barrel, then toward his feet, where Heller had crumpled to the floor.

In desperate need of air, Wessner inhaled deeply. He had never killed a man before, but he couldn't stand by and watch the senseless execution of an innocent girl.

With a quick look to his left, he saw the armored truck park alongside the house. In what seemed like slow motion, the young Swiss woman moved to Kristina's side. She sat on the floor and held her in her arms while the other two men gathered around the sobbing girl.

As the shock began to pass, his mind refocused. It was clear what he should do. Training his pistol on Gabi and the girl with the *Mona Lisa* in his free arm, he stumbled backward toward the deck, keeping his attention and pistol aimed in the interlopers' direction. His shoulder jostled the doorjamb that supported the shattered window, where Schaffner's still body lay.

The impact caused a large triangular shard of glass to swing like a pendulum, free from its wooden bond. Gravity took control and pulled the heavy fragment to its final destination. The heavy quarter-inch plate passed across Wessner's extended right forearm, scything through skin and muscle. The surgical blow was initially painless but caused Wessner to lose strength in his hand.

With a grimace, he looked at the pulsating rivulet of blood that soaked his tenuous grip on the heavy semiautomatic, now dangling from his bloody fingertips. With an intense, aching pain building in the mangled limb, Wessner knew he had to hurry. The banker rushed across the deck and down the stairs to the idling armored vehicle parked in his driveway.

Thoughts of a hefty reward from the French government for saving the *Mona Lisa* fueled his steps. Better yet, he would be acclaimed as an international hero, and now only he had access to Heller's fortune. As he approached the rear of the armored truck, the back door swung open and a uniformed guard offered a hand and relieved Wessner of the painting.

"The Dolder Bank in Zurich, Herr Wessner?" the driver asked.

"No, the branch office at the Limmatplatz." Wessner squinted up at the guard and into the blinding sunlight. "Do I know you?"

"I don't believe so."

"Who are you?"

"Ernst Mueller. And this is my colleague, Allen Dulles."

As Wessner's eyes adjusted, he saw the double barrels of the shotgun pointing at his head.

Visions of his hero status as rescuer of the *Mona Lisa* evaporated into the pale blue Swiss sky.

27

"I apologize that this is taking so long, sir. Your escort should be here any second."

Eric noticed the MP admiring the classic Rolls Royce. "Not a problem. The plane won't leave without us."

A white bar across the entrance to the Dübendorf military airfield outside of Zurich blocked their path. Eric turned in the driver's seat to address Kristina, who sat between Gabi and her father in the back. "You'll be going home in no time, honey. Gabi's dad will pick up his wife and before you know it, you'll be driving through the gates of your home."

Kristina beamed as Gabi gave her a reassuring squeeze.

Three minutes later, the crossbar was raised, and the polished sedan was waved through the checkpoint of Switzerland's largest military airfield. Eric was quite familiar with the home of the Swiss Air Force, charged with defending Swiss airspace from intrusions by Luftwaffe planes as well as Allied bombers and fighters. When battle-damaged RAF and United States planes approached Switzerland, however, they were escorted and allowed to land at Dübendorf instead of crashing in Nazi Germany.

A lead car guided them past more than a half-dozen rows

of Flying Fortresses, B-24 Liberators, and British Lancasters parked wingtip-to-wingtip in orderly precision. They continued past the control tower and terminus building toward a section of the quadrilateral-shaped airfield where a row of Swiss Me-109 fighters were lined up. Eric's eyes followed the lead car, which led them past the attack aircraft to a bulky tri-motor with a low cantilever wing. Stamped on the corrugated duralumin metal skin was a white cross painted over a square red background.

"Recognize the plane?" Eric looked in the mirror at Gabi, sitting behind him.

A look of surprise swept her face. "That's a Ju-52."

"Dulles must have called in another favor from General Guisan." Eric was referring to the head of the Swiss Army. When Gabi had flown into Germany three weeks earlier as the Swiss courier, General Guisan had put his personal aircraft at her disposal.

"It looks like the same plane."

"And the same pilot."

Standing in front of the fuselage door at the rear of the passenger plane was Captain Bill Palmer of the United States Army Eighth Air Force, a warm smile creasing his lips.

"What are you talking about?" Bernard asked.

Eric spoke up. "The American pilot is Captain Palmer. Back in January, his bomber limped into Swiss air space and landed in Dübendorf. He was interned in Davos with other Allied pilots and would still be up in the mountains, but he volunteered to fly Gabi on a top-secret mission a few weeks ago. Trust me, he's a great pilot."

Eric eased the Rolls Royce to a stop. Palmer walked across the grassy tarmac toward them, and Gabi hustled out of the back door to give him a warm hug. Introductions were made all around.

As Ernst moved Kristina to the front seat, Eric opened the trunk. He and Bernard carefully lifted the wooden crate containing the *Mona Lisa* out of the back of the car.

"We got her!" Eric called out.

Ernst shot him a thumbs-up and hugged Gabi. "See you soon, and God go with you," he said, letting go of his daughter. Then he hopped in the driver's seat of the Rolls and drove off with Kristina.

"Looks like you've come up in the world." Palmer nodded toward the stunning luxury car leaving the airfield.

"The *Mona Lisa* travels in style, Bill. Must be why they asked you to fly her," Eric said with a chuckle. "Let's get her on board."

He and Bernard slowly shuffled toward the fuselage door. The American pilot bounded up the four steps and held out his arms.

"Let me give you a hand," Palmer said.

Eric positioned his side of the crate into Palmer's arms and then helped Bernard up the steps and into the passenger plane.

"Where do you think we should put her?" Eric deferred to the Frenchman on board.

Bernard looked up the relatively steep fuselage of the passenger plane, outfitted with seven rows of leather seats, one on each side of the center aisle.

After a long moment, Eric understood the delay in a decision. Bernard had never seen the inside of an airplane before.

Eric turned to Palmer. "What do you think, Bill? Where would you put the *Mona Lisa*?"

The American pilot, dressed in khakis and wearing a beige United States Eighth cap, rubbed his face. "I'd put the crate on the floor between the front seat and the bulkhead. I think we can wedge it in there so that it won't budge on takeoff or landing."

Palmer was right. There was just enough room to lay the wooden crate on the floor.

"She'll sleep like a baby all the way to Paris," Eric enthused.

"Not me." Bernard wiped his brow from the exertion. "I won't rest until we're on French soil and the *Mona Lisa* is back in the Louvre."

———

"Are you going to need any help with these engine controls?" Gabi dropped into the copilot's chair and looked at the center console, where three sets of levers controlled the throttles, mixture, and fuel cocks. "They're still in German, you know."

Palmer's eyes scanned the instrument panel. He touched several electrical switches and set his feet on the rudder pedals. "I'll be okay. Like riding a bike, right?"

"If you say so." Gabi regarded the clusters of dials, indicators, knobs, levers, and switches crammed into the cockpit area. "I have no idea how you get this ship off the ground."

"Don't let a hair on that pretty head of yours worry about a thing. Looks like a milk run to me. Plenty of daylight left, no anti-aircraft guns to worry about, and a full tank of gas to get there."

Palmer smiled. "You're an amazing young woman, Gabi. I'm proud of what you've done for our country, especially helping the French get back the *Mona Lisa*. Your father briefed me on the phone about what happened in Lucerne. I'll want to hear the full story."

Palmer turned toward Gabi and set his right hand on the center console.

"I've gone through the preflight and haven't forgotten how to fire up this puppy, so you can go back and visit with

Eric and your French guest. Maybe you can practice being a stewardess. I hear that civilian aviation is going to take off after the war."

"Stewardess? I think I'll have better things to do than serving highballs to boorish businessmen on expense accounts."

———

Gabi settled into the first seat on the right side of the aircraft, while Eric and Bernard took places in the second row. Bernard said he felt more comfortable sitting right behind the *Mona Lisa* so he could keep an eye on the wooden crate.

Sitting on the right side afforded Gabi a direct look at Captain Palmer through the open cockpit door. He tripped a couple of levers, and then she heard an electrical whine. The number one engine on the left side of the aircraft caught lustily, and a robust vibration shook the plane. Palmer then turned his attention toward engines two and three, which kicked into gear. The decibel level rose dramatically inside the fuselage.

Palmer lifted the leather helmet hanging from a hook next to the captain's seat. He turned on the radio and set the frequency to ground control. A voice in English crackled through the earpiece, clearing him to taxi short of the active runway, and gave him the tower frequency to call when ready for takeoff. The American military pilot reached over to the center console and pushed forward on the throttles.

The plane lurched forward, and the butterflies in Gabi's stomach jumped. To distract herself, she looked outside her window as the plane lightly bounced along the tarmac. They passed hangars, parked planes, and personnel riding in jeeps when Palmer made a broad, sweeping turn, pivoting the plane toward the west. He ran up his engines, checked his pressure gauges, and completed his preflight checklist.

After resetting his radio frequency, he called the tower and received clearance to take off.

"Everyone got their seatbelts on?" he yelled over the din.

She held up a finger. "Wait a second."

Bernard wasn't looking outside his passenger window. His eyes were transfixed straight ahead, as if he was gazing at something in the distance. Gabi reached over and tapped him on the shoulder.

"You need to use your seatbelt."

"A what?"

"Your seatbelt." Gabi lifted hers, which was wrapped around her lap.

He searched his seat and found the two straps. He didn't know how the two ends went together . . . but then figured it out.

Palmer looked back toward Gabi and gave her a thumbs-up. "You're halfway to being a stewardess," he shouted over the propellers' roar.

The RPMs of the plane's engines increased rapidly, and the plane began its takeoff roll. The noise level drowned out any chance for communication.

The plane lifted in the air, and Gabi looked down on the village of Dübendorf, off to the right.

The Junkers continued to climb as Palmer set a westerly course that would take them over the Swiss lowlands before angling northwest into France and on to Paris. The view from the air was exciting. She enjoyed seeing her homeland from an entirely new dimension. The farmlands resembled a green-and-gold checkerboard, and pastoral villages dotted the verdant landscape like shimmering jewels. Flying was an act of boldness, and only a few were given this new view of the world.

She glanced behind at Eric, whose mouth was agape. He

thoroughly enjoyed the view of Switzerland from the eyes of an eagle.

"Having fun on your first plane flight?"

Eric looked away from the window with a huge grin.

He leaned over and gave her a kiss. When Gabi pulled away, she looked in Bernard's direction to see if he had been watching them—or sightseeing.

The answer was neither. This time, he was leaning on the seat in front of him, eyes locked on the wooden crate containing the *Mona Lisa*.

The hum of the engines and steady progress lulled Gabi into closing her eyes. A sudden dip jostled her.

She looked at her watch. They had been in the air for nearly two hours. She unbuckled her seatbelt and stepped into the cockpit.

Bill Palmer looked up from the controls. "You're probably wondering when we're going to arrive."

"Sorry. I've never been on a *normal* flight before." Gabi flashed a smile.

"That makes two of us. Maybe I will fly for some airline after the war. At any rate, we're a bit more than a half hour out of Le Bourget. Won't be long now."

"I'm really excited to be flying into Paris. Should be quite a sight."

"What about that boyfriend of yours? Are you excited about him?"

Gabi blushed. "Very much so—more than ever."

She turned and looked back to the passenger area. Eric wasn't there. He must be using the lavatory before they landed. She hoped he wasn't airsick and decided to go check on him.

Gabi stood up to walk toward the rear of the plane. This time Bernard was watching her, his eyes intent. She just passed him when she heard the command, "Stop."

"Stop?"

She turned around, and standing in the aisle was Bernard. A pistol was pointed at her forehead.

Gabi gasped. "What are you doing, Bernard?"

"You'll find out soon enough." His steady voice and steely resolve surprised her.

With his free hand, he reached into his knapsack and took out a set of chrome handcuffs. "Lock yourself to one of the seats."

"Why?"

He didn't answer.

"The *Mona Lisa*?"

Bernard nodded. "This doesn't concern you. This is a matter for France to decide. I don't want to kill you, especially because you risked your life to save *La Joconde*, but what is happening right now is far bigger than you or me—or a Renaissance painting for that matter, no matter how priceless it is. So do me a favor and lock yourself to a seat."

It only took her a second to see through Bernard's plan, and then she understood. He was making a play for the *Mona Lisa* to give *his* side a bargaining chip. The French Communists planned to use the revered portrait as some sort of public relations weapon against de Gaulle.

"The French people will not come to your side."

"We won't know until we try." Bernard waved the gun. "Oblige me, *s'il vous plaît*."

Gabi sat down and slipped one handcuff over her right wrist. Then she shackled herself to an opening in the armrest. "Satisfied?"

Before he could answer, Eric stepped out of the rear restroom—and Bernard planted his gun on Gabi's temple.

The Frenchman opened his free hand to Eric. "Your weapon."

Eric looked up, visibly stunned. "What's going on?"

"I'm running out of patience. Kick your gun in my direction."

Alarmed, Eric lifted his hands. "I'll do what you say. Just don't hurt Gabi."

"End of the barrel."

The Swiss reached into his pocket, and gripping the pistol by the end of the barrel, handed it over.

Keeping his eyes on Eric, Bernard stuffed the gun into his waistband, then pulled another set of handcuffs from his pocket. "Take the row behind Gabi and lock yourself up."

Eric followed his instructions.

"For you, for your cause, and for the *Mona Lisa*, I hope you've thought this through," Gabi said.

"Don't worry. I have. Now your American pilot. When I get his attention, I want you to tell him two things. First, I want him to handcuff himself to the cockpit. Second, land this plane at Orly, not Le Bourget. Remind him that I know my Paris landmarks."

"Everything all right back there?" yelled a voice from the cockpit. They were far enough back that Palmer couldn't see them from the captain's seat.

Rousseau moved quickly up the aisle, and in an instant trained his pistol on Palmer.

The American pilot glared at Rousseau. "What are you doing?" he demanded in English.

Gabi answered for the Frenchman. "He's hijacking the plane! We're handcuffed to our chairs."

The plane suddenly dove, and Rousseau hit the ceiling of

the fuselage. The Ju-52 continued to gyrate and lose altitude, eliciting screams from Gabi. When the plane leveled out, Rousseau slammed to the floor and leaped toward Gabi. Once again, he placed the business end of the cold pistol on her temple. "Tell him I start shooting if he tries that again."

Gabi glowered at Rousseau but obeyed. "He's promised to kill us if you try that again," she yelled out. "You're to land the plane at Orly. No tricks. He knows his Paris landmarks."

Rousseau reached into his satchel for another set of handcuffs and jangled them at Gabi, who understood what Rousseau wanted to say.

"Bill, another thing. Rousseau wants you to handcuff yourself to your seat or something. He's coming up now."

Rousseau approached the cockpit and tossed the pair of handcuffs at Palmer, who released his grip on the wooden control wheel and caught them in mid-air.

The pilot's face was a frozen mask. "I don't like this, but I really believe you're crazy enough to take everyone down." He chained his left wrist to his steering column.

"Satisfied?" he demanded.

Rousseau, who didn't understand, ignored him and stepped back into the cabin.

Gabi looked at the rings of sweat darkening the armpits of Rousseau's button-down green shirt. Desperation reeked from every pore.

"What happens when we land?" Gabi asked.

"I leave with the *Mona Lisa*, and you remain in the plane."

"It won't be long before half of Paris is looking for you," Eric barked.

Bernard wiped his free hand across his brow. "Then I better work fast."

As Gabi listened to the exchange, a gut feeling came over her. *Don't rock the boat—or the plane. Let Rousseau take the Mona Lisa and play his little game*. Like a house of cards, it would all come crashing down. She gave Eric a knowing look, and he understood.

They both knew Rousseau wasn't going to win in the end.

Bernard took Gabi's old seat and looked down upon the rural landscape. Ahead, still a ways off on the horizon, he could make out a warren of densely packed buildings that signified Paris proper. Given that overarching landmark, he got his bearings. They approached Paris from the southeast.

The geographical difference between the Le Bourget and Orly airports was stark. Le Bourget was located a good distance north of the Seine—twelve kilometers. He was just a boy when he and his parents joined 100,000 rabid Parisians to greet American aviator Charles Lindbergh after his history-making solo flight across the Atlantic.

He turned and looked at the pilot, who concentrated on his gauges. Using the Seine as a line of demarcation, they would be landing at Orly.

Bernard took no pleasure in what he was doing. He realized that he had jumped the Rubicon regarding his relationship with Colette. She would never speak to him again.

He was taking a huge gamble, but life was a risk, was it not? He was risking everything, not for himself, but for an opportune moment—a chance to reshape postwar France into a Communist society, where everyone was treated equally. No longer would the rich and titled call the shots. The proletariat would prevail.

Gabi was right. He would have to move quickly.

The Ju-52 lowered in the sky until the wings dipped, and the plane seemed to float for the longest time. Finally, the aircraft landed on the pavement with a soft bump. The Ju-52 rapidly lost speed.

Through Gabi, he informed Palmer to taxi the plane toward one of the abandoned hangers. Orly had been a strategic base for the Luftwaffe, but the Nazis were long gone.

The plane pulled up near a fence, and Bernard heard the engines cut. That was his cue. He turned to Gabi and Eric. "Sorry the trip had to end this way. I know you don't understand, but this is for France."

The Swiss didn't reply, which surprised Bernard. Strangely, he had expected some sort of rejoinder. It didn't matter.

He had the *Mona Lisa*. Colonel Rol and his comrades would be glad to see him. He'd become the hero they longed for.

With a short wave, he picked up the wooden crate and disappeared into the gloaming.

28

WEDNESDAY, AUGUST 30, 1944
PARIS, FRANCE

Marcel Bertille studied his black leather address book, which contained a list of newspaper reporters, radio commentators, and opinion makers. He had worn many hats for the French Communist Party over the years, but on this Wednesday morning, he played the role of media liaison. He was relying on newspapers and radio outlets to get the word out.

"Salut, Jean-Louis. How is Libération treating you?"

Bertille listened to the blowhard at *Paris-Soir*—one of the notorious collaborationist newspapers—blather on about de Gaulle's triumphant walk along the Champs Élysées and how that epoch represented a new day in France. At the opportune moment, Bertille tickled his ears with a dainty morsel of information.

"Listen, I have a blockbuster story for you, and you're going to want to be there."

"Where?"

"In front of the Louvre entrance. Colonel Rol will be

making an announcement at two o'clock today—a very important one. You don't want to miss it."

"Are Rol and your Communist pals making a play for political control of France?" Jean-Louis scoffed. "Because if you think the people are going to turn to you instead of de Gaulle—"

"Now is not the time for politics," Bertille interjected. "That national discussion will happen someday, but not today."

"So what's Rol going to talk about?"

Bertille paused. It was better to let the line out a little longer and wait for this ink-stained fish to strike. "It involves a matter of national pride."

"National pride? I think de Gaulle cornered the market in that department."

"I'm really not supposed to say more."

"C'mon, Bertille. You have to give me a little more than that. I'm a busy guy."

Bertille paused again to signify that he was thinking when in actuality he was waiting for the right time to set the hook.

"Okay, I suppose I can trust you. Colonel Rol will be talking about the disappearance of the *Mona Lisa*."

Bertille heard an audible gasp. "*La Joconde*? Wasn't the painting evacuated with the rest of the Louvre treasures?"

"Correct, but it seems that a pair of German operatives got their hands on the portrait."

"When?"

"Yesterday at a chateau near Annecy. We believe they took the painting into Switzerland."

"This is unbelievable. How do you know?"

"Because one of our men was at the chateau when the thieves broke in and carried her off. His name is Bernard Rousseau. He will be at the press conference to tell his side of the story. Sorry. I wish I could share more details, but at this time . . ." He let his voice trail off.

Bertille could feel a tug on the line. Any moment, the *Paris-Soir* columnist would bite—and he did.

"I will be there," the reporter said. "I was a boy when the *Mona Lisa* disappeared for two years before the Great War. My parents took me to the Louvre and we looked at the dark spot on the wall. Paris and the world went into spasms of aesthetic agony. So you're saying this disturbing event happened yesterday?"

"Yes."

"Why wasn't the *Mona Lisa* secured? And what about the rest of the Louvre collection? Are our Monets and Delacroix riches in jeopardy as well?" Jean-Louis rattled on. "If the Nazis can't have Paris, will they continue to loot our treasures and cart them off?"

"All important questions, *mon ami*. Colonel Rol will be happy to supply the answers this afternoon. That is why I'm calling and suggesting you be there."

After a closing salutation, Bertille settled back in his chair with a satisfied look.

Then he opened his address book again.

He had many more phone calls to make.

Gabi and Eric, along with Bill Palmer, were eating a late breakfast inside the mess tent on the grounds of the École Militaire, where they had spent the night. The trio had received red-carpet treatment after Gabi successfully picked the locks on the handcuffs with a hairpin. All they could do now was wait.

"Do you think the police will find Bernard Rousseau soon?" Palmer asked.

Eric set down his piece of toast. "He could be anywhere in a huge city like Paris. I think he—and the *Mona Lisa*—can't stay under wraps for too long. He and his comrades are probably figuring out how they can exploit this situation to maximum advantage."

After a second coffee, an aide to General Leclerc approached.

"Word is getting around Paris that Colonel Rol and Bernard Rousseau will be in front of the Louvre at 2 p.m. to make some sort of 'major announcement' about the *Mona Lisa*."

"Thank you, Lieutenant." Gabi turned to Eric. "We were expecting something like this."

Nervous energy soared through Bernard's body as he stood at the bottom of the stone staircase leading to the Louvre entrance. Situated in the large palace courtyard, Bernard—along with Colonel Rol and Marcel Bertille—were surrounded by a legion of reporters and photographers ready to record their history-making announcement. A hundred or so tourists and locals who happened to be in the area pressed closer to learn what the fuss was all about.

One hundred meters away, the *Mona Lisa* lay in her crate inside a Peugeot double-parked on the Place du Carrousel. Bernard turned and looked at the four armed men surrounding the vehicle. It was Bertille's idea for the bodyguard quartet to ceremoniously carry the *Mona Lisa* the length of the courtyard while photographers snapped pictures that would be transmitted around the world.

The four men awaited their cue to begin the procession, but that would only come after Colonel Rol hectored the Gaullist government for allowing the *Mona Lisa* to fall into

Nazi hands. After railing against the malfeasance, Rol would tell the courageous story of how he—Bernard Rousseau, Resistance hero—risked his life to single-handedly free *La Joconde* and bring her back to her home at the Louvre.

Bernard knew it was all a bald-faced fabrication, but he and the French Communists were operating under the Churchillian axiom that a lie gets halfway around the world before the truth has a chance to get its pants on. His side needed to do something to knock de Gaulle off his pedestal, and right now, the *Mona Lisa* was their biggest club. Sure, the Gaullists could produce Gabi and Eric as well as the American pilot, but it was his word—a Frenchman!—against theirs. It also helped that Bertille could obfuscate with the best of them.

Bernard regarded his wristwatch, battered and scratched from his underground missions. Only a few minutes remained until nearby church towers heralded the arrival of the two o'clock hour.

The plan was for Colonel Rol and Bertille to do most of the talking until Bernard delivered his eyewitness account of the Germans' heist at Chateau de Dampierre. He planned to embellish the story of how the hated *boches* threatened to cut off the girl's fingers one by one. He was certain that this detail would be highlighted in tomorrow's newspaper stories. Then the *Mona Lisa* would be produced, procession and all, and together the three of them would escort *La Joconde* back to the Louvre, where future generations would enjoy that famous smile.

Bells pealed in the distance, prompting Bertille to mount two steps and address the media crunch.

"Welcome, everyone, and thank you for coming today on short notice. It pleases me to see so many reporters from newspaper and radio stations on hand. Freedom of the press was lost when Nazi boots occupied Paris, but those of us in the FTP gave our blood to see that liberty returned," Bertille said.

There was polite applause, and Bernard joined in the clapping.

"But a serious situation has arisen that I want to bring to your attention today, and to help me do that, I've asked one of the real heroes of the Resistance—"

Bertille's introduction of Colonel Rol was drowned out by the sound of police sirens and honking horns barreling into the Louvre's palace courtyard. All eyes turned to a fast-moving motorcade of four black Citroën sedans with minia-ture French *tricolores*, escorted by a pair of police motorcycles. Mothers reached for hands of little ones, and couples made sure they got out of the way. The parade of shiny cars rolled to a stop not far from the entrance staircase where Bernard and the others had gathered for the press conference.

Cries of "It's de Gaulle!" rose into the air. Bernard took a step to gain a better view and saw the regal general step out of the car wearing his trademark *képi*, a cap with a flat circular top and visor.

A clamor arose, and the bystanders surged toward the general. Chants rose from their lips. "Vive de Gaulle! Vive de Gaulle! Vive de Gaulle!"

The pool of reporters deserted their press conference and rushed over to see what was happening.

What Bernard viewed next was unbelievable. Stepping out of the same rear seat was Colette, dressed in a yellow sun dress and dark sunglasses to shield her eyes from the hot August sun. The raucous crowd immediately engulfed her as well.

"What's going on?" Bertille demanded, as if Bernard knew the answer.

"I don't know, sir."

Bernard's world was thrown into a faster tailspin when Eric and Gabi exited the second car. They fell into a group that followed de Gaulle to the top step of the entrance stairway. Photographers chased after the entourage, angling for a shot of the general marching into the Louvre. Bernard saw flashbulbs go off and cameramen winding film in their cameras.

The crowd noise intensified and bordered on chaos. De Gaulle, in that imperial manner of his, turned at the top of the steps and faced the throng.

"Mesdames et messieurs, la *Mona Lisa* est arrivée!" *Ladies and gentlemen, the* Mona Lisa *has arrived!*

Bernard's head throbbed, and he felt a shortness of breath.

"What is the meaning of this?" Colonel Rol demanded.

"I have no idea, sir." How could de Gaulle say he had the *Mona Lisa* when *they* had her? He looked back toward the parked Peugeot. The four men, with guns drawn, still surrounded the vehicle.

De Gaulle spread his arms to signal that he wished to continue. "She will now be hung in the Salle Carré and restored to her place of glory. I invite you to witness one of the first important steps that show France getting back up on her feet after the national humiliation of German occupation."

The doors to the Louvre—which had been closed for better than ten days—suddenly swung open. The crowd pressed forward, and Bernard found himself following Rol and Bertille through the front entrance. The ticket booths were unmanned, and Louvre personnel were on hand to direct the sudden flood of visitors.

Bernard and his comrades fell in behind the army following de Gaulle and his former girlfriend. The throng marched along several long *halles* whose walls were lightly populated with works of art along with sawhorses and carpenter's tools.

They entered the Salle Carré, where men in white lab coats and white gloves waited with their own set of work tools. Six Free French 2nd Armored Division soldiers flanked them with rifles resting across their chests.

And then everything came into view.

Sitting on a table against the far wall was a wooden transportation crate—but made of different wood than the one from the Chateau de Dampierre.

De Gaulle took his place in front of the table. "The *Mona Lisa* arrived from her summer home in southern France early last evening, and we only thought it was appropriate that she be immediately shared with the French people. Her presence today is a national reminder that art inspires the soul, uplifts the human spirit, and creates unity among its people."

Reporters scribbled in their notebooks, and photographers' flashes filled the grand hall. De Gaulle stepped aside as two men in white lab coats meticulously unscrewed several screws around the perimeter of the wooden crate.

Bernard moved closer, holding his breath the entire way. Underneath the lid was the same purple slipcover that covered his *Mona Lisa* . . .

The two men untied the drawstring and carefully worked the velvet pouch down the frame to reveal *La Joconde*.

How could this be? Impossible!

A gasp circulated through the crowd, and a flurry of flashes filled the room.

"Mesdames et messieurs, I present you . . . the *Mona Lisa*!" De Gaulle, a rarely seen smile creasing his taciturn face, pulled both arms behind him and then stepped back.

He appeared to be content having the spotlight taken off him—which had to be a first.

Anger and confusion wrestled for control of Bernard's mind.

He turned to say something to Colonel Rol and Marcel Bertille, but they were already beating a hasty retreat. Instead of chasing after them, though, Bernard chose to step closer as de Gaulle stood for a photograph with the *Mona Lisa*. If the general was trying to match her impish smile, he fought a losing battle. Then the French general waved Colette to stand next to him as more flashbulbs popped inside the grand hall.

"And now, ladies and gentlemen, I present you with the heroine for the *Mona Lisa*'s return—Colette Perriard."

De Gaulle's introduction set off a torrent of questions from the reporters.

"Mademoiselle Perriard, is it true that the Germans tried to steal the *Mona Lisa*?"

"Can you give us more details about what happened yesterday?"

"What did the *boches* look like?"

General de Gaulle stepped in front of Colette and asked for politeness and decorum. "Mademoiselle Perriard is prepared to provide more details, although there are some facts that must be withheld because of the wartime situation. Mademoiselle Perriard?"

Colette cleared her throat. "Yes, the rumors are true. The Nazis tried to steal the *Mona Lisa*. She had been secured during the last six months of the Occupation at a chateau outside of Annecy, away from prying hands. But the attempt was foiled, and the decision was made to immediately bring the *Mona Lisa* back to the Louvre, where she will resume her reign as the world's most famous painting under the watchful eye of the Louvre's security detail."

"How did the Nazis try to steal the *Mona Lisa*?" shouted a reporter from *Le Petit Parisien* newspaper. "How many were involved?"

Colette looked to General de Gaulle, who bestowed a faint shake of the head.

"I'm sorry, but we are not prepared to discuss those details at this time."

For the next few minutes, Colette doled out bits of information—and devoted most of her answers to explaining why she couldn't answer further, which raised the frustration level with the press.

"Thank you for your attention, but that is all we are prepared to discuss today." With that statement, Colette stepped back as her eyes scanned the room.

Bernard thought about departing, but like a moth drawn to a flame, he could not look away.

———

"I can't believe what happened. I really can't."

For the fifth time in the last half hour, Bernard bitterly railed against the events that had transpired at the Louvre. If he expressed enough vehemence, he thought, maybe Colonel Rol and Marcel Bertille would forget that it was him who was at the epicenter of *l'affaire Mona Lisa*.

Bernard looked at those gathered inside the crowded living room of Bertille's third-floor apartment tucked away in the Marais neighborhood. Filling couches and sitting on chairs were more than a dozen men—the senior leadership of their organization. A heavy pall hung over the room, reminding Bernard of a reception hall at a morgue.

Bertille took the floor, building a case that the French Communist Party had been pushed to the fringes of political discussion and would likely remain that way in postwar

France. As Bernard listened glumly, he wondered how such a hoped-for prize had slipped out of their hands.

At every juncture, de Gaulle had been a step ahead. And if what he had witnessed with his own eyes was true, then Colette had the real *Mona Lisa*.

Or did she?

He stood up from the settee and walked into Bertille's formal dining room where three armed men, unshaven and sweating in the unyielding heat of August, sat around a mahogany table. The *Mona Lisa*—at least the painting that he thought was *La Joconde*—was still lying inside the uncovered wooden transportation crate. She was exposed to the world; her protective purple slipcover had been taken off and placed underneath the painting.

He sidled up next to the crate and regarded the monotone palette of yellows and browns that defined da Vinci's genius. Time had aged and darkened her complexion, and upon closer examination, he could easily view cracks caused by differential shrinkage of traditional oil paints.

Then a staggering thought hit him like a thunderbolt: They still had the real *Mona Lisa*!

"Marcel, come here!" Bernard called to the other room.

Upon his colleague's arrival, Bernard rapidly explained his theory. Colette and de Gaulle had pulled off an elaborate ruse with a reproduction—and they would take back the *Mona Lisa* from them!

Bertille buried his chin in the palm of his right hand. "Sounds entirely plausible to me. I wouldn't put it past the old goat. Let's get more men stationed inside and outside. We have to be prepared for—"

"Sir, a man is approaching the building." The report came from one of the Resistance members on lookout.

"Is he armed?"

"I don't think so. Doesn't look the type, either."

Bernard followed the partisan to a bay window overlooking the street. To his surprise, he identified the lone figure right away—Henri Rambouillet, the senior curator and Colette's boss. After a knock on the door, Bernard warily welcomed him inside Bertille's apartment.

"I didn't expect to see you," Bernard said. "So why are you here?"

Rambouillet took off his hat. "To talk about the *Mona Lisa*."

"What's there to discuss? I have the original *Mona Lisa*, and you fooled everyone today by hanging a copy in the Louvre."

"Please, Bernard. I come here as a friend. I could have sent the police to recover the property you've stolen from the Louvre, but I wanted to save you a shred of respect by not exposing you to further humiliation."

"Don't try to deceive me, as you did the press and General de Gaulle today. It is you, Colette, and that pompous general that need saving from humiliation!"

Rambouillet offered a sad smile. "Please, don't mistrust me. I'm grateful for all you have done to free France, and because of my gratitude for what you have done as a member of the Resistance, I'm asking you to do the right thing now."

"Colette should be the one asking. Or should I say *begging* that I give back the original *Mona Lisa*."

"You disappoint me, Bernard. She risked everything to save you—her professional career and her life. She came to me after Heller threatened her and then promised to have you tortured if we didn't comply. Together, we devised a plan to foil any Nazi attempt to steal the *Mona Lisa*. We never expected da Vinci's masterpiece to be stolen by a fellow countryman, especially someone in the Resistance. You have hurt Colette deeply. How could you expect her to come back here and beg you to save yourself? Do you not have any self-respect?"

Bernard was convinced he was right. His only confidence was in the Communist party, and Rambouillet represented the part of society he wanted to grind out of France with the heel of his boot. He was destined to be defiant to the end and would have nothing left to lose if Rambouillet was telling the truth.

Colonel Rol, Bertille, and many of his fellow comrades watched Bernard in silence.

"If you've come to claim the real *Mona Lisa*, then we have a problem," Bernard replied in a condescending tone.

"There won't be a problem."

Gaining confidence, Bernard let his arms fall to his side. "And why do you say that?"

"Because you have the copy."

Bernard remained resolute, jutting out his chin and looking down on Rambouillet. Bertille and several witnesses whispered among themselves.

"Prove it." Bernard crossed his arms across his chest, the picture of arrogance.

"Shall we have a look at your '*Mona Lisa*'?" the senior curator asked.

"Be my guest."

Rambouillet tilted up the *Mona Lisa* and inspected the backing of the painting. "Do you see the Louvre seal, right here in the center, as it should be?"

"The official wax seal. I see it."

"Did you notice the inscription on the bottom?" He pointed toward the lowest point of the picture frame.

Bernard regarded the scribbling, in golden paint, at the bottom of the right-hand corner. "It's some sort of writing, but it looks indecipherable. Are those numbers?"

The Louvre director reached inside his coat pocket and took out a small hand mirror. "It's written backwards, a trick da Vinci liked to use. Place this mirror against the back of the painting. Read for everyone the writing you see in the mirror."

Bernard held up the mirror to the back of the painting. "So what does it say?"

Bernard's heart sank.

"Copie par Gilles Simon, 1932."

29

"You look absolutely beautiful tonight, Gabi."

Eric took Gabi's gloved hand in his as they followed the maître d' to their white-linen table in the sky. A single-stemmed pink rose in a glass bud vase had been placed in the center of the table.

They had taken the private elevator inside the Eiffel Tower's south pillar to the landmark's second level, where Le Jules Verne restaurant reigned over the alluring city. The sleek contemporary décor, with striking views of the cityscape and impressions of the tower's intricate metal latticework, was several levels up on the refinery scale. An aide on General de Gaulle's staff had secured a reservation for Eric—a difficult endeavor since tonight was the grand reopening following the departure of the German occupation force.

The tuxedoed maître d' deftly pulled out Gabi's chair and reached for her cloth napkin as she settled in. In one seamless motion, he unfolded and set the napkin across her lap.

"Welcome to the Jules Verne. A waiter will be with you shortly," the maître d' said in a clipped manner before departing.

Eric blew out a breath. The relief of the moment hit him, releasing tension that had been building ever since they had set out for Paris before Libération. Now finally relaxed, he wasn't looking over his shoulder for the first time in nearly a week.

This promised to be quite a night—dining high above Paris's darkened skyline just days after the city renewed its love affair with freedom. Gabi looked elegant, chic, and smart on this perfect summer evening. She had brought up her shoulder-length tresses to create a more formal chignon hairstyle by coiling her blonde hair into a classic bun and inserting hair sticks in a crossed design. Hair strands curling next to her ears softened her look. She was the most beautiful woman in Paris and he was the luckiest man alive.

Gabi had borrowed the long black evening dress from Colette's closet. The V neckline and draping, along with glittering sequins, gave the black satin gown a sophisticated feel. Eric almost felt underdressed in a black suit, white shirt, and pencil-thin black tie.

A waiter appeared with leather-bound menus. Eric looked across at Gabi and embraced her smile, lingering in the warmth he felt within. Never happier or more in love.

"Everything looks delicious. What about this one—*Cervelles Au Beurre Noir*?" Eric said enthusiastically.

Gabi had a wide grin. "Are you sure? Veal brains cooked in dark brown butter?"

"Ah . . . no thanks." Eric returned to the menu.

"I think I'll have the *Supreme de Volaille*—flambéed chicken breasts in a cream sauce. That's an entrée that will hit the spot after a rather amazing day."

"I'll have the same."

Eric closed the menu, happy to now focus completely on Gabi. He reached across the table and held her hand.

315

"It's wonderful that we have this moment together. More than once, I was afraid that I might lose you. You are the brightest light in Paris."

Gabi blushed but held Eric's gaze.

Eric's heart skipped. Everything felt like fireworks.

They smiled into each other's eyes, then Eric squeezed her hand. "I'm so happy to be alive and here with you."

———

Gabi returned the squeeze. Then she looked out past the panoramic view of the enchanting city. "I imagine that Kristina is home and snuggled up in bed with her mom about now. I'm so thankful she's safe."

"She was one brave girl," Eric said.

"The last person I expected to save her was that Swiss banker."

"He saved our lives too. But running off with the *Mona Lisa* wasn't the best idea."

"But Wessner thought he had the real *Mona Lisa* in his arms, just like we did," Gabi said.

"That's true. Did you feel duped after finding out we put our lives on the line for a reproduction?" Eric asked.

"I'll admit it was a shock to find out about the copy, but as Colette explained this morning, to protect the real *Mona Lisa* she was forced to keep absolute secrecy and those who knew of the painting's exact location to the barest minimum. Even Colette didn't know about the reproduction until she confessed to Rambouillet that Heller had forced her to reveal the location of *La Joconde* in order to save Bernard's life."

"Yeah, that was interesting," Eric said. "Rambouillet earned his keep, working with the Count to hide the real *Mona Lisa* down in the wine cellar for safekeeping. Even

Kristina never knew a reproduction was mounted above her bed."

"Their plan worked," Gabi said. "But what's amazing to me was how the Countess handled this. The Countess knew the Germans would have taken the girl anyway to ensure a safe escape. So to answer your question—*Did I feel duped?* No, not really. I put my life on the line to save Kristina."

With an almost imperceptible nod, Eric took a deep breath. "You're right. It really didn't matter, I suppose. We had to save Kristina. We can always console ourselves with the thought that if the Germans hadn't kidnapped her, Colette would have stopped us from chasing the reproduction. Even the best plans are unpredictable, especially in times like these."

Gabi switched from Swiss-German to French. "C'est la guerre."

"Oui. C'est la guerre." *That's war.*

From their lofty perch, Eric looked toward the bejeweled city and thought about the irony of those who had died yesterday in a vain effort to steal a copy of the famous painting. He and Gabi had put their lives on the line as well.

Few, if any, would know of their shared sacrifice. Certainly, the French people would never be told how close they came to losing the *Mona Lisa*. Whatever the reason, the outcome was what he had hoped for, and he was thankful that he and Gabi had survived.

———

The dinner had been sumptuous, the view beyond description, but Eric's genteel companionship helped Gabi glow with a luminescence of inner contentment.

When the waiter presented her with the dessert *carte*, Gabi initially demurred, but Eric playfully urged her to order her favorite dessert—*mousse au chocolat*.

"C'mon," he prodded. "We're in Paris, atop the Eiffel Tower, celebrating . . . everything."

"Okay." She raised her hands in mock surrender and ordered the chocolate mousse.

"And a dessert for the gentleman?"

"Nothing for me," Eric protested. "Couldn't eat another bite."

Gabi stared back, mouth agape. "What?"

Turning back to the waiter, she lifted two fingers into the air. "Bring two spoons. We'll share."

Five minutes later, the *serveur* returned, bearing a plate covered by a silver dome. He set the covered plate before her, and with a flourish, lifted the silver cover.

Instead of *mousse au chocolate*, Gabi saw an oval-shaped navy blue jewelry box poised in the middle of the ceramic dish. She looked back at Eric, her eyes glistening.

Eric moved from his chair onto bended knee. "Will you marry me?" he asked earnestly.

Gabi looked at him, sincerity and love written all over her face.

"Of course, I will. I'm so in love with you!"

Eric rose to his feet and took her hand. Gabi stood and stepped away from her chair. They embraced as the sound of applause rippled through the restaurant. Gabi blushed from embarrassment as well as happiness.

"Can I be the first to offer congratulations?"

Gabi turned toward the voice.

"Colette! What are you doing here?"

Gabi reached for her with one arm, and the three shared an embrace.

"Woman's intuition." She winked at Eric. "Aren't you going to open the box?"

"The box?" Gabi was puzzled.

Colette nodded toward the table.

"Oh, the ring."

Gabi put her head on Eric's shoulder and held him tight. "I've got all I want, right here."

EPILOGUE

PRESENT DAY AT THE LOUVRE MUSEUM

A group of California high school students broke into spontaneous applause as their tour guide, Caroline Tanvier, finished the tale of the *Mona Lisa*'s return to her place of honor.

"So, did Eric and Gabi get married?" asked one of the teen girls.

Caroline smiled as she led her tour group out of the Salle des Etats, where the *Mona Lisa* welcomes thousands of visitors each day.

"Yes, they had the ceremony the following May at a fourteenth-century castle outside of Zurich. Very romantic."

"Whatever happened to Reichsmarschall Göring?" asked another student.

"Even though an organization known as ODESSA smuggled Nazi war criminals to Latin America, Göring was never able to escape following the war. You see, Göring was the highest-ranking Nazi still alive after Germany's surrender. When capture was inevitable, he made sure that he was taken prisoner by the Americans since he feared the Russians would kill him out of hand. He was tried at the Nuremburg

Trials and sentenced to death by hanging. The Americans were reputed for not using enough rope at the gallows, so instead of their necks snapping after the trap door opened, several Nazi generals slowly strangled for many minutes before dying. Göring asked to be shot, but he was refused. Two hours before his execution, while on suicide watch in his cell, he bit into a cyanide capsule and died. How he was able to poison himself remains a great mystery, but he cheated the hangman's noose."

"What about all his art?" another student asked.

Caroline gathered herself for a moment. "In the closing months of World War II, with the Russians bearing down on Berlin, Göring knew he had to evacuate his beloved Carinhall. He ordered his art collection to be loaded onto a succession of private railway trains and delivered to Burg Veldenstein, another one of his properties deep in the Bavarian heartland. Then Göring dynamited Carinhall, and the country lodge burned to the ground."

Gasps escaped the lips of the enthralled students who hung on her every word.

"As the Allies closed in on Burg Veldenstein, Göring's trains reassembled and moved his art even farther from the front lines to Berchtesgaden, a small German town on the Austrian border. Göring was captured nearby, and his collection of paintings was secured and inventoried by the Allied Forces. More than 1,800 paintings were recovered, and his collection would be worth several hundred million dollars today."

Caroline looked down at her watch. "Listen, we're losing daylight, so we better keep moving. Next up, the Venus de Milo in the Sully Wing."

A blonde-haired teen raised her hand. "How did you know this story?"

"Because . . ." Caroline paused. A smile tipped her lips. "Because Gabi and Eric were my grandparents."

Looks of astonishment greeted her.

"Are your grandparents still alive?" asked another student.

"No, they are no longer with us. Eric passed away four years ago, and Gabi just last year." Caroline paused for a moment, a bit overcome with emotion.

"Growing up, I always wondered why my grandmother liked to take us for long walks in the mountains overlooking Lucerne. Later, when she told me this story, I understood. I think those hikes were a reminder of her adventures and most important, of saving Kristina. She was most proud of that."

"What became of Kristina?" another student asked.

"Well, she's in her late seventies now and still lives at the Chateau de Dampierre with her son and his family. For many years, she would come to visit the *Mona Lisa*, right at closing. She was always allowed to have a private audience, just as Colette promised. I think that was her way of dealing with those awful events as a young girl.

"Kristina once described *La Joconde*'s smile as a knowing expression, like she understood her and the way she felt. In recent years, though, she wasn't able to travel to the Louvre because of failing health, so the museum sent her the actual reproduction painted in 1932 by Gilles Simon—on loan of course—but for her to keep as long as she wished.

"I'm told the *Mona Lisa* still hangs over her bed today."

ACKNOWLEDGMENTS

We (Tricia and Mike) are thankful for all those who've supported our efforts and cheered us on while writing this book. Tricia thanks her wonderful husband, John, and her houseful: Cory, Katie, Leslie, Nathan, and Alyssa. Mike thanks his patient Swiss-born wife, Nicole, who read and reread chapters as they were written. We also appreciate our wonderful agent, Janet Grant, and our editors, Vicki Crumpton and Barb Barnes—three of the best people in the business!

This book could not have been written without Jon Shafqat, who devoted untold hours to reading chapters, offering plot ideas, and making editing suggestions along the way. Jon—a friend of Mike's from Encinitas, California—had some amazing twists that are woven throughout the story. A doff of the chapeau, as the French say, and this is why the book is dedicated to him.

When I (Mike) was in Paris doing research, John-Paul Fortney, who conducted a World War II walking tour of Paris for Classic Walks, was a fount of information regarding the Gaullists' takeover of the Préfecture de Police during the insurrection leading up to Libération. John-Paul, an

American from St. Louis, had conducted more than two hundred World War II tours since 2008, but he patiently listened as I peppered him with questions about the Resistance and the Nazi occupation. He has since left Classic Walks to form his own tour guide company called Culinary Tours of Paris (www.culinarytoursofparis.com).

Bob Weimann, a retired United States Marine Corps Lieutenant Colonel living in Raleigh, North Carolina, provided much of the background for tank scenes in Paris during Libération. He also advised us on the story's military details.

Keith and Karen Cunningham of Birmingham, Alabama, were super-sleuths for pesky typos. Keith, a corrections officer, said he loves correcting manuscripts. Karen's mother, Judy Doyle, grew up in Lausanne, Switzerland, in the 1950s. The Cunninghams hope to take their three children on a family vacation in the Swiss Alps someday.

Swiss residents Carol Bieri of Geneva and Philip Djaferis of La Conversion helped make sure the Swiss sections of *Chasing Mona Lisa* were up to Swiss precision regarding landmarks. Stephan Stücklin of Basel proved to have a real editor's eye for French history during World War II as well as Switzerland's role in that conflict. The Turrian family of Villars, Switzerland, as well as Nicole Yorkey, helped with the French and German dialogue.

Nate Dickinson, who owned an art gallery in Portland, Oregon, helped with the description of how the *Mona Lisa* was packed in a wooden crate. Nate grew up with Mike in La Jolla, California. Keith Proctor, a friend from Mike's church who reads one hundred novels a year, offered some great insights. We also loved the ideas shared by Debbie Lambert of Buda, Texas, and Kari Benirschke of Del Mar, California, both early readers. Mike's aunt, Sandy Smith of La Jolla, proofed the final galleys with eagle eyes.

Finally, we would like to acknowledge several books that were instrumental to our understanding of what Paris was like during Libération as well as the Nazis' plundering of art. *Is Paris Burning?*, written in 1966 by Larry Collins and Dominique Lapierre, is considered the quintessential book on the topic and was made into a popular '60s movie with the same title. *The Rape of Europa* (1994) by Lynn H. Nicholas described how the Louvre took steps to keep their treasures out of Nazi hands during the dark days of Occupation as well as what happened to the *Mona Lisa* from 1939 to 1944. The documentary movie of the same name is also well worth viewing.

Göring: A Biography (1989) by David Irving was a fount of information about the German Reichsmarschall. *Liberation of Paris 1944: Patton's Race for the Seine* (2008) by Steven Zaloga described how the various Resistance organizations maneuvered for position in the weeks leading up to the liberation of Paris.

And last, *Vanished Smile: The Mysterious Theft of Mona Lisa* (2009) by R. A. Scotti told the fascinating story of how the *Mona Lisa* vanished from the Louvre on August 21, 1911, which shocked the world until the most familiar and lasting portrait of all time was returned to the Louvre.

So, yes, that century-old story of how authorities were chasing *Mona Lisa* was completely true.

Tricia Goyer is the author of twenty-eight books, including CBA bestseller *Beside Still Waters* and *Remembering You*. She lives in Little Rock, Arkansas, with her husband, John, and they are the parents of four children. She loves talking with World War II veterans, doing drama in children's church, and mentoring teenage mothers. Visit Tricia's website at www.triciagoyer.com.

Mike Yorkey is a veteran author or coauthor of more than seventy-five books, including the *Every Man's Battle* series and *The Swiss Courier*, the prequel to *Chasing Mona Lisa*. He lives in Encinitas, California, with his wife, Nicole, and they spend part of the year in her native Switzerland. They are the parents of two adult children. Visit Mike's website at www.mikeyorkey.com.

"I enjoyed everything about *The Swiss Courier*...
the wonderful characters, the rich atmosphere,
and the truly exciting story. A winner!"

—Christopher Reich, *New York Times*
bestselling author of *Rules of Vengeance*

Gabi Mueller is a young woman working for the newly formed American Office
of Strategic Services in Switzerland. When she is asked to put herself in harm's
way to safely "courier" a German scientist who is working on the atomic bomb
out of enemy territory, the fate of the world hangs in the balance.

a division of Baker Publishing Group
www.RevellBooks.com

Available Wherever Books Are Sold

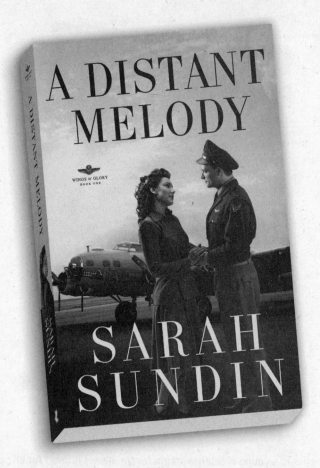

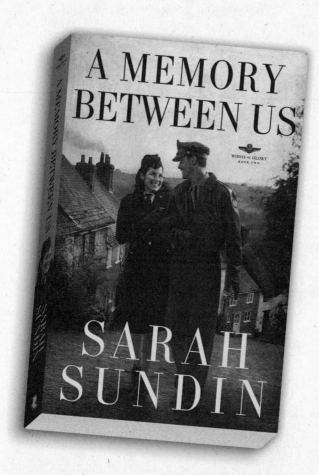

"Sarah Sundin is a master at lyrical writing, and she has that rare talent of being able to combine humor with heart-pounding action. I couldn't stop turning the pages."

—Melanie Dobson, author of *Love Finds You in Liberty, Indiana* and *Refuge on Crescent Hill*

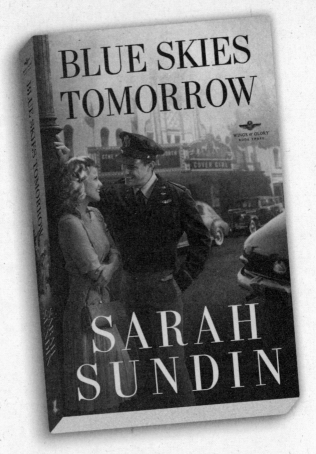

A young war widow covers her pain with the frenzy of volunteer work until the spark of her romance with a WWII pilot propels them both into peril.